Little Moscow

To Niki,

With gratitude

for tonight

Best wishes

Mick Scully

12.06.07.

Little Moscow

Mick Scully

Tindal Street Press

First published in June 2007
by Tindal Street Press Ltd
217 The Custard Factory, Gibb Street, Birmingham, B9 4AA
www.tindalstreet.co.uk

Versions of these stories first appeared in the following publications:
'Little Moscow' in *Birmingham Noir* (Tindal Street Press, 2002)
'Abstract' in *Dreams Never End* (Tindal Street Press, 2004)
'Ash' in *Tell Tales* (Arts Council, England, 2006)
'The Night of the Great Winds' in *CrimeWave* (TTA Press, 2006)

A CIP catalogue reference for this book is available
from the British Library

ISBN: 978 0 9551384 4 7

Typeset by Country Setting, Kingsdown, Kent
Printed and bound in Great Britain by Clays Ltd, St Ives PLC

For Sheila and Jennifer

Contents

Little Moscow

Out. A week now. I have waited a full week before heading here, the Little Moscow. A basement bar on the edge of the Tyseley Industrial Estate. Not that there's much industry left, just a lot of broken down factories nobody needs any more. Crumbleville.

The Little Moscow has always been a villains' bar, although in the sixties it doubled, briefly, as a trendy Mod bar. That's when I first descended its narrow flight of brick steps – in my Crombie and Ben Sherman shirts. I've always cared about my appearance. Even inside I take a pride in it. You can these days. The clink isn't the place it used to be.

Tonight my purpose here is different. Then it was to be admired, to get a shag. And I usually did. I was a good-looking boy.

I've always been a criminal, and a good one, efficient. If you're around long enough you get a reputation; and a name. Mine is Office.

I'm independent too; usually worked alone. Small jobs, but plenty of them. Of course I'm talking about some time ago, when cash was king. People got paid weekly – cash, in fat little brown envelopes. I did wages jobs. Thursday nights, Friday mornings. They were my busy times. A cosh swung above the head of a wages clerk; a few threats.

Easy. People didn't swear so much then either, so a few curses scared the shit – *Fill the fucking bag, you tosser. Or I'll spread your fucking brains all over the fucking walls.* I wonder how many times I've used that line. And I could always judge just how it needed to be said. Sometimes you lean in close to the face, so they can feel your breath, and hiss the words out, other times you scream them out like a fucking lunatic.

My old fella was a villain too, but not so successful. A team player, he called himself. Meaning he had no ideas of his own, no initiative. And he always chose the wrong team. Even supported the Albion and what the fuck have they ever won? Banged up most of his life. Died inside.

There's hardly anyone in the bar, but it's early yet. I look around. It's the same old place all right. A few tables and chairs. Photographs of Moscow pasted on chipboard, Athena-style, still hang from the walls. Faded now and to-bacco stained. The Kremlin. Some cathedral. Red Square.

I see Fat Alex is still here, behind the bar. He's taking bottles from a plastic crate to fill a low shelf. His big arse sticking up above the bar. It was his father who opened the Little Moscow in the fifties. A Pole who came over here in the war. There was a big Eastern European community in Brum at the time – Poles and Czechs mostly, a few Hungarians. Fuck knows why he called it Little Moscow, given what was happening in his country at the time. A joke? Maybe. A lot of gambling went on then. Alex's dad did a spell inside for it.

Eventually Alex rises, wheezing, boots the empty crate under the bar and turns towards me. 'Yes, mate?' Then his face does a squiggle as recognition comes. 'Office! Well fuck me. Good to see yow, man.' His podgy fist grasps the beer pump and he squints, taking me in. Then comes the usual crap. 'You're lookin good, kid. No doubt about it.

Yes. Lookin very good. Nice suit. I eard you waz clear. Wondered if yow'd pop in. Yeh. It's good to see yow, mate.'

I bet it is. I let his awkward pause hang for a minute. Watch his eyes shifting uncomfortably. Then I help him out. 'You haven't lost any weight, I see. Ya fat bastard.' And I give him a bit of a smile.

Relieved, he laughs and slaps his bulging belly in confirmation. 'Shit. It's been a long time, Office.' I say nothing. 'How long is it?' Not the right question.

Still, I'm here for a reason, so I answer the man. 'Sixteen years.'

'Fuck me rigid, Office. Sixteen years. Bloody ell. So. What yow drinkin?'

I scan the pumps. Same pumps, different beer. Each shield bears the name of an unfamiliar brand. 'No Ansells any more, I see. Or Double D.'

'Fuck me. It as been sixteen years, asn't it? Ere.' He flicks the little knob of an electric pump. 'Try one of these fancy Belgian lagers. We're in the Common Market now, ya know.'

He places the foaming lager on the bar before me. 'On me. Free sample.' Then he drops a double whisky into a tumbler. 'Chase it down, Office. Welcome ome.' Yeh. I bet.

The trouble with returning to a place like this is the ghosts. Before I've had more than a gulp or two of lager, a shot of whisky, they start to appear. Taking their places at the empty chairs. They hang around the old upright juke-box that's been shifted out now. They are leaning on the bar, heads close together, whispering. One ghost is missing, of course. And as I think of him my eyes flicker towards the door to the Gents. Still there. Where it was then. There's been no reconstruction in Little Moscow – of any sort.

Fat Alex is still jawing away, telling me things, as if he can fill me in on sixteen years in the time it takes to down a few drinks. Or maybe it's nerves. I'm not listening to

3

him. Just nodding, making the right noises. Every now and then he mentions a name from the old days. I look around and there they are, sitting at a table, lolling in a chair, walking across the dirty wooden floor, sharpening cues at the pool table in the big alcove.

Gradually a few bits of real flesh and blood start turning up. Nobody I know, of course. Youngsters, a lot of them. But all part of the Brotherhood. Or apprentices. Sitting together, gassing. One or two standing alone. Moody. Watching. For someone or something to turn up. And as they arrive, gradually filling the place, they evict my ghosts.

Second pint. Third. And I start to get comfortable. Assam, a lad I knew inside, arrives and comes across, a piece of skirt hanging off his arm, and we exchange a few words. Buys me a pint. 'Are ya lookin for work? Might be able to fix ya up wiv somethin. Small it would be. But it's money.'

'You're all right, mate,' I reply. 'I'm okay for a bit. Thanks for the offer though.'

Assam pisses off with his woman and it's time to make my first move. I've waited till it's busy but not packed. Now I catch Alex's eye with a serious look, raise my finger and curl it, beckoning. 'Over here, mate.' His eyes flicker to my glass but he sees it's still near full. He squints as he shuffles towards me. I lean forward across the bar, speak softly but firmly. 'I need to have a quiet word with you.'

A shifty look that he drags into a smile. 'Imran, lad who helps out, e'll be in about nine. We'll talk then.'

A few minutes later I spot him on the mobile. He's turned away from the bar, trying to make himself small. Some fucking chance.

I've rehearsed tonight. A thousand times at least. On the bunk, in the gym, on the bog. In the long sleepless nights – and I've had plenty of those over the years. And here I am. Walking the dream. Back in the Little Moscow. It's still here, and so am I.

Now there's a moment of panic. I pull hard on my fag. You stupid fucker, I'm telling myself. To believe in a promise made from the other side of a gun all those years ago. 'There's bugger all honour among thieves, son,' my old man used to tell me. 'Remember that.' Well, we'll see. I'm here, aren't I?

I'm careful about people. That's why I worked alone. I took only cash, so I was always my own man. But you get known. Like attracts like. I hung around this place like a flag – was on nodding terms with everyone. And when business was bad, or I needed to keep my head down, I did a bit of work for the Sanchez brothers – door work, spot of driving, sometimes a bit of back-up for a heavy job.

I'd been working for myself all that year, 1984. A good year. My pockets were full. It was a few days before Christmas. Pissing down outside and cold. The usual Christmas crap pouring out of the jukebox and hardly anyone in here. But there was this kid. He was in here when I arrived. Eyeing up everyone who came down the steps. Standing at the bar with a pint he wasn't enjoying much. Thin. Pimply. In an old-fashioned overcoat, sizes too big for him. I notice he keeps looking over. Apprentice, I reckon. Looking for a bit of work over the Christmas period. Now there's certain things you can work out straight away from a bloke's eyes – and his are strange. Watery, too old for him. Greeny blue. Like the marbles I played with as a nipper. He's as nervous as fuck. Like a schoolboy outside the headmaster's study. Knows he's up for six of the best and just wants to get it over with. Doesn't care how bad it will be. Wants to get on with it, that's all.

The eyes slide towards me again. Lips tremble slightly. I nod. He nods back. What the fuck, I think, and push my glass a bit closer along the bar.

'Not seen you in here before.'

'No,' he says. Sort of breathes it out. And his voice is funny. An accent, foreign.

'You're not English.' A bit stupid really, but I'm not a natural conversationalist, don't find small talk easy. Better at listening.

'No.' He's not giving much away. Sensible.

'Where you from then?'

'Poland.'

'Fuck. You're a long way from home.'

He thinks this is funny and laughs.

There's a pause. I tap my finger to the stupid music. The kid can't take it. He moves closer. Shoves his watery eyes up at me and blurts out, 'Are you interested in buying something?' This is no apprentice. A complete bloody novice. Does a job and can't take the heat. 'Something valuable. Very rare. Expensive.' Mistake Number One: I feel a bit sorry for him. He's got no nerve, blurting it out like this.

'I might be. What is it?'

'Jewellery.'

'Not really my bag, son.' I was about to leave it there, but he was pissing himself with fright, so Mistake Number Two. 'I might be able to sort something out for you though. I know a few people.' At this point I have him down as a novice climber. He's just shinned up his first drainpipe, nicked some rich tart's Christmas present and wants to unload it quickly. I'd had a good year, plenty of cash; it might be worth a look. 'Have you got it with you?'

He straightens up. 'Follow me. In a minute.' And with that he turns and marches off towards the door marked *Gentlemen* – always a bit of a joke in the Little Moscow. Just like a little soldier.

I give it a couple of minutes, stub my fag and follow.

But he hasn't gone into the bog. There's a small lobby with a double fire exit door leading out on to the towpath.

Tonight there's a mangy-looking Christmas tree blocking the exit, a few tired lengths of tinsel stretched across it. The kid's standing by the tree, pretending to admire it. He's got an envelope in his hand.

I stand beside him. Take out the fags, offer him one, but he shakes his head. 'I do smoke. But not now. Thank you.' He's calmer now he's out of the bar.

'Let's see the stuff then. How hot is it?'

He takes two photographs from the envelope. They're old pictures. Fawn with age. He hands one to me. It's a woman, about thirty, smiling into the camera. There's a cigarette on its way to her lips.

'Do you recognize this lady?' the kid asks.

She's glamorous, done up to the nines. I don't know who she is. Think maybe she's some film star from the thirties or forties.

'No. Can't say I do.'

He points to her hand. 'This is the ring I have to sell.' I see now there's a big sparkler on one of her fingers. 'It is a square-cut sapphire. Here in the centre. Large, yes? And these are rubies around it. With small diamonds, tiny ones, in between.' He's starting to sound like a salesman. 'It is a very beautiful ring.'

'Where is it?' I ask. 'Let's see the real thing.'

But he just hands me the other picture. It confuses me for a second. All I take in is it's a picture of Hitler. In uniform. There are some other blokes with him. One a fat, bald bloke. I ought to know his name. Then I see, in the middle, with old Adolf's arm around her, the woman in the first photograph. Another fag on its way to her mouth. The ring singing out from her finger. You can see the flash of the stones in the light.

'What is this?'

'The lady. Her name is Eva Braun. You know of her? She was Hitler's mistress. He gave her the ring. He had it specially made. A Christmas present for her. It is a very expensive ring. Very beautiful. Very, very special. No?' He reaches for the photographs and replaces them in the envelope, which he puts inside his coat. 'I have this ring. I wish to sell it. For twenty-five thousand pounds. So I can get to America.'

Fuck me, I thought. You must be planning to go by Concorde if you need that sort of dough. 'That's a lot of money, kid. Well, let's see it, then.'

He gives me a look as if I'm the novice. 'You do not carry such a thing. But I have it. I can quickly get it if you wish to purchase it.'

My brain's turning somersaults.

'Not me. This isn't my territory. Look, let's go back inside and talk about this.'

We carry our beers from the bar to a table in one of the small alcoves. He hasn't touched his, but I take a hefty swig from mine. This could be a big one, I'm telling myself. There's the chance for some real money here. A Big One. Mistake Three.

The kid must trust me, for he opens up. Apparently this bird, Eva Braun, was Hitler's favourite piece. They killed themselves together, which I sort of knew. The kid's grandfather was one of the soldiers who discovered the bodies. They'd been burnt. But the ring had survived the amateur cremation and this kid's grandaddy had pocketed it. It'd been a sort of insurance for the family and a huge secret.

When the kid decided to make a run for the West he stole the ring from his father; it was his 'collateral'. He made me laugh as he said that word. So careful. With so much effort. A bright lad.

'I think I can help you out,' I told him, 'but I need the photographs. Without them it's just a ring.'

'Yes. It is its antecedents that make it so valuable.' Bloody hell. A bright kid, all right. He knew more words than I did. 'But it is a beautiful ring. Exquisite.'

8

'Yeh. Well, you wouldn't expect old Adolf to give his missus something from Ratner's, would you?' He didn't understand.

The next days were busy ones. While the city grew frantic with Christmas shopping I set about finding a buyer for the ring. It took some thinking about – this was big stuff. I decided to go straight to the top – Big Eric Scudamore. Then I thought, No, the Sanchez brothers. Of course. They were pretty much running Birmingham at the time. Two big clubs in town and a host of other business interests – property, porn, who knows what.

Ramon sat quietly behind his desk at the Candystrip looking intently at the photographs laid out before him.

'You say you haven't actually seen the ring, Office? Touched it? Given it the once over?' His fierce little eyes burned at me, but Ramon didn't scare me. The brothers were businessmen. If they went for this they'd be serious. No messing. The brass was there. And they had the back-up if anything went wrong.

'No, Ramon, but my source is totally legit. Not local. European.' I thought he would like this. 'And you know me, Ramon, if the goods aren't up to scratch, then the deal is off. No problem.'

He thought for a moment. Sighed heavily. Then burped loudly. An unfortunate habit of his. 'Have you approached anyone else?'

'No. You were the first people I thought of.'

'So. No one else knows anything about it.'

'No one. Just you, me and the supplier.'

'Who is?'

'Oh, come on, Ramon. You know I can't tell you that. But you know me. I don't take risks. I wouldn't be anywhere near this if I wasn't sure it's absolutely kosher.'

He leaned back in his comfortable leather chair and

spoke slowly in his soft Spanish accent. 'It certainly seems a very interesting investment. There's all sorts of . . . er, weirdos, who'll pay well over the odds, yes, very big sums, because of this ring's antecedents.'

Fuck me. That word again. I was beginning to think I ought to read more. Starting with a dictionary.

Ramon sighed, scratching his chins. Then he fixed the eyes again. 'You say the price is fifty grand?'

'Yep. That's it. On the nose.'

'Can't you bid it down?'

'Already have, Ramon. It started at nearly twice that.' The breath whistled out of him and I prepared myself for another burp. 'So it's come down a lot.' I paused. Let him think. 'The thing is, if we don't bite, it'll go abroad.'

'And yours?'

'I'm asking a couple of grand from you and the same from the vendor.' Vendor. Not a word I use a lot, but I was beginning to feel a bit touchy about my vocabulary. All these foreigners using words I didn't know.

'So. That will bring our investment to fifty-two thousand pounds.' He spoke the words with slow care, as if he needed to hear them to believe them. 'That's a lot of money, Office – that's a house.'

Not where you live, I thought.

'Yeh, but as you said, Ramon, it's a hell of an investment. When will an opportunity like this come up again? The ring itself is top notch. Worth that money. Then there's the intercedence. It's money in the bank.'

His finger was tapping. Head bent, looking at the photographs again. Then he carefully replaced them in the envelope.

'Give me a minute, Office.' He was off to see his brother. But I knew it was a done deal and was cheering inside. If Ramon was happy, then brother Manolo wouldn't argue. Ramon was the gaffer.

All I had to do now was bid the kid down to twenty grand. Things looked as if they were turning out nicely, as my old man used to say. Poor sod.

I met the kid on the towpath of the Tyseley Canal. Small patches of ice formed a seasonal patchwork across the filthy water. He was still wearing his old overcoat. A red scarf round his neck now and bloody great workmen's boots. Not the trendiest youngster in the world.

'I wish you'd brought the ring. I've got to be sure the merchandise is up to scratch – for my clients.'

He didn't flinch. Right little soldier. 'Your clients will not be disappointed. The merchandise is magnificent. I will produce the ring when you bring the cash.'

He was a puny little bastard. Shaking now. But he was no pushover. Skinny, but determined as fuck. Still, you don't climb out of a country unless you've got guts.

'The problem is, kid, twenty grand is the total tops they'll go. I tried hard as I could for the full quarter. But twenty's all I can do.'

His breath was making small clouds of white smoke in the frozen air. A little dragon. He turned his wet eyes straight on me. 'Then I must thank you for your help. But there is no transaction.' Shit. What sort of school did he go to? I thought they were all piss poor in Poland.

'Come on, kid. Think about it. Fifteen thousand pounds will give you a great start in the States. Easy.'

'You said twenty.'

Time to toughen up. Let him know where he stood. 'I'm not doin this for nothing, y'know. I want something for myself.'

'You should add your commission to the purchase price. I told you I wanted twenty-five thousand pounds. Or a quarter as you say. That is the price. I will sell for nothing less.' And he meant it. I could see that. 'I thank

11

you for your efforts. I must leave now.' And he held his hand out for me to shake.

Tough little fucker. I liked him. You have to admire guts.

'Okay. Let me have another try. I'll see if I can push them up another couple of grand.'

'Another five.'

I laughed. 'All right. Another five. I'll see what I can do.'

Mistake Number Four. I always claimed I wasn't greedy. I saw too many take the drop because they got too greedy. But somehow I managed to convince myself it was the kid who was the greedy one. He was the one pushing too far.

I was still there, standing with frozen feet beside the canal, watching him climb the towpath steps towards the station when I decided. I'll go for the lot. Take the cash myself. Top the kid. I know I shivered a little, but it was a cold day. Brutal.

I had never even considered killing before. Rarely used any sort of violence. Didn't have to if you scared them enough. But the decision wasn't a surprise to me. I suppose I always knew I would. If it was worth it. And fifty grand was.

I met Black Andy Crawford in here. He was the Sanchez brothers' front man in those days, took over from them in the end. Sharp-suited lad. Not much more than a kid then. But confident. Going places. Always beautifully turned out.

'Have you actually seen this ring yet, Office?'

'Yeh.'

'And?'

'I'm no jeweller, Andy. But it looks fucking fabulous to me. Never seen anything like it.'

'Well. The brothers are very interested, but only if it's the real thing.'

'There's no doubt about that.'

'I've been down the library today.'

'Bloody hell, And. Didn't know you could read.'

'I've been looking at pictures – of this Eva Braun tart. And I turned up two more showing this ring. Are you sure – absolutely sure –' and here he gave me one of his hard looks, meant to be sinister, but I've seen every look in the book – 'that it's the ring in the photographs?'

'Absolutely fucking certain.'

'You understand that if it turns out to be paste – we get our money back, plus expenses, or . . .'

He didn't have to go on. Now it was my turn for the look. Cold as that fucking canal freezing out the back. 'Andy. How long have you known me? I've been around a long time. I do all right – and I know my place. I don't fuck with the Sanchez brothers. I want to keep my bollocks.

'I said I'm no jeweller, but I can tell paste from stones. I know quality. You've seen me walk away from a dozen chances. I wouldn't be here if I wasn't certain.'

He was convinced. I could see. That's the beauty of a track record. He licked his lips. 'I'll get us another drink.'

The deal was done. The set up was this. I would meet Black Andy here on the night before New Year's Eve. It would be quiet. Everyone saving their dosh for the festivities the following night. Andy would pass me the notes and leave. But wait in the car outside. When I had the ring I'd take it out to him in the car. Everything was sorted.

My plan was, I'd do the kid. Hand the ring over as arranged. Keep the money. Get out.

I thought the kid would be pleased. He probably was. But all he did was nod his head. He was seeing America, I suppose.

'Now look, kid. I'm sticking my neck out for you. If you don't come up with the goods we're both dead. These are big-timers we've got involved. There's none bigger in this city.'

'You do not need to worry. I will be there with the ring.' He gave me a look. 'The merchandise. Once I have counted the money it will be yours. Thank you for your work. I hope you have negotiated a good commission for yourself.'

Cheeky little ponce. With his big words. Suddenly I didn't feel sorry for him any more.

It was Christmas Day when I changed my plan. I'd picked up this bird in the Locarno Christmas Eve and was shagging until dinnertime. Then all of a sudden she noticed the clock. 'Bloody hell! Me mum'll kill me if I'm not there for the turkey.' With that she had her knickers on and was away. I rolled a Chrissy joint, a great fat bastard, and got greedy.

This was the Big One. Of course it was. Everyone talked about the Big One. The one that will change everything; the retirement job. I knew it was a myth. Just kept the blokes going. Always thought I was too realistic to swallow it myself.

Then by the time the ads for summer holidays started on the telly, about teatime, I was saying to myself, This is the Big One. It is. It's just tumbled into your lap, son. A gift from Santa. And I laughed. Go for it. Go for it all. You'd be a prat not to. It was then, watching the ads for holidays in Spain and Portugal which punctuated *The Great Escape*, that I decided. Okay. I'll go for the whole fucking lot. The money. The ring. And piss off for ever. I'd do the kid in the toilet. Out through the fire exit. Along the towpath. Have a motor by the bridge half a mile up the water. And away.

*

The festivities were over. Or at least there was that lull, dead time, before New Year's Eve. I decided to use a knife. Planned it meticulously. Wondered if the kid knew that word. When the time arrived there I was. Standing here. Right here, where I could see the stairs. First down was Black Andy. Immaculate as ever.

'Have a good Christmas, Office?' He smirked.

'Quiet, And. How about you?'

'Quiet.'

We were both on shorts. Mine a whisky mac to keep out the cold. Andy's a rum and black. A couple of these and a bit of football talk, when he says, 'Couldn't get your pressy round for the big day. But here it is,' and he pulls this thick package, all shiny and glittery with little snowmen on it, out of his overcoat pocket.

'Happy Christmas, Office. This is from the family.'

'Cheers, Andy. I've got yours, but I'll have to give it to you later.'

'I'm lookin forward to it.' He finishes his drink and pushes off. 'See you later, mate.'

He wasn't late. I knew he wouldn't be. I saw the boots first, trudging down the steps, then the overcoat, the red scarf. It had started snowing. A few flakes were melting on his hair and shoulders. He spotted me straightaway.

I bought him a beer. He seemed as nervous as fuck, but I knew him better now.

'Have you got it?'

'Of course.'

'We'll have a bit of a drink. Then, as before – the bog.'

'That was my idea too.'

He took the tiniest mouthful of beer. 'Did you enjoy Christmas?' he asked.

'Quiet. You?'

'It was quiet for me too. I am alone and without money.

But it was the last Christmas that will be this way. Next year I will be in America.'

'Why d'you want to go to America so much?'

'It is a great land. Free. I am a musician. I will join a band and become a rock star.'

So that was it. The dream that had dragged him out of his land. Led him to do whatever he had to do to get the ring, to get here. Dreams. Dangerous things.

He took a swig of his beer. A surprisingly long one. Emptied half the glass.

'Thirsty?'

He smiled, which was something I hadn't seen him do much before. He looked even younger. 'No. It is part to celebrate and part to give me the courage of the Dutch. In a minute I will sell what has been in my family all my life. Our secret. Our security.' He saw my look. 'Do not be afraid. I will do it. But it will be my final betrayal. I drink to my treason. I hope one day I will be able to make amends.' He took another swig which emptied the glass. He was still reading my look. 'Do not look so worried. I will give up the ring readily. It is the price. I will pay it.' He shuffled on his seat. 'I will go to piss now. Really. I need to piss.'

I nodded. 'I'll give you a minute. Go into the lock-up when you've finished – but don't bolt the door. I'll be in soon.'

He turned and marched off across the bar. The little soldier. This was it. I felt the beautiful adrenaline start to flow, glow through me. He pushed open the door unsteadily.

Slowly I count to twelve, like the twelve days of Christmas. Then action. Swiftly to the door. In the lobby I kick the tatty Christmas tree away from the fire exit, my hand reaching into my jacket for the knife taped inside.

Knife in my hand, I boot open the bog door. The kid is still pissing. One leap and I'm on him. Grab his head, jerking it into the crux of my shoulder, exposing the full throat, twisted back. His hands reach for mine and his cock springs upwards, piss shooting into my face. I tug his head further back, pulling him up on tip-toe. Lower my own head into his neck to avoid the splash and plunge the knife into the centre of the throat. The gush of blood splatters like rain against the ceiling. In a stroke I push the knife left towards the ear then drag it back right. Grab the hair back, and the throat opens up with a gurgle. I hear cords tearing apart. I let go. The kid flops down like a puppet. I skim him over. Go for the pockets. Fuck. Nothing. Check again. Fuck. Then I see it. A plaster at the base of his dripping cock, like a garden hose still seeping water. I rip it off. And there it is. Eva's sparkler. Slipping it inside my jacket I'm away.

I shoulder-charge the fire escape. The doors flap open easily and I'm out into the freezing darkness. The reflected lights of factories and high-rise flats twinkle dismally in the black canal. The cold air filling the lungs is a treat. Out. And now to the motor.

Near the bridge, a bush at the side of the towpath suddenly expands into a suit shape. Just a suit. Then a mouth opens. Black Andy. Sneering. 'Silly boy, Office. Very silly boy.'

I sense, more than see, another figure behind me. Then hear his breathing. I'm transfixed by the small glint of the gun in Andy's hand. Waist level. He hadn't even bothered to raise it.

So this is it, I thought. The Big One. This is the end of the story. And I realized that always in a life such as mine there is the knowledge that this might be the way it ends.

'The ring!' Andy muttered. 'Hand it over. That's right. Now the money.' A touch of Christmas glitter on the package catches the light reflected on the canal and sparkles briefly, before disappearing into Andy's coat. 'Good boy,' as I hand it over. 'Now. Turn round.' Just like a film. I did so. Thinking of the firm courage of the little soldier. Scared. Yeh. But they wouldn't have known. No noise. No shaking or twitching. No begging. I was pleased with myself.

I didn't recognize the other guy. Saw his gun. Fuck. Back? Front? Both together. That's simultaneous. Wonder if the kid knew that word.

Head. I felt the small nudge of the barrel touch my neck, just below the skull. Then Andy leans close and whispers in my ear. 'Walk. We're going back.'

Inside the bog the kid lies red and mangled on the floor. 'Now. Don't be a stupid fucker twice, Office. This is your job. Not a word.'

'I'll get you for this, Crawford. That's a promise.'

I can see Fat Alex shuffling up behind him, keys jangling from his fist. And you, you bastard, I think. The door banged shut and I heard a key turn in the lock. When it turned again half an hour later it was the filth.

For half an hour I was alone with my handiwork. The kid's body was curled, knees up. The head, almost off, faced the door. Eyes open, but no longer watery. Hard and glazed like boiled sweets. A small stream of blood still trickled into the urinal. Splatters of blood across his face had hardened into rusty scabs. I smashed the lights so I wouldn't have to look at him. Sat in the lock-up, eating fags, listening to the hiss of the urinals. Knowing he was lying there. And smelling the stink. The astringent combination of piss and disinfectant. And rising above it, clawing its way into my churning belly, the metallic odour of fresh blood.

Life sentence, of course. Served sixteen. And now I'm back. Back to the scene.

I make my way to the bar. There's an Asian lad serving now. Scar down the side of his face. Order another pint.

He knows who I am. 'It's on Alex,' he says tersely, as I reach for my pocket.

I'm bursting for a piss. This is the moment. I can't put it off. I go back in there, or I piss myself here in the bar. Just for a second, as I make my way, I see him, the nervous little fucker, standing hunched over his untouched beer at the bar. Just for a second. The blink of an eye.

It's the same stinking hole. Graffiti on the walls. That's new. Jesus! There's still some Blues supporters left. Everything else is the same. The piss streams out of me. Relief. I'm back. Back in Little Moscow. Of course, I've returned here many times in the last sixteen years. I've been a good lad. Kept my nose clean. Gone to psychology sessions, talked to the God Squad, repented my crime. It's the only way to get parole. In my bunk at night I've relived it – time and again. I put my dick away. Turn and take a proper look. I stoop down. It was here. Touch the tiles. Trace my finger across them. This is where he lay. This is where his feet would have been when I pulled him up onto his toes.

I'm sorry, kid. Sorry it was you. Inside, sometimes, when I was watching telly and something in America came on, or a rock band full of young kids, I would think of you. And I dreamed about you. We are here. We go into the lock-up. You open a wooden box. 'Here's the ring,' you say. 'Eva's ring.' And it's there all right. I can see it sparkling in the darkness. But as I reach for it, it's still on a charred finger. I feel the hard, burnt flesh and I recoil. You start to laugh, a real belly laugh. Throw back your head. And your throat opens up.

I trace the tiles again. This is the place you died. Where I killed you. Sorry, kid.

Close my eyes. See it again. How many times have I seen it? Felt my head push against his neck. The give of flesh beneath the blade. The tension in his bony body, then its collapse. Like when a woman yields in your arms.

And how many times have I wanted to do it again? Wanted to. Do it again. And again. Once is not enough.

I stand up. My chest is sore where the shooter chafed it as I stooped. It's time for my chat with that fat bastard Alex. Alex the Key.

The door swings open right in front of me. Crawford. And behind him, just like before, Fat Alex.

'Hello, Office. We must stop meeting like this.'

Abstract

Sure. Murders happen in Birmingham, like everywhere. Hamid knew this. But it isn't every day you see a man hanging from a lamppost, his spectacles shattered three feet beneath his shoes. In other places, yes.

And in the afternoon too. Long after noon. Four p.m. to be precise. It was November, and that grey–orange light – so familiar in England at that time of day, at that time of year – suffused the decaying street, gracing the boarded-up houses and broken gates with an undeserved romanticism.

When Hamid saw him, hanging simply and still, like a pendant, he knew he would never have to work in Durscher's Eight till Late Convenience Store again. The sweeping and packing, the grovelling, were over.

The hanging man was a gift and Hamid knew he was a gift meant for him. He shinned the lamppost to the point where he could lean across and unravel the rope. The carcass fell in a heap.

It had been his intention to use the rope to drag the dead man into the cover of a doorway or down that passage between two derelict houses. But this would ruin the clothes. And they were clothes of such good quality. Fashionable.

He had risked much in his life. And for what? Well, he was here. What was one more risk? He heard the hum of traffic from the nearby motorway. One impatient driver seeking a shortcut and he was undone.

He raised the dead man to a sitting position, lolling against the lamppost. He was young, about thirty. A similar age to Hamid. But even in death the face contained the remains of a youth Hamid felt he'd never had. He's a little heavier than me, Hamid judged, but that won't matter. And he started to strip the corpse.

For those who have long given up hope of fortune smiling upon them, when luck arrives it is accepted circumspectly, without shock or celebration. So when Hamid felt the weight of the jacket and discovered the wallet with its credit cards and wad of notes, when he heard the rattle of keys in the trouser pocket, he wasn't surprised; it was as if he were receiving his due.

For Hamid, it was a pleasure to remove his own clothes. Even here in the cold, darkening street. To feel the cheap, warm garments, stiffened by sweat, fall away from him into a pile at his feet. Then to bend slowly to the expensive clothing resting in the dead man's lap. The shirt first. Then shorts. Striped. He didn't check to see if they were stained. It was possible. But he didn't look. Blood. Piss. Shit. He didn't care. If they were, then he would carry the relic of his benefactor with him. The trousers were looser than he would have liked, but he would get a belt. The touch of the sweater. Soft as a woman. He stroked it before taking possession of it. Cashmere.

When all the dead man's clothes were upon Hamid's back, he picked up the shattered spectacles and, folding them, placed them carefully in the top pocket of his jacket. Something else was in there too. Four condoms. Hamid smiled. His first smile for a long time. Then he stooped to the rags beside the dead man and started to dress him.

Getting him back up the lamppost was more difficult than releasing him. After all that hauling and tying of knots, the rope had scoured strips of skin from his fingers and palms.

Inside the wallet, tucked behind banknotes, a card reminded Mr Martin Burrows of Flat 46, St Nicholas Towers, Bell Tower Grove, Edgbaston, Birmingham, that he should visit his dentist on 2 December. Hamid read the dead man's address again.

There was purple in the sky, indicating imminent darkness, when Hamid started to make his way towards Edgbaston. He listened to his footsteps on the pavement. Good leather shoes make a satisfying sound. Better than the humiliating slap of worn rubber from his trainers that had echoed his every step for months now.

As he walked, Hamid was aware that he didn't know what he might have to confront upon his arrival. A wife. A family. An elderly mother, perhaps. It didn't matter. His destiny was held in the elegant click of his shoes.

He thought he knew the way to Edgbaston. He was sure he did. First, make for the city centre. Down to the busy streets. Moving against the traffic, which nosed in follow-my-leader formation, as if attempting to escape a catastrophe or a war zone. A creeping trail of paired lights, moving minutely. Stopping. Moving again. He was faster than they were. He was unafraid of catastrophe or war zones. He had met these devils before. His stride lengthened. There is always a cave, a hollow tree. I need no map. Shoes as expensive as these know where to go.

He stood for a moment, held by his reflection in the large glass doors of St Nicholas Towers. I am a new man. Within his own reflection he saw the lights of the apartment blocks behind him. The city's expensive streets were contained within his shadow on the glass. Inside, a brass plate revealed his apartment was on the fifth floor. The elevator zoomed him soundlessly to it.

He placed the key in the lock and turned. There was no

hesitation. No fear. Nothing to be gained by pause. But there was a tension within his limbs – a coil, ready to spring if action was required. The feeling pleased him. It was the closest he had come to power for a long time. He felt strong again.

The apartment was in empty darkness. Beyond, he recognized a change in the quality of that darkness as a door stood ajar at the end of the hallway. Banging the door behind him, he marched towards it. This is the lounge. The sitting room. A Venetian blind produced stripes of light and lesser darkness against a large window. He found a couch to sit on. This was good. He had come a long way. It was time to sit down and rest. The lights of the city outside sparkled between the slats of the blind.

As he sat at ease on the comfortable couch the shapes in the darkness became distinct. A chair over there. A lamp here beside him at the end of the couch. Of course, such darkness prompted memories. The darkness of his long journey to this country. The sound of the lorry returned to his ears, that constant, relentless drone, which continued for suffocating hour after hour. There were eight of them jammed into the small compartment. Lying flat out. No one spoke. Just the drone of the engine. The stench of themselves.

But the blackness was a joke. There were a lot of jokes. Release. That word could make him laugh. Release from his country that had sunk into darkness. Release from the lorry into the dark days that followed. The hovel they shared. The long hours of drudgery in Durscher's Eight till Late Convenience Store. Unpacking. Stacking. Sweeping. Cleaning. For almost nothing. It was a joke and his pain was the knowledge that it was the end of the road, there was no way out. 'Complain if you wish,' Durscher jeered. 'You'll get not a penny more, you bastards. You're lucky to be here.' He lifted a fat finger and waved it at them in warning. 'Remember. One word from me, to the right people, and you'll be in a cell. Then back home.' So, day followed day like the turning of a millwheel.

'But it is finished,' Hamid whispered to himself. 'Hanging from a lamppost in the dark.'

But when the darkness eventually became intolerable, as darkness does, Hamid reached out and flicked a switch. Instantly the room filled with yellow gloom, a mocking reminder of the bright days he had once known. But he saw there were other lamps in the room and went to them one by one, increasing the light with each flick of a switch; like turning up the sun.

'This is a rich man's apartment,' Hamid muttered as he looked around the room. Large and comfortable. There were pictures in the room that were images of nothing – abstract is what they are called. Their jangled colours spoke of chaos and confusion and it was right they should be here in such a modern room.

In the kitchen a stark strip light made him blink. Such a kitchen. Empty and full at the same time. Smooth steel surfaces reflecting the brightness. There were no handles, but indentations. Perfect finger spaces in the shining flatness. Hamid rested a finger in one and pressed. The door clicked and swung open on a cupboard full of more metal. Pots. Pans. Machines. Another depression produced a drawer of cutlery, another the refrigerator. It held a plate covered in foil. Hamid peeled it back, revealing pink fish. Fresh. Two pieces. Bottles of beer too, lots of them.

Back to the lounge: racks of CDs, a large television, a pile of magazines. But no books, not even a Bible. And certainly no Koran. Hamid looked at the formless rioting colours of the pictures again.

He went into the bedroom. A double bed. This will provide me with great comfort tonight, he thought, and was about to praise God for the blessing bestowed upon him – but he did not, could not. The wheels had turned endlessly in the darkness and here he was in the light. Electric light.

He returned to the kitchen where even the floor shone. The gleam of temple tiles. He pressed his finger into the depressions of the disguised cupboards. One contained bottles of wine. I will drink alcohol tonight in my new home, he thought. He found a corkscrew, large and viciously dangerous, but changed his mind. I will drink beer, as Englishmen do. And he selected a bottle from the refrigerator.

Two pieces of pink fish. He re-covered them. Vaguely, they worried him. The beer was called Budweiser. The label proclaimed it 'The King of Beers'. He had seen bottles of beer like this in Durscher's Eight till Late Convenience Store. There was a large glass-fronted fridge which hummed loudly at the back of the shop filled with different beers, Budweiser prominent among them.

The beer was gassy and very cold. It had little flavour. But after the first gulp it was easy to drink.

Hamid sat on the polished wooden floor of the lounge, flicking through CDs. So many of them. Who had time to listen to so much music? Lots of pop bands he had never heard of. Then some classical music. This he was more familiar with. He selected one: Mozart's Clarinet Concerto, a picture of a castle wreathed in mist on the cover. Through trial and error he discovered how to use the remote control and it pleased him when the music took possession of the room.

He took a second beer and went to the window. It was raining now, a silly indecisive rain. The weather here is like the people, without passion or determination, he thought. The lights of Birmingham were smeared like an abstract painting into white and gold streaks by the weak indecisive rain.

The phone rang. Tension coiled in him again. Four rings. Five. Decisively he moved towards it. But a voice halted him. 'This is Martin. I can't take your call right now. Sorry.' The voice of the dead man. 'But leave a message after the tone and I'll get back to you just as soon as I can.' After a pause, another voice, a man's. 'Martin? Are you there? I thought you'd've been back ages ago. Are you there? I wanted to know how it went. No. You're not there, are you? I'm coming over anyway. See you.' A click, followed by a tone that repeated and repeated. A button on the phone shone yellow. And the tone repeated over and over. It was impossible to ignore. It was destroying the Mozart.

Hamid stooped beside the phone and pressed the yellow button. The phone clicked, then, 'Martin. You greedy, cheatin bastard.' Hamid recognized the tones of a Birmingham accent. He recognized, too, the anger and hostility in the voice. He had met these things before. 'How the fuck did you think you could get away with a stunt like this? You dozy bastard. Listen. Be at the Moscow at two. And bring the stuff with you. And no tricky business. Got that?' Then a woman's voice: 'You were called today at eleven fifty-nine a.m. The caller withheld their number.' The message from the young man who was coming over anyway repeated, before the woman's voice announced tersely, 'End of messages.' Then there was only Mozart.

Hamid went to the kitchen. He selected the largest, sharpest knife he could find. 'I will have to kill him when he arrives,' he said. A statement of fact unaccompanied by any sentiment.

In just a couple of hours Hamid had taken occupancy of Martin's life. He was not going to lose it easily. This is the way things are done. He had never killed before, but he had thought about it many times. It is a pity it is not Durscher, he thought, as he laid the knife behind a cushion and went again to the window. In the watery light he saw the soldiers drag his father and his brother from the house, heard the shots. He heard the screams of his wife and the hungry grunts and chortles of the soldiers. 'I have come so far,' he confided to the city. 'I can do whatever I have to do. I belong to you now.' And once again he had to quell the desire to thank God and to pray. Instead he looked out again onto the weeping city and, as he slurped his beer, the impulse disappeared. Hamid's breath on the glass obscured the lights and he wiped it away to retrieve them.

He replayed the CD as he sat waiting. 'I am a warrior. I will kill as a warrior. I am fighting for the lights out there.' He turned off the lamps and, when the music died, silence and darkness regained the room.

He knew that he had changed. In these clothes he wanted what he had previously despised. This comfortable room. The aggressive kitchen. What else was there now but the gleam of possessions and power? I am here. And his toes stretched in his expensive leather shoes.

When the key turned in the lock he was fully prepared. He was the soldier in the hills ready to rain down terror. He heard the rush of movement through the hallway, but did not move or turn his head until the light sprang on.

The woman stood frozen in the doorway and Hamid thought of the two pieces of pink fish waiting in the refrigerator. Of course.

'What? Who are you?' The voice husky with surprise. 'What are you doing here? Where's Martin?' She was pretty. Blond hair, glittering as it caught the light. Tall and thin. Her pink skirt was very short and she wore a grey furry jacket.

He rose. He would have to move quickly. The man who was coming over anyway would be here soon. I will have to kill twice tonight. So be it. The words came easily to his mind and as he heard them he was convinced by them. Surely she would be too. 'I am to stay here. For a day or two. I am a friend of Martin's. He said he was taking some stuff. He didn't know when he would be back.'

She seemed to be accepting this. She looked him up and down. He felt calm. She might be afraid; he was not: he was a warrior.

Then, suddenly, a cry. 'Why the fuck are you wearing his sweater?'

Still he was unperturbed, though he did not like a woman swearing. But, maybe, this will make it easier. 'I have nothing. He has given me clothes to wear. He has done much for me.'

Cautiously she came further in to the room. 'Where is he?'

What could he say? 'I know only that he has taken the stuff to the place. The Moscow. To meet with the man he has cheated.'

There was a slight gasp. She was weighing the words. They had not been wrong. But Hamid knew they were only purchasing him a little time. They were a currency he was not rich in. Soon she would want more. So, he thought, it will be as it must be.

He was smiling confidently as he sat down. She, unsure what to do, turned, first back towards the hallway, hesitated, then back into the room. Hamid's hand rested on the cushion. He tapped it. His composure reassured her and she took the gesture as an invitation to sit beside him, which she did. Closer than he expected. His nostrils filled with her perfume.

He lifted the bottle of beer towards her. She smiled as she took it, but he did not like the way she guzzled it back. 'Thanks.' She leaned further back, stretching out her long legs.

It was already decided. His erection hurt as it forced itself against the fabric of his pants. He would have her. Two or three times. At least once in the clean bed where he could stretch out above her, here on the couch, on the floor, perhaps across that low table over there. On the magazines.

She was pretty. Painted pretty, but pretty nonetheless.

Her make-up was very heavy. Her lips pink and glossy. The light reflected in her dark eyes. A tiny lamp in each. He let his knee push against hers and she did not object.

'Has Martin told you about me?'

'Yes.' He lifted the knife from behind the cushion and leaned towards her.

'Fucking Jesus!'

Such profanity. Gruff and harsh. She should not speak like this. Her shiny pink mouth was curved in shock. He liked this look on her face. She made to cry out as he moved further towards her, but no sound came. Her eyes darted. She was young and pretty, but wore too much make-up. She was breathing deeply and her skirt was far up her legs. She was frightened but she would relax, he knew it. He could do this for her.

He placed his hand upon her knee, which held steady rather than jerking in alarm. A slight push opened the legs. No resistance. Easy. He knew what he was going to do and pleasure was dripping through him. She averted her eyes – she could not look the enemy in the eye at her moment of surrender. His hand travelled smoothly up the thigh heading for the crotch.

His fingers touched the satin of her pants. He trembled. But then – confusion. A hard obstruction. A shocked realization whipped his hand back, and in that moment a fist reared up beneath his hand, sending the knife hurtling across the room while a punch to the side of his face knocked him from the couch to sprawl upon the floor. With a clatter the knife lodged within the slats of the Venetian blind. She was up and away, high heels kicked to fly across the room. Vaulting the arm of the couch, she made for the door.

Hamid sat blinking on the floor, the feel of hard cock beneath the sweet satin still on his fingers, the knife jangling in the blinds. He heard a door bang.

Waiting for the room to right itself, he stroked his jaw where the blow had landed, then rose, steadying himself against the couch, and made his way towards the window to retrieve his knife. He would return it to the kitchen. Then he would leave.

He tugged at the jammed knife and the blind pulled away from its fixing and jangled to the floor, exposing the city of glinting lights. Their patterns merely hinted at shape – a galaxy of smeary twinkles and glints in the rain. Then her reflection reared up behind him. He turned. She jabbed the corkscrew towards him.

The battle was over. He knew it. He came from a place of certainty, a land of rocks and mountains. Here was the chaos of the abstract; a map in turmoil. She was part of this. He was not. He could not win.

The defeat lay within his dull eyes. She knew, he thought. Understood that for her the threat was gone. She held the power now.

She poked the corkscrew at him as if it were a gun. 'Sit down. There. Now, tell me what's happening.'

It was an impossible command. He didn't have enough words. But he told her what he knew as well as he could.

She was pressing towards him. Listening hard. But there was more. He felt her attention like body weight upon him.

He knew now, however, that he was not to be ripped by the curled metal spike she held. She would not gouge deep holes in his flesh, like those made by bullets, through which his blood would leak to extinction.

But he understood, too, by her breath on his face and the tilt of her body towards him, the look in her eyes, hungry as his people, that there was a price to pay. He had stumbled, fallen. She would exact her price. And he would pay it. Gladly, perhaps. For this is the way things are done here.

He could see her cleavage. Real breasts. Flesh. She had real breasts and a cock. What type of creature is this?

Outside the rain was fierce now. Decisive. It pounded the window viciously, obliterating all but the most eloquent squiggles and daubs.

He had been taken, so obediently he followed her to the bed. It would not be so bad. No. There were those of his countrymen who had chosen a similar path in order to survive, and prospered. It was cash in the pocket for them.

He walked behind her. This was some trust. A compliment from the conqueror. He felt some power returning. He would do it well. He was here. It was his destiny.

In the bedroom he made himself look, watch. The pink skirt fell. He saw the obscure bulge of the satin pants. Pink too. 'Leave them on,' he said. The hips were fine and the painted face so very pretty.

In bed she leaned across him. He could feel her cock hard against his thigh as she reached for the lamp. 'No. Leave it on,' he said.

'Yes, Martin. If that's what you want,' she replied.

Yes, Martin. It is the price we pay. The abstract confusion. But it is okay. And he moved himself on top of her, his cock pressing on hers, and closed his eyes. Tomorrow I will shave my beard. I will cut my hair, he thought.

There came a moment while he was in her, looking down at the pimples on her back, that everything became clear. He had turned his eyes towards the lamp, its light blurring his vision, so that he saw again the pictures in the lounge, his pictures now, the abstracts. He understood that such art could only come from lands where there exists endless electricity, false light, where things collide in it, brutally, but where it is possible to survive such collisions.

Prague Blonde

The barman placed a beer on the counter in front of Matt Fuller and took the proffered piece of paper. His lip curled as he read the address written on it. 'This is a poor area,' he said sadly. 'It is not so nice. It is modern.'

The cold beer tasted good and Matt smacked his lips. 'Great beer.'

'Thank you,' the barman responded politely with a nod of the head and a pleased smile, as if acknowledging a personal compliment. He took a pen from the breast pocket of his white shirt. 'I shall write the metro station you need on here for you. Then, when you turn left out of the metro you will be in this street.' He indicated the third line of the address. 'But it is a long street and the place you want is at the other end. You must walk fifteen minutes at least. Or take a taxi; there will be taxis outside the metro.'

'It's going to be a nice evening. I'll walk.'

The barman nodded sagely. 'Okay. You will know you are close when you come to the tall apartments. Look for this one,' and he tapped the second line of the address: *Rechziegel 4*. He handed the paper back to Matt.

A poor area: he should have expected that. When he had explained to Madame Lubzec last night that he wanted to see the girls she had become dramatically offended. Her long diamond earrings had swung energetically as her

33

initial charm turned to cold disdain. 'I arrange only high-quality girls, very good ones. Mr Crawford will be very happy. There is nothing to worry about.' But Matt had insisted. Crawford had insisted he insist. Whatever you said about Crawford, he was a good businessman. No point in bringing a load of women into the country that (a) aren't attractive, and (b) don't know what they're coming for. No stupid stories about being au pairs or secretaries. These girls were going to be whores and if they weren't that already they needed to know the score.

A young man in a smart blue suit, carrying a leather briefcase, came in. The barman knew him. Matt watched the two men clap hands across the counter in greeting. The barman pulled two beers, one large, the other small, from the swan's neck pump and carried them to the other end of the bar where the man had seated himself on a stool. He loosened his tie and put the briefcase on the floor. The barman placed the large glass before his friend and, leaning against the counter, took the smaller for himself. They touched glasses before drinking. Matt took another long pull from his own glass. It was good: beer with a bite, a tang to it. Better than that Prague Special rubbish he had spent all morning organizing shipments of. Crawford was delighted with the price when he rang him to confirm the deal – just wait till he tasted it. Crawford would have to re-label the bottles. What was he going to call it? Prague Piss?

Matt lit a cigarette. The two men at the other end of the bar were chatting and laughing; good buddies, he decided. He wished he had someone to talk to.

Crawford had made it sound as if he were fixing him up with a free holiday when he told him he wanted him to come over here and sort these deals out. If there's not a beach, palm trees and lots of girls in bikinis then it's no holiday, Matt had told him, but he knew he would have to come. 'That's what I have a lawyer for, Matt. Check these things out for me. Make sure I sign the right pieces of paper. Check the merchandise.' He couldn't argue. He was bloody lucky to have this position with Crawford, he knew that. His fabulous legal career hadn't quite turned out as he had imagined it would. Oh, he was a good lawyer, knew his stuff, had style, anyone would agree. He had just got a little bit greedy in the early days. Poor judgement meant his track record wasn't all it could have been. Shit, who was he kidding? The straight stuff wouldn't touch him now, which was why he was lucky to be with Crawford.

This town was unreal – a fairytale, a stage set, a pop-up book. Through the long window beside him he saw buildings so ornate and decorated, so cutely constructed, they belonged in children's picture books. He had walked around for a while after he had sorted the lager deal, as far as the other side of the river and back, and had felt uneasy at the presence of so much painted history, so much prettiness and gilt, so many churches and clock towers, weathervanes and spires. Give him Birmingham's straightforward concrete and glass any day. He had crossed the bridge through a gallery of huge statues, all saints apparently. He had never been in a town with so many streetlamps, each one like the lanterns on Christmas cards.

He had chosen this bar, Metamorphosis, because it was modern, glass and chrome, the only place he had seen where lines, rather than curves, dominated; the only place that didn't look like an antique shop. But even this place wasn't immune. Attracted by what he saw through the large plate-glass window, he had opened the door expecting cool, modern sounds. Like Whites, his favourite bar in Birmingham. But no: opera was playing, not too loudly, just there in the background, reminding you where you were.

You'd sure never need an alarm clock here, Matt thought as he heard clocks striking the hour outside. He folded the paper and returned it to his wallet. This city full of statues and bells was having a disquieting effect upon him. It was like fetching up in a graveyard.

A young woman was peering through the plate-glass window into the bar. She had a pretty face and her spiky blond hair gave her a pixieish quality. Was she looking for someone? Perhaps she was another of the barman's friends. Would she come in? Matt wondered what the rest of her looked like, and when she turned and moved away he swallowed the remains of his beer, took his cigarettes from the counter, shouted goodbye to the barman and left.

Following the girl for a few minutes would be a pleasant distraction, although he hoped she wouldn't travel too far or too fast; it was a bloody hot day. He realized just how strong Czech beer was when, quickening his pace to catch up with her, his balance faltered for a second. Yes, he would enjoy following her for a while, watching the stride of her long legs. She was stylish. Above black jeans she wore a white top that exposed her midriff, printed with bold black flower shapes: some round like daisies, others trumpets, like lilies. He wondered what she did for a living. She was good-looking and elegant enough to be a model, or a whore. He wanted to see her face again and when she stopped to look into a bookshop window he carried on so that he could position himself further along the cobbled street and watch her walk towards him.

She was striking; yes, decidedly so. Her skin was pale and her features finely chiselled. She was tall and thin, with small breasts, a woman of lines and angles rather than curves, which pleased him. Her eyes were blue and she wore very little make-up; she didn't need it with a complexion like that. As she passed him, Matt saw she wore a stud in her belly. He followed. They turned right and quickly right again. Then left into a street of small pink houses, still storybook houses; cottages where the good witches live.

Matt was starting to formulate a plan to get talking to her. Asking directions was probably the easiest. Let her get me lost and then ask her to show me the way home.

It was a surprise when she suddenly disappeared into a wall a few metres in front of him. Where she had vanished he found a simple wooden door with a latch handle. A metal strip read THE CHURCH OF ST JOSEPH. Matt stepped back to take his bearings. The curved wall was the back of the church. He returned to the door, lifted the latch and entered. He was in a lobby. Empty. Labelled coat-pegs reminded him of schooldays. There was a wall-font where the faithful could bless themselves with holy water before entering the church proper. He pushed through the swing doors and found himself standing between two stone columns that reached up and became sinuous stone fingers supporting the vaulted ceiling. The enormous, cavernous church smelt of incense and candles; holy smells, he guessed. Making his way between carved oak pews to the central nave he scanned for the black-flowered shirt, the blond hair.

Further up the long nave, in front of the gilded high altar, a group of musicians was preparing to give a recital. People sat in the first rows of pews, waiting. He couldn't see her. He let his eyes travel again, more slowly this time, along the pews, like a panning camera. No, she definitely wasn't there. He checked the musicians: she hadn't joined them. He looked down the aisle to the large central doors with their brown glass panels.

Perhaps she had just used the church as a shortcut. As he made for the main doors he saw her, kneeling in a side chapel. He continued down the aisle towards the doors, but turned left before them and doubled back up to the chapel, which he entered side-on so he saw her in profile, kneeling in candlelight before some saint: a young nun with a serene face holding a wooden cross and a bouquet of pink roses.

The eyes of the girl in the black-flowered top were closed; a rosary hung from her fingers. She had placed a square of black lace on her head. Quietly Matt took a seat near her. At first he was repulsed by this vision of the woman at her devotions. Peeping into the bar, swinging her hips through the streets, browsing the bookstore window, she had seemed so modern and carefree, so very attractive and exciting. Now, seeing her kneeling in submissive worship, Matt was unsure how he felt. He looked at the plaster statue of the saint and then again at the blond girl: both were beautiful women, but only one was flesh and blood, and she was very beautiful flesh, her alabaster complexion as faultless as the saint's. Matt watched the beads move through her fingers. Occasionally her lips moved too.

Matt wondered, as he often had before, how young people could buy into all this. He wanted to go up to her, place his hands on the black lace square, feel the press of her spiky hair beneath it and slide his cock into her mouth, nudging her head back and forth on it. He hardened immediately and awkwardly he had to stand to adjust himself. His movement made the girl's eyes flicker open, but only for a second. Before Matt was seated again they were closed.

In the church behind them the musicians were tuning their instruments. Matt's desire was so strong now it was hurting and the trail of fantasies occupying his mind demanded some resolution. If the church were empty he could just walk up behind her . . . He stopped himself. There must be a toilet in this place. He rose quickly, heading for the main doors. Beyond it, in the entrance, two women sat at a green baize table like card players, collecting entrance money for the concert. 'Toilet?' he asked, and one pointed to another door.

After his jerk-off, Matt took one of the hotel cards he had been given when he checked in and wrote on the back:

My name is Matt Fuller. I am English. You are very beautiful. Better than the saint. Can I take you to dinner? Tomorrow would be good. Ring me if I can. Matt. Room 217.

She was no longer in the chapel when he returned but Matt saw she had joined those listening to the recital. A woman played the piano, another sat in front of her playing the cello. The others held their instruments still, awaiting their moment. She was sitting alone at the end of a pew. When he tapped her shoulder she jumped.

'Excuse me.' He tried to sound upbeat. 'Can I give you this?' And he handed her the card. As she bent to read it he turned and left, resisting with difficulty as he marched down the aisle the temptation to turn and see if she was looking after him. When he reached the doors he slowed, just in case she had risen and was following him out, but she hadn't, she wasn't.

He was right. Central Prague is a stage set, nothing more; for an operetta, or a camp nineteenth-century tragedy. It is not real. Matt emerged from the metro and it was as if he had pushed through the ornate scenery into the wings of the theatre beyond where the grubby stagehands work; where cables and wheels and discarded props and all the mundane sweaty mechanisms that create the fantastic illusion lie in disorderly heaps.

In the bright early evening heat Matt sweated his way along the disconcertingly straight street, lined on both sides with row upon row of cramped metropolitan housing. Beyond rose factory chimneys billowing purple, black, grey, yellow smoke which gave a chemical sourness to the air and coated the inside of his mouth. This was real all right. Not a gothic church or baroque tower in sight. No gargoyles or coats of arms or mannerist graffiti. You would find no princes or princesses here, no fairies or goblins.

The mundane urban spell cast by so many houses packed so closely together was broken occasionally by a group of shops, a petrol station, a concrete playground or a small brown door stamped, like well-travelled luggage, with stickers bearing the names of a variety of beers, indicating a bar.

The houses stopped abruptly as if halted in their progress by a tall gaggle of tower blocks through which ran a railway line. Washing hung from balconies. Children played noisy football on the strips of dried grass between them. Boys on skateboards, young men on mopeds sped in and out of the darkness at their stilted bases.

Matt located the block signed *Rechziegel 4* and looked up at the towering concrete pocked with metal balcony guards and square windows glittering blackly in the bright sunlight. Crimson geraniums trailed optimistically from a few balconies. From one hung a white sheet, a slogan in Czech scrawled across it in red.

This was it: *Rechziegel 4*. He was seized by disgust. This huge grey tenement, this whole area, disgusted him. He wanted to be away from it. The business he was about to conduct – yes, that disgusted him too, but he was used to that feeling, he had come to terms with what he was now, Crawford's agent; the dreams of a fine legal career turned to ashes long ago. This feeling now was something more. Deeper. It was the blonde. What he had wanted to do in the Church of St Joseph. Something like trembling was happening inside him.

He needed a drink. He moved away from *Rechziegel 4* and continued down the unending road until he came to another group of shops: a hairdresser's, a grocer's, a pharmacy, a haberdashery; and sure enough a small brown door covered in beer stickers. He opened it and descended the brick steps.

It seemed at first, with its low, beamed ceiling, like a bar set up in the cellar of someone's house. A large television set fixed to the far wall. In a corner, surrounded by stools, a small bar. As Matt's eyes adjusted to the gloom he saw there were alcoves along the other wall, each with leatherette-padded fixed seats and a table. At the other end of the room was an arch through which he could see a pool table. He smiled. Not unlike the Little Moscow. He wondered if this place attracted a similar clientele. British punk rock from the seventies was playing, fast and furious, but not loud enough. You wouldn't hear that in the Little Moscow. From the beams behind the bar hung several dusty string puppets like the condemned on a medieval gallows. Matt took one of the bar stools.

A fat, middle-aged barman wearing nylon football shorts and a striped waistcoat over a T-shirt trundled towards him, expertly avoiding the hanging puppets. Matt ordered a beer. Card players at a table near the bar raised their eyes from their hands when they heard his English accent. There was a cuckoo clock behind the bar, a poster of Michael Schumacher, a trophy cup on a small shelf and another clock, an old one with roman numerals and a pendulum. The barman delivered Matt's beer in a heavy glass jug. A rack of similar jugs hung behind the bar, each with a name on a grubby label beneath it.

In one of the alcoves a fat girl in a short black skirt was asleep, her head resting on the shoulder of a man in blue overalls. His hand was up the girl's skirt; like a mole it formed hillocks in the fabric as it burrowed around. Now Matt saw there was a different sort of clock in each alcove. Then he noticed three framed drawings of wristwatches on the wall beside the stairs down which a group of middle-aged men in the same blue overalls as the man in the alcove was now descending.

The man in the alcove removed his hand from beneath the girl's skirt. The barman took labelled jugs to fill with beer for the workmen. This was Friday evening, Matt remembered; the end of the working week for these guys. They were laughing and joking with each other and making fun of the man with the still sleeping girl. A middle-aged woman in sunglasses, wearing a ra-ra skirt and a football shirt, came down the steps. She pushed her shades up into her dyed blond hair and peered round. One of the workmen called to her and she made her way towards the group.

Someone touched Matt's shoulder, making him jump. It was the fat girl. She laughed at his reaction, then spoke to him in Czech, pointing at the pack of Benson & Hedges lying on the counter beside his jug of beer. 'Oh, sure.' He handed her the pack and lit a cigarette for her. She inhaled deeply and exhaled into his face. This, he guessed, was supposed to be a come-on. A large thigh pressed into his knee.

'You English?' she asked breathily. Definitely a come-on.

Matt turned his head. Her companion was watching from the alcove. 'Yes, I am,' he replied.

'I love English cigarettes very much,' she said slowly and huskily. 'I love everything English.' Oh boy, this was going to lead to trouble if he wasn't careful. She beamed a smile and brought her face closer to his. 'I like Man-ches-tah U-nye-ted. And tea. I like Shakes-peare. Row-meow and Joolet. Row-meow. Row-meow.' And extraordinarily, and in such broken English it was difficult to understand exactly what she was saying, she continued to recite lines from the speech.

Matt could feel the eyes of her man drilling into his back from the alcove. He saw that the barman was watching them too. He stopped her. 'That's very good. I am very impressed. You know it better than I do. Here,' he said, handing her the cigarettes. 'Take the pack. I have another.'

She didn't follow all of the words, but she understood the gesture, although she was going to make a meal of it. 'For me?' She smiled coquettishly.

'Sure.' Matt was careful not to smile back, not to look directly into her face at all: just be polite and hope she goes away.

'Tank yer. Ser merch.'

'Don't mention it.'

As she moved away she rubbed her arse against Matt's leg.

Once she was safely back in the alcove the barman winked at him, the first friendly gesture Matt had received from him, and ran his finger across his throat. Matt responded by finishing his beer in one and heading for the stairs. Back to *Rechziegel 4*.

The building stank. It had been a ferociously hot day yet this building still smelt damp. A battered number board told Matt that apartment 104 was on the fourteenth floor and a metal arrow directed him towards the lift in the centre of the building. The concrete floor had once been covered with green tiles; now only a few remained.

He hadn't wanted to come on this bloody job organizing cheap lager contracts. Then when Crawford had mentioned the girls, sorting out this deal too, the idea became more appealing. What a fool he was. He should have known it would be tacky and sordid: what else could it be? But, if he was honest, wasn't it this that excited him?

The lift was currently at the ninth of eighteen floors. He needed the fourteenth. Matt pressed the downward arrow beside the doors. In a corner a young woman with very black hair eyed him as she smoked a cigarette and pushed a grizzling infant back and forth in a buggy.

At his command the lift rose noisily to the eleventh floor and returned to the ninth. Matt pressed the arrow again, more forcefully this time. The lift hummed and buzzed; the lighted indicator moved from nine to ten to eleven. Matt heard metal clank hollowly somewhere high above. Then the light reversed to nine. He tried again: the process repeated. He tried the upward arrow but the response was the same. Matt looked across to the black-haired woman. She stared coldly, threw her cigarette end to the floor and looked away.

There was no alternative; it was the stairs. He located a blue fire-door that gave him access to the cold and smelly stairwell. He looked up and saw the stairs ascend in four sections to make a turn of each floor. Fourteen floors. Fuck it! They went on for ever. He started to climb. High above, a woman was crying, sobbing hysterically. A man shouted. A door banged. The urge to get out of this hole was strong. But what was he getting so worked up about? There were places like this in Birmingham. Every city in the world probably. He'd been on the estates: Frankley, Pool Farm, the Vale. So what was the problem? This city? Like chocolates in a beautiful box, yet you lift the lid to find them all rotten. Or was it the blonde in the church? Or the way he had felt about the blonde in the church? What he would like to have . . . might have? Enough. Get on with the job. He concentrated on counting each blue door as he reached another floor. Eventually he arrived at the door marked 14 and was surprised that he had sufficient energy to pull it open.

104. The zero was missing; beneath the gap a fish-eye spy-hole. Matt sucked damp air into his lungs, made a fist and rapped on the door.

It opened slowly to reveal a stretching security chain and beyond it a slice of a guy in shades and a baseball cap.

'I'm here to see Madame Lubzec,' Matt told him.

Through the narrow space the guy lifted a finger and closed the door. Matt heard the chain being released. It opened again and the guy waved Matt in and led him along a narrow hallway to a sitting room. In the middle of the room, behind an office desk, sat Madame Lubzec. Next to her, looking ready for the beach in a T-shirt and baggy shorts, stood – Matt blinked – yes: Prince William.

Madame Lubzec saw Matt's expression of disbelief and laughed delightedly. The long earrings, ebony today, swung noisily and frantically. Like a chandelier in an earthquake, Matt thought.

'Ah, Mr Fuller, I see you have noticed the resemblance between Ion and your Prince William.' Madame Lubzec beamed. The W of William was pronounced as a V, giving the word an ugly, aggressive sound.

Ion pushed back his fringe and smiled shyly.

'Yes,' Matt muttered. 'Remarkable.'

Madame Lubzec's ring-studded hand reached out and touched Ion's thigh just inside the leg of his shorts. Her eyes rolled. She *was* in a good mood today. 'Already he does look-a-like work here. When his English is better I will take him to London, America. We will make a lot of money, don't you think?'

'Yes, I'm sure you will.'

There was a pause. Madame Lubzec's hand remained inside the leg of Ion's shorts and it seemed she was deciding whether to withdraw it or let it travel further upwards. Ion spread his legs a touch providing her with more room if that was what she wanted. The guy who had let Matt in was sprawled in an elderly brown leatherette armchair, watching, and Matt could see two other guys drinking coffee and smoking in the kitchen behind Madame Lubzec.

'The girls. Business.' Matt reminded Madame Lubzec that he was still there.

*

Madame Lubzec's set-up occupied several flats on this floor. He was taken by her and the guys from the kitchen, Lukas and Pavel, into the flat next door where the current crop of girls had been assembled. There were eight of them, all in bras and pants. First impressions were good. They all seemed pretty enough, one or two exceedingly so. Matt looked each one over carefully. The girls smiled at him enticingly.

Matt pointed to one, a girl whose coarse black hair was tied behind her head in two tails. Her eyes smouldered as black as the ebony of Madame Lubzec's earrings. Her small pink mouth pouted provocatively, but it was rehearsed and uncertain. 'How old is she?'

'Elizabeth is just eighteen.'

'No,' Matt contradicted emphatically. 'Thirteen. Fourteen at the most.'

'She is very pretty. And experienced,' Madame Lubzec said. The girl was starting to remove her bra. Her look was defiant.

'No. Not her.' Madame Lubzec accepted this, clicked her fingers and one of the guys took the girl away.

Matt surveyed the others again. All had black hair except for two sandy redheads. 'Are those two sisters?'

'Dorothy and Kylie. Yes.' Matt knew that back home plenty of men would pay premium rates to screw a pair of sisters. These two were definites.

'Where are these girls from?'

'Bulgaria. Romania.' She pointed to the most beautiful girl. 'Jessica is from Slovenia.' Madame Lubzec watched Matt's expression. 'She is very nice, yes?'

'Yes.'

Madame Lubzec leered at Matt, poked his arm. 'You would like to see more of her? There is time.' The girl had risen from her chair and was swaying her hips.

'No. Not right now.'

Matt looked at the girls a final time. 'Yes. We'll take all of these,' he confirmed.

He expected trouble from Madame Lubzec when they got down to business, not over money – that had been settled the day before – but over the security of Crawford's investment. When Matt photographed each girl's face and left hand with his phone, she tutted, clicked her tongue in irritation and said this was very irregular and quite unnecessary since she had an excellent international reputation, but made no more of it than that. Matt keyed each girl's name in with her photographs. They had all been given ludicrous English names: Josephine Smith; Audrey Burton; even Dorothy Perkins. The sisters had different surnames. Lucas and Pavel in turn led each girl away as Matt finished with her.

'We will go back next door to finish our business,' Madame Lubzec told him when the last of the girls was gone. As they were leaving the flat, she snapped a comment at Pavel. He nodded. Matt narrowed his eyes. He disliked it when people he was conducting business with spoke to each other in a language he didn't understand. Madame Lubzec saw this. 'I am telling him to bring the mothers back,' she explained. 'This is their room.'

'The mothers?'

'I have a number of girls who aren't attractive enough for entertaining – not for the higher levels of income. They provide a surrogacy service for childless couples. From all over. America. France. Sweden. I even have a Russian couple waiting now.'

'They live here?'

'I have six flats on this floor where they come for the final weeks of pregnancy. So we can look after them. The girls in transit are on the floor above.'

Back in the flat with the missing zero Matt rang Crawford, who told him to go ahead and conclude the deal. Matt handed over half the money, the other half to be paid when the girls arrived in Folkestone.

Madame Lubzec said that Ion would drive him back to his hotel and offered to let him take Jessica with him for the night as a token of goodwill, but Matt didn't feel any goodwill towards Madame Lubzec and though tempted by the thought of Jessica, he declined both offers.

Matt woke covered in sweat, his mouth parched. He peeled back the sheet. He had been dreaming. He was falling down a lift-shaft or a stairwell or some combination of the two.

The room was baking hot. Its windows did not open. He wished he had had the presence of mind to buy some bottled water. He had got drunk. That was stupid. After leaving Madame Lubzec he had wanted company. He had wandered back to the clock bar and played pool with some of the blue-overalled workmen. There was an electricity plant near by where most of them worked. The more he drank the better he seemed able to make sense of what they said. They had taught him some Czech words, but they were all gone now. He remembered the fat girl in the black skirt draping herself round him as he sat on a barstool after being beaten at pool. The man from the alcove had disappeared. She'd kissed Matt and he'd rubbed his hands across her arse. He had considered taking her upstairs and out into the street, finding somewhere to screw her – the stairwell of one of the tower blocks, he thought – but he hadn't. She had been sticky with sweat as she clung to him.

Now a couple were humping in the room next door. The bed squeaked rhythmically. Matt heard occasional sighs and gasps from the woman; mumbled words. He lay back down on his bed and listened to their noise, slowly jerking himself. He spat on the palm of his hand and smeared his cock. He thought of the girl in the church and wondered if she was in bed with someone right now; bound to be. He wondered if she would ring. He imagined her here with him. When the bed next door went crazy and he heard grunts and calls, he shot his load too. He wiped himself on the sheet and threw it to the foot of the bed.

In the bathroom he swallowed glasses of tap water. Sated, he stepped into the shower and let the water run cold. He dried off and returned to bed. The guy next door was snoring now, as rhythmically as he had been fucking a few minutes before.

But for Matt Fuller sleep wouldn't come. He was plagued by imaginings. The wank hadn't worked, merely got some motor running he couldn't stop. How long would he be able to keep this thing caged? It was there, inside. Just waiting. Shit! He was sweating again. It was pouring out of him. His mouth was dry as fuck. Stop this. Take control. Think. Okay, he had ended up on the shady side of the street, but he was young, intelligent, good-looking, rich and getting richer.

It was futile. He was out of bed and getting dressed before he realized the battle was over.

In daylight he hated this place. Now, outside, in the smoky blue shadow of summer darkness, he felt at home. It seemed that these dim narrow passages were where he had wanted to be all his life. Loneliness and shame counted for nothing now. He was comfortable with the tension within him. A good ache. An exciting throb. The city wasn't empty; he could hear noises, voices, cars, shards of music, but all outside the capsule within which he walked. He lit a cigarette, enjoyed the burn of hot smoke in his chest. Held it there for a long time before exhaling. Watched it circle and twist away from him into the Prague night. His hands were slimy with sweat. He recalled the fat girl in the clock bar. He knew why he had not pursued her, why he had turned Jessica down: it was the blonde he wanted. He threw his cigarette to the ground and moved on. Nothing was more exciting than this.

It was by the church that he heard the click of high heels. Click, click in the warm night. He followed the curve of the old walls, honey-coloured in the dim streetlight. Sweet.

She was alone. Walking slowly. Wearing a skirt now. And high heels. Click. Click. He saw her hair in the lamplight: the Prague blonde. You make a wish in some places and it comes true. He knew he would find her here. The image of the plaster saint she had prayed before swayed through his mind like the flicker of candlelight. He was overwhelmed. This was real, true, it was happening. He took off like a sprinter towards her, taking her off her feet and up against the church wall. The screaming was fuel to the engine of his desire. He covered her mouth with his hand, tugged her head back towards him. It wasn't her. But it was a Prague blonde. Angles, lines, like her. He could feel the layers of deception and repression fall away, allowing him to meet himself in the fearful gleam of the woman's eyes. She bit hard into his chin, tugged viciously at his ear, spat. It was wonderful.

Fuck. The skirt was leather. He pulled at her top, which split in one. She spat again. It dripped down his face and he licked it into his mouth. His hand was up her skirt, dragging her pants down. Hers was in her top pulling out a whistle. Matt took her off the ground, sent her pants flying. A powerful tug ripped open his jeans, his dick striding out as they folded to his feet. The whistle rang out authoritatively, like the start of a football match. Then again and again. It meant nothing. He pushed her beneath him to the ground. He thanked God when he saw the look in her eyes. Nothing. Everything. Everything was worth it for this. He grabbed her legs. Hoisted them. The whole city fell away. Time, the universe, this blonde: they were all his. Lord of it all. He was going to bang into the soft flesh at the heart of this woman. Fuck this whole fucking city. Thrust it away to sparks of light and dust. Even the siren squealing was no more than another visceral colour in the tableau.

His throat constricted. Air? There was no sound either, it seemed. Something gripped his throat. His head hit the ground. The cop rammed his boot onto Matt's chest. The blonde fizzled away. Sound was back: he heard bells, chimes, marking the hour. Lonely sounds, he thought.

As he was dragged to the car, the old stones scouring the skin from his knees, his arms pulled achingly high above him, the angels of mundanity and consequence, not always natural companions, arrived. How quickly it all happened; the chimes hadn't finished by the time he was cuffed and thrown into the back of the police car. Two capped officers sat in the front. The car roared away. He could hear the men in front of him talking in a language he hadn't a hope of understanding.

It was over. He knew. He had glimpsed – more, he had reached in and felt. He knew what he was. But it was over. Beyond the car window the sickly lights of the city, brown as old skin, held their peace. It was nothing. They were heading for darkness and going fast. Matt did not care. The best he could hope for was that it would swallow them all. Swallow everything.

The car stopped in an area of tower blocks. He was backstage again. Beneath a modern streetlight: blue cold. And in that light the officer in the passenger seat turned. He smiled. Matt blinked. Yes. It might have been a thousand years ago, but yes, it was – Prince William.

Pavel turned. 'Get out, Mr Fuller.' He reached over and flicked the catch. Matt shuffled but his jeans were as good as cuffs round his ankles. Ion came round and pulled; Pavel, still inside the car, gave his arse a shove.

It did not feel like shame to Matt. In fact he felt nothing. Standing there, exposed and pathetic in blue light in front of the two policemen. Then feeling returned. As if someone had shouted 'Action', or lifted a spell. His brain clicked into gear. Shit! These two, policemen. Working undercover. Madame Lubzec? Perhaps she was a cop too. Christ! What a mess. At least Crawford wouldn't be able to get at him in a Czech jail. At least, he didn't think he could.

'Where are your credit cards?' Pavel asked him.

'In my hotel safe.'

He smiled at him. 'You should have accepted Madame Lubzec's offer of the girl. Not gone round the streets try-ing to rape our whores when they are tired and only want their beds.' He laughed. 'Well, Mr Fuller, it will cost you twenty thousand dollars to get out of this. Is your credit that good?'

Matt didn't hesitate. 'Sure is.'

'I thought so.'

Ion said something to Pavel in Czech. 'Oh, and Ion likes your wristwatch very much. Your Rolex.' The watch had been pushed up his arm.

'Sure. As soon as the cuffs come off it's yours.' Ion understood and smiled.

They uncuffed him and Matt pulled up his jeans. The button was gone and the zip broken so he had to hold them up. He felt the sagging fabric sticking to his bleeding knees.

'We will take you back to your hotel,' Pavel told him. 'Ion will stay with you until the banks open. Then we will take you to the airport. All your business here is done, I believe.'

*

When they had their dollars, Ion brought Matt back to the hotel to collect his things. Matt had to check he understood. Knowing Ion's English was poor he spoke carefully. 'You are a real policeman.'

Ion laughed loudly. 'Oh yes. Real.'

'And Pavel?'

'All who work for Madame Lubzec are policemen. We are still a poor country. We all have two jobs.'

As he was checking out, the receptionist handed him a card with the hotel's name and logo on. 'You had a telephone call last night.'

He looked at the card. On it was written: *Your friend from St Joseph's rang at 7.15. Her number is 0942 79700.* A line ran through the final zero so Matt wasn't sure whether it was part of the number or not.

Matt Fuller looked from the cheesy grin on Crawford's mouth to the honey-coloured liquid foaming in front of him.

'Looks the part,' Crawford said. It was true, it did. Crawford took a heavy pull on the lager. 'This is good stuff, Matt.'

Matt took a swig and pretended to like the drink. Still tastes like piss, he thought.

'Just get the new labels printed,' Crawford said, 'and we're away.'

Matt wiped his mouth. 'Blonde,' he sighed. 'Prague Blonde. That's what you should call it.'

Crawford cheered. 'I like it. I fucking like it, Matt.' He lifted his glass. 'Prague Blonde.'

Ash

Ashley lit up when he reached Harold North's grave. He didn't know why he always did it here, but he did. He inhaled deeply. The hot smoke hit his chest and he held it there for as long as he could before exhaling. He looked at his watch. Nearly eleven. Halfway through break.

He made for the area of trees and benches beyond the long stretch of graves. Sometimes when he came here a scattering was happening and he had to hold back, but today all was clear and it was too cold for anyone to be sitting with their memories or their grief on one of the benches. He had the place to himself.

He headed for the laurel bush, squatted and let a finger touch the frozen ground. The ashes of his mom, and later his nan, who had looked after him for a while, had been scattered here. He inhaled again. Stroked the ragged tufts of grass. Green. But not summer green. This was the harsh, dull, metallic green of winter. Perhaps the cigarettes would kill him. He hoped so. That's what it promised on the pack.

Shivering, he stood and pulled his blazer tighter round himself. He wished he wasn't so skinny. He wished he was clever and good-looking. He wished he was good at football so he could become a professional and be rich. He was good at snooker, but not good enough for it to come to anything. The same with darts. He hated school. Hated it. All talk about the future. Promises. Lies more like.

Sometimes when he came up here he talked to his mom and his nan. But not today. It was too cold – and it was pointless anyway. He stamped his feet as he took a last hefty pull on his cigarette, dragging the fire right down to the nub. He flicked it away, held the smoke in his chest until it hurt – someone had told him it was the same burn you felt when you got cancer, better get used to it – then exhaled. He could do a ring, but he wondered if anyone could do a question mark. He had tried to work out how you would have to position your lips, what you should do with your tongue, how much suction was needed in the cheeks. He had got somewhere near a few times but not close enough for it to be recognized as a question mark. He lit another cigarette. If he could get it right perhaps he could work out how to do lots of other shapes, writing even, go on telly and be famous. Tour the clubs.

A procession of black cars was making its way through the gates. Ashley wondered what that would be like as a job. Last summer he had talked to some of the undertaker blokes as they stood smoking at the back of the chapel waiting for the funeral to end so they could drive the people home. They were okay. They had joked with him about wagging school, about smoking at thirteen, said what he needed was a bloody good hiding – like they'd had as kids when they'd done those things. But they were all right. He liked the way they were fooling around, swearing and joking one minute, then becoming all serious and kind the instant the chapel doors opened and the mourners filed through. Like his dad changed when the cops turned up and changed in another way when the lads came round.

His phone toned. A message from Karl. *U bin spotted. Maddocks bin looking 4U. Whitlocks just taken a register. I got your coat in my bag.* More trouble. So what? Ashley didn't care. They couldn't do anything, not really. Last night Maddocks had kept him behind. Pointless. Just standing there in his office while the headmaster got on with reading and signing a whole stack of forms. For an hour he had just stood there, being deafed out, like he was invisible. Stupid.

On the way home after his detention Ashley had stopped at a greengrocer's and bought a banana. He spent ages in the bathroom trying to stuff it into his arse, using soap as a lubricant. He remembered a joke about gays using soap. His plan had been to ram it all the way in, make his arse bleed, then go to the cops. Tell them the headmaster had shagged him. He had formulated the plan while standing, jam-packed with anger, in his office watching him sign forms. It was the perfect plan. If he could get Maddocks sent down for a long stretch Ashley knew the Criminal Injuries Board paid out huge amounts in abuse cases. He'd probably be able to sue the Education too. And if he made out he was so messed up by it he couldn't work he could probably claim invalidity benefit for a few years as well. A master plan.

But the banana hurt too much. Like fire. Less than a fingertip length in and he thought he was going to pass out. He gritted his teeth and pushed. The pain consumed his entire torso. He tried again, and then again, but it was useless. Then his dad was banging on the door. 'What you doin in there, Ash, avin a fuckin wank? I need a shit.'

The house was empty when Ashley got back. He went across to the Highbury. His dad was in the bar with Kieran.

'What you doin ere? You should be in school.'

'Waggin it.' Ashley sat down on the padded bench beside the men. Baz was behind the bar. He squinted across at Ashley, but Baz was all right, he just raised his eyebrows.

'Can I have some crisps?'

The Weasel fished in his pocket, produced a pound coin and banged it down on the table in front of his son who lifted it and made for the fruit machine, where he turned the single coin into three. He went to the bar and bought two bags of crisps.

'I've got enough for two scratch cards now,' he smirked as he rejoined the men. 'What you over here for anyway?'

'Shurrup and eat your dinna,' the Weasel told him.

'You never fed the dog,' Ashley accused. 'She's starvin.'

'Greyhounds are supposed to be thin.'

'The fucking thing can hardly stand.'

'Same again, Weeze?' Kieran lifted the empty pint glasses. The Weasel nodded. 'Ta.'

'D'you want a drink, Ash?'

'I'll have a Coke.'

MTV was on the big screen in the corner of the bar but the sound was low. Michael Jackson was singing 'Thriller'. Ashley hated Michael Jackson. He was a freak.

While Kieran was at the bar the Weasel turned to his son. 'I'm pleadin guilty, Ash.'

The boy stopped eating. 'Oh, fuck.'

'It's for the best. There's no point going to trial. They've got too much on us. We're goin for guilty.' Ashley was fighting back the tears. 'Ere,' his father said, 'ave a fag.' He pushed his pack across the table.

'How long will you get?'

'Between three and five. Most likely three though.'

'Oh, fuck.'

'Ere. Now don't go gettin upset.' The Weasel tapped a cigarette from the pack and handed it to the boy. 'Ere.' Ashley put it in his mouth. His father struck a match. Ashley inhaled.

'That's better. It'll be all right, son.'

'All right? Of course it won't be fuckin all right. What's goin to happen to me? They'll stick me in care.'

'No. No, they won't. I promise. I'm workin somethin out.'

When Kieran returned with the drinks, Ashley was shaking. 'What's wrong with the kid?' he asked the Weasel. 'Cold?'

'I've just told him. About the guilty plea.'

Kieran sat down and leaned towards Ashley. 'It's for the best, Ash, honest. It'll save him two years.'

Ashley couldn't speak. He had stopped the tears, but he couldn't control the trembling or the snot running from his nose.

Kieran pushed a plastic sachet to the Weasel.

'Go and blow your nose, son.' He dropped the sachet in Ashley's lap beneath the table. 'Ere, but only a line, mind. Just to make you feel better.'

'You should do something about his spots, Weeze,' Kieran said, as the two men watched the boy make his way towards the Gents. 'Take him to the doctor before you go down.'

The Weasel lifted his beer and took a gulp. 'Fat chance. E won't even let me squeeze em for im.'

After school Karl brought Ashley's coat round for him. 'Come in the kitchen,' Ashley told him. 'It's warm in here. I'm making my tea. Want some toast?'

Karl shook his head. 'Maddocks had me,' he told Ashley. 'Asked if I knew where you'd gone. Said he's going to ring your dad.'

Ashley snorted. 'Phone's off.' St George snuffled round Karl's feet. The boy stroked her head.

Ashley lined fish fingers up on a slice of toast, poured tomato ketchup over them and put another slice on top. He bit into the sandwich. A fish finger slipped out to the floor. The dog pounced on it. Karl laughed.

'Me dad's pleadin guilty.' Karl felt awkward, so he said

nothing, just patted the dog's head. 'E'll get three years.'
Karl still didn't know what to say. 'So I'm in the shit.
Don't know what to do.' There was no point beating
about the bush. 'D'you think your mom'd let me stay at
yours? Till I'm sixteen. A sort of foster. She'd get benefit.
Some sort of allowance. At least fifty quid a week.
Probably more, I'm Special Needs.'

Karl had to say something. 'Dunno. I'll ask her.'

'Thanks.'

'Are we going to nick some radios tonight?'

'Yeh, all right. When I've finished my tea. D'you want
to see *Neighbours*?'

'Might as well.'

When the programme was finished and the boys were
leaving the house Ashley grasped Karl's arm. 'If your mom
won't have me, d'you think she'd let you look after the dog?'

'Dunno. I'll ask her.'

Then there was the pigeons. What to do about the
pigeons?

Taking the tin of feed from under the sink he walked
down the narrow strip of garden to the shed. He drew the
bolt. The hungry birds swooped around him. Ashley made
the squawking sound, *chorkee*, *chorkee*, *chorkee* as he
cast the feed in arcs around the shed.

This was stupid, he might just as well let them go, just
leave the door open, let them join up with the street
pigeons, give them their freedom. There was one week to
go till the trial. There would be no one to look after them
then. Not that his dad did much of a job of looking after
them. He used to, years ago when Ashley's mom was alive.
He had good pigeons then, looked after them properly,
raced them seriously. Ashley remembered when he was a
little kid watching his dad taking them, one by one, and
thrusting them away, sending them tumbling upwards, as

if thrown by a juggler into the sky, their great highway. Ashley used to love watching that.

When he returned to the shed none of them had left. They couldn't be bothered. All instinct was gone now. Standing in their midst, he gently lifted the nearest grey bird, a collar of white around its neck, from a perch, stroked the length of the head with his fingers, then quickly grasped, tugged, felt the quick jerk of the body, a fluttering of the wings, then stillness. He dropped the bird to the floor, reached for another and repeated the action, then reached for another until a dozen birds lay dead on the shit-encrusted floor of the shed.

Soon he would have to do something about the dog.

Ashley did churches on Sunday mornings, sometimes with Karl. It was easy. If the alarms went off people were slow to return to their cars. You can't just rush out of a church service. He could do half a dozen in a morning, no problem.

Ashley took the radios round to Easy Ted Nicholls for a fiver a time. Ted flogged them at car-boot sales. 'You're a little bastard,' Ted told him.

'Oh yeah?'

'Yeah. What you did to your dad's birds.' Ted cuffed the side of Ashley's head.

'Piss off.'

'Then you let the fuckin dog eat em.'

'She was hungry.'

'Fuckin loon, you are. Broadmoor's waitin for you, mate. Got a bed with your name on it.' He put a mug of tea in front of Ashley. 'Want some toast with that?'

'Go on then.'

When Ashley had eaten his toast and collected from Ted, he confided his fears. 'Social worker keeps coming round.'

'Trial's Thursday?' Ted checked.

'Yeh.'

'And?'

'I'm in the shit. She keeps goin on about fosters.'

'They're not gonna let you stay in that house on your own, Ash.' Ted could see the tears in Ashley's eyes. 'Fag?'

'Ta.' Ashley took the offered cigarette from Ted and lit up.

Ted watched him. He felt sorry for the boy. 'It's for the best, kid. You get the right family, they'll look after you.'

'No way.' It was almost a wail.

'Ash, you can't stay in Cecil Road. The house'll be repossessed in a couple of months.'

'No. Crawford's going to look after that.'

'Bollocks. For four years. There's . . .'

'Three. He'll get three.'

'Ash, you don't know. Anything could happen.'

The boy said nothing. Ted could tell he was thinking; he let him be.

Ashley finished his cigarette, drained the remains of his tea. He was calmer now. 'Ted, any chance of me stayin ere for a bit? Just kippin, like. I'll get the radios for rent. Other stuff too. I can do the clothes shops easy. Good stuff.'

'Sorry, mate. Marilyn'll be out in a coupla months. We should get the kids back. It'd be too much.'

'Till then. Till she comes home.'

'Sorry, Ash. No can do.'

'What about the dog then?'

'Same. Sorry. What about that black mate of yours?'

'Karl? His mom won't let him.' Then quietly, as if to himself. 'No can do.'

Fuck it! Fifty quid's worth of lottery tickets and all he had made was twenty quid. It wasn't fair. This had been his last chance. He knew his dad had agreed with the social worker that he should go into care. That's why she was coming round tomorrow before his dad left for court. No.

No. No. He wouldn't. He wouldn't be here when she came. No way. Some poxy family telling him what to do. Making him sit down for meals. Being all nice. *Just think of Richard as your brother. You can call me Mom if you'd like.* Well he wouldn't fucking like. He'd been there before. He hated it. No. No. No. He'd lamp Richard or Darren or whatever the next one was called and he'd be back in the home waiting for the next on the list to come and collect him. No.

Ashley wondered why there was never any smoke coming out of the big crematorium chimney. Perhaps they burn them at night. No, the undertaker blokes had told him they do it straight after the funeral, that's the law, they said, it must be done straight away.

Ashley stood before the laurel bush. The cold wind brought tears to his eyes. 'I won't be back for a bit,' he explained. 'I'm not going in no home, Mom. Nor a foster neither. I'd rather do time. It'll be better that way. Don't worry, I'll be all right. And I won't hurt anyone. I'm going into school tonight. Just Maddocks' office. Torch it. I won't do it till late, when everyone's gone. No one'll get hurt.' He took a cigarette and lit it. 'All I got to do now is keep out the way till it's dark. I've done the dog. Well, there was no choice. She's in the shed, but I'll take her in the school if I can. Leave her in the office.'

He crouched down and let his fingers dance on the cold earth. The shrivelled grass. The hot smoke in his chest was a comfort. When he had ditched the nub he rose. 'Oh well. I'm going now. I'll be all right. I'll be back one day. Promise.'

There were other words – he wanted to say them, but what was the point? And it was too cold anyway. But he'd be warm tonight. As he reached Harold North he popped another cigarette into his mouth.

Tattoo City

The tattoo parlours came under Crawford's insurance scheme at the same time as the saunas. This type of scheme was new for those establishments but nobody objected, at least not out loud – until Tattoo City opened on the corner of Kent Street.

'Give it a month,' Crawford told Kieran. 'Then pay them a visit and sort things out. Who is it anyway?'

'Don't know really. Not one of the usual chains. Some kid. Opened up on his own account.'

'In the city centre. Must have a consortium behind him.'

'Don't think so.'

Some kid – well, Nathan was twenty-five. As soon as he and Pricey walked through the door of Tattoo City Kieran recognized that he wasn't the usual easy fodder. All the blokes who run the parlours have tattoos, but not like this. Nathan stood six foot two in boots laced to halfway up his calves. The right side of his shaven skull gleamed a startling white while the other bore an extravagant swirl of blue curves, like snakes fighting or mating, that travelled down the side of his face. The other side was thickly covered with studs and rings, chains and small silver bolts – ears, nose, eyebrows, lips. Everywhere.

Nathan stood looking at the two men. He knew

immediately they weren't customers. He knew about the racket and had been expecting a visit. He knew too that he wasn't going to play into it.

Kieran and Pricey had seen all sorts, but this head, reminiscent of some tribal god, was something new. Then Kieran noticed the right arm. Blue. All of it. Like it had been dipped in ink. The man's appearance was so unexpected there was a moment's hesitation. Kieran took a breath.

Nathan took in the situation. His mouth opened to reveal bejewelled teeth. The teeth parted. A studded tongue curled and flicked. 'You two can fuck off.'

It's not form but Kieran and Pricey shot a glance at each other – for just a moment – before their eyes returned to Nathan. But he saw it. He saw too beyond the stony glares they were forcing at him. These were just routine. Behind the glares they were processing: *What the fuck have we got here?*

No point in messing around. This was a test. He had been expecting it. Make it fancy, Nathan told himself, and he whooped as he spun like an ice-skater before jumping into the air, kicking out into Pricey's gut just above the pubic bone. He let the momentum carry him round and the fist at the end of his extended blue arm smacked into the side of Kieran's face.

Kieran staggered against the wall, dislodging a poster of Bruce Lee. It floated down, blocking for a second the light from Kieran's eyes.

Dignity is important to the work in which Kieran and Pricey were engaged. You have to stay on top. Both men were trying to figure out how they could retrieve it. For Pricey retaliation was instinctive, but he'd need a moment to regain his wind. For Kieran getting out of Tattoo City in one piece was the pressing concern.

Nathan solved the problem. 'Now do what you're told. Fuck off. I've got a customer. A sea-horse to finish.' He turned his back and went into a cubicle at the back of the shop.

'You should have smashed the place up there and then,' Crawford said. 'Cheeky little fuck.' It was almost funny. But he wouldn't laugh. At least not in front of these two. Anger was pointless too. These were good men. They had never come to him with a negative before. 'What's this kid's background?' he asked.

'Not local,' Kieran told him. 'Southerner. Sounds like a cockney, but a posh one.'

'I didn't know there was such a thing.'

'Looks like something you see in a museum,' Pricey added.

What would you know about what's in museums? Crawford thought. He leaned back in his chair. Tapped the buckle of his belt. The two men eyed him and waited. Then, a slow snarl: 'Why are you telling me this?' There was no reply. 'If you can't sort this out what good are you to me?' Still no reply. 'So you'd better get it sorted.' They turned to go. Crawford stopped them. 'And get yourselves a fucking poppy each.' A finger touched his own, fastened to the lapel of his suit jacket. 'It's Remembrance next week. Show some respect.'

Kieran didn't like this. He was Irish. At least his family were. Pricey didn't care. He'd wear a fucking chrysanth if it kept Crawford happy.

It's funny how things turn out, Crawford thought, as he turned Carle over and saw the row of Chinese characters running the length of her back. 'Babe. They're beautiful,' he told her, running his finger down her spine. She arched her back and raised her head. Purred her pleasure. He grabbed her hips. Pulled her to him. Entered in one. Carle sighed. Her head dropped into the pillow. Beautiful work,

67

Crawford thought, as he got into his stride. Craftsmanship.

He leaned forward so that his head was beside hers. She pressed her cheek to his. He reached round and caught the rings in her nipples. 'The tattoos are brilliant, babe,' he whispered. 'Brilliant. Where d'you get them done?'

'Tattoo City.' He tugged at the rings. She gasped. 'The new place. Had these from there as well.'

'Well, he's good at his job.'

'So are you,' she said, as Crawford knew she would, and he let his tongue trace the first Chinese character in the sequence at the top of her spine.

In the Moscow Kieran and Pricey discussed tactics. Pricey knew from his days in tree surgery that tools impress and his more recent experience working for Crawford had done nothing to undermine this belief. 'We walk in there with a pick-axe,' he told Kieran. 'Wham it into the counter, a couple of cubicle doors, then threaten to put it through that tattooed head. That'll do the trick.'

Kieran felt a more reasonable approach should be taken first. 'I don't like the painted little bastard any more than you do, Pricey, but let's try talking to him first. Explain the situation. If that doesn't work we'll do it your way.'

From the bar Fat Alex watched them plotting. It was always good to see Crawford's boys in here; gave the place a bit of class. Both men wore smart dark suits and Pricey was even wearing a poppy. Must get one myself, Alex thought, and then wondered why no one from the Legion ever came in with a box for the counter as they did in most bars in the city.

'This is what we'll do,' Pricey said. 'We'll go in with the axe. I'll keep it under my overcoat. You start the chat. I'll let the overcoat slip open so he can see it, and we'll take it from there.'

Kieran went to the bar for refills. He watched the lager

fizz and foam into Pricey's glass. 'Yow two don't look appy today,' Alex said. 'Things not running smoothly?'

Kieran looked down at his Guinness – which was running smoothly – rising darkly up the glass. 'Some little cunt trying to be awkward, that's all. You know how it is.'

'Insurance?'

'Yes.'

Alex skimmed the cream head off the glass and offered it back to the pump. 'Must be crazy.'

'He's new. Don't think he can have heard about Crawford.'

'Don't be a ponce, Kieran. Everyone's heard of im. Anyway, shouldn't take you too long to sort im out. Ow is Crawford, by the way? I ear e's screwing is way through every lap-dancer at the Spotted Hippo.' He placed the Guinness beside the lager on the counter.

Kieran tapped the side of his nose. 'Careful, Alex. Careless talk costs lives.'

Alex snorted and the thin foam on the lager quivered.

Roberts was flat on his back holding his bollocks out of Nathan's way with a piece of white tissue he had been given for the purpose. He closed his eyes – the neon above was shining into them – then quickly opened them again; he didn't want the tattooist to think it was the pain.

'It's a compliment,' Nathan said as he worked, 'you coming all the way to Brum. Finding me out.' The back of Nathan's hand brushed Roberts' balls.

'You got a girlfriend up here yet?' he asked Nathan.

'No.'

'You're slow, mate. Women.' He breathed the word out like cigar smoke. 'I just love em.' It was enough. 'The Afghanistan you did on the other leg. It's perfect. No one else was going to do Iraq for me. No matter where you were I was going to find you out.'

Nathan completed the curve of Iraq just above Mosul. When the man stood up the city would be in line with the fall of his left testicle. 'So, what was it like? Iraq?'

'Not good, mate. Not good. But not as bad as the fucking papers say. Are you still doing the karate, Nathe?'

'I've found a good teacher up here. Go four times a week.'

'Good man. I'm here for the week. I want you to do the gun before I go.'

'The Kali. I'm looking forward to that. Give it a couple of days. Come in Thursday. I want to sketch it out. Get the scale right.'

'You're a fucking genius, Nathe. You know that? Seriously you are. An artist. No fucking patterns with you.'

'I do the patterns, like everyone else,' Nathan explained. 'You have to. I love this though. It's a challenge. Most people just want butterflies, dragons, a bracelet of barbed wire round the ankle. Chinese writing's all the rage now. Or kids' names scripted in a curve just above the arse. These one-offs are great. Where you staying up here?'

'Messin in with a mate. Frankley. You know it?'

'Heard of it.'

'Served the last tour with him. So why d'you leave, Nathe? To come up here?'

'I like it up here.'

'Everything going well for you, is it?'

'Mostly. Trade's good. Excellent, in fact. A few teething problems with the shop,' he added cautiously.

People were intrigued by him, Nathan knew this. He used it when necessary. Roberts was no different. Nathan knew this protection business wasn't settled – not by a long way. And he had a strategy. He would finish the map of Iraq. Get Roberts to come back tomorrow so he could script in the five cities he wanted labelled – all in red, except Basra where he had served; that was to be in blue – then when he came in on Thursday for the Kalashnikov on his back he would talk to him about guns – the real thing.

Crawford liked this Czech lager he was knocking back. Two good things about that country: beautiful women and strong lager. Both cheap and both hit the spot. He must go and have a look at that place one day soon, instead of letting his lawyer conduct all the business over there; have all the fun. This Prague Blonde was the best seller in the Spotted Hippo, had been for several weeks, and cheaper than piss to pick up.

Crawford ran the back of his hand across his mouth. The staff were working well tonight, but then they knew he was watching them. Darren, the chief barman, was carrying through another crate of Prague Blondes to fill up the cooler. Crawford noticed the tattoo on his right arm. That was new. Naked bird with tassels on her tits, just like the dancers in the club. Darren crouched and started to fill the cooler. Fuck me! The bird's tits quivered every time he flexed his biceps, just like she was jiggling them.

'Daz, mate,' Crawford called. 'Over here, son.' He knew the answer to his question before he asked it. He lifted Darren's arm. 'Fucking brilliant tattoo, kid. Where d'you get it done?'

'Thanks, boss. The new place. Off Kent Street. Tattoo City.' As if Crawford didn't know.

'Tasty work, that.'

'He's bloody good, the bloke there.' Darren stroked his arm proudly. 'Busy as fuck though. Had to make an appointment. Wait a week. Like the bleedin dentist.'

Crawford could see Carle looking across at him as she went through her routine. He ignored her, keeping his eyes focused on the new girl, Tiffany. The shiniest hair you've ever seen. Glowing beneath the stage lights.

Darren saw him watching her. 'That Cardiff piece is tasty, eh boss?'

Crawford said nothing, but smiled for a reply.

Carle was on the pole now. She was good, acrobatic. Crawford watched the blue Chinese script on her back flow and ripple, like a flag. She looked across to him and he looked away. It was no good letting these girls get too close. He'd had Carle twice. He turned his attention to Tiffany. 'Send her a drink across when she comes off,' he said to Darren.

Behind Crawford at the bar, a man lifted his bottle of Prague Blonde from the counter and walked across to stand closer to the stage, get a better look. He too was fascinated by the moving Chinese characters on Carle's back. In fact everything about her fascinated him.

She noticed him looking – well, it was her job to see these things. It was pretty obvious that Crawford was no longer interested, so she might as well get back to business. She smiled as she danced past him. Roberts raised his bottle towards her in salute, then brought it to his lips.

His eyes trailed her as she left the stage and went among the seated men, wriggling between their legs, pushing her tits into their faces, teasing with a casual stroke of their hard-ons as she moved away. When she came close he caught her wrist. 'I'd like to buy you a drink.'

The small talk didn't take long. He'd already made his mind up. 'How much?' he asked.

He was staying with his mate Kirk over in Frankley. He wouldn't mind him bringing a tart back. But three fifty for the night was a lot of money. The alternative was an hour in some grotty room round here, the back of a taxi rank or somewhere like that.

'I thought I'd seen every fucking thing under the sun down ere,' Alex told Kieran as he pulled his Guinness. 'E makes the Elephant Man look like Prince Charming. What freak show did you pick im up in then?'

'He's a client.'

'Well we don't do Diet Coke. E'll have to ave full sugar. Can't be any enamel left on those teeth anyway. Looks like e's eaten Ratner's.' Alex filled a glass from a plastic bottle of cola.

Kieran was working on his own initiative. After all, he had been hired by Crawford as a talker not a fighter. When he did door work at one of the clubs it was his role to persuade those not welcome to turn round and go somewhere else, go home. All friendly. Everybody's mate. Only got their interests at heart. He'd even call them a taxi if it'd help. Like his mad Auntie Bridie used to say, 'Kieran, you could talk the angels into hell.' It was only if his skills of persuasion failed, which they did too often for Crawford's liking, that the heavies standing behind him moved in. A lot of the time now he was just a messenger, he had to admit, but here was an opportunity to show what he could do. Get the thing sorted before Pricey, the mad axeman, stole the show.

The cola was flat but Nathan sipped at it anyway. He knew the game: talk him round before they needed to come up with the brutals. Okay. Why not? he told himself. Know your enemy.

Kieran wanted to get this right. No point in going straight into gory details of what would happen if he didn't cough. And he'd got him to come for a drink with him. That was a positive. Showing him this place might help him to see what he was up against, though there weren't many in right now. Psychology was what was needed. 'How long have you been in Birmingham, Nathe?'

'A few months. Three or four.'

'Ever been to the Spotted Hippo?'

'Heard of it.'

73

'Another of the boss's outlets. Some beautiful women in that place. Best in the city.' He took a card from inside his jacket. 'A free pass. Try it out.' He took a pen from his pocket. 'I'll tell you what. I'll put a little note on the back. First girl you want is on the house.'

'I'm not into women.' Nathan looked Kieran straight in the eye. 'They're not my thing.'

Shit! Kieran thought. Still. Okay. He returned the card to his jacket pocket. He was trying to think quickly. 'Go down the Nightingale, do you? Route 66?' Kieran wasn't sure he could do anything for him in the gay clubs – not his patch – but he could try.

'I'm not queer,' Nathan sneered.

Kieran didn't know where to take this. 'No. Sure,' he muttered. Give it a second, he told himself, then get back to the matter in hand. Explain to him the logic of doing business. He knew where he was with that.

Nathan was still looking directly at Kieran. 'I'm a bestialist,' he said, and watched the confusion rise in the other man's face.

Kieran was trying to remember what the word meant. He'd heard it before. Something to do with whipping?

'I'm sexually attracted to animals,' Nathan continued. 'Very sexually attracted if you want to know the truth.' He watched the mouth across the table fall open.

Kieran wanted to ask Nathan to repeat himself, just so he could check. But he knew that would be a bad move. He watched as Nathan's head tilted forward in shame. His voice dropped. Kieran had to listen hard.

'Don't worry, I don't go round fucking dogs and cats. People like me have specific species we're attracted to.'

Kieran took a hefty pull on his Guinness. Let the words replay in his head. Waited for Nathan to continue, but he said nothing.

Kieran couldn't stop himself. 'So what are *your* preferences?' He asked the question quietly. Sensitively, he thought. Although inside his head there was a lot of shocked shrieking going on. He noticed Alex looking across at Nathan. He'd drop down dead if he could hear this, Kieran thought.

Nathan raised his head to look at Kieran again. It looked like there were tears in his eyes. 'Penguins,' he said. 'Penguins and giraffes.'

This had got to be a wind-up. Had to be. But looking across at this strange head, so weird and so tough, now fighting for control, it seemed obvious. Why else would you do all that to yourself? His head alone was a horror story. God knows what the rest of him was like. It had to be disgust. Self-hatred.

'It's not just sex,' Nathan was continuing. 'Well, yes, of course it's sex. I've got a whole collection of pictures, you know, out of wildlife magazines, that I wank over. And I go down the zoo whenever I can. But sometimes it's too much. You see I really like these animals as well. It would be all right if it was cats or dogs, sheep or pigs even, I could have one as a pet. Build a relationship. But . . .' His voice trailed away.

Yes, Kieran saw what he meant. 'Penguins and giraffes.' Kieran spoke the words slowly, thoughtfully. 'Yes. I suppose Birmingham's not the place to be really.'

At the bar, waiting for Alex to pull him another pint of Guinness, Kieran knew it wasn't going to work. Bloke like that, as weird and perverted as that. Nothing would make sense to him. Things that would scare other people. He understood his determination now. Bloke like that, he's got nothing to lose. Goes out looking for penguins and giraffes to shag. Gets off on David Attenborough. Hopeless fucking case. Oh well, he'd tried. 'I'll have a chaser with it, Alex. A double.'

*

Tiffany couldn't believe her luck. She'd only been in this city a week and she'd just had the shag of her life, and from the boss, too: Crawford – not just the boss of the Hippo, the boss of everywhere from what she had heard; the city boss. She went down again. But Crawford had had enough for one night. He pulled her up and kissed her briefly on the mouth, eased her head down to rest on his chest.

'You're beautiful, Tiff.' He stroked her lustrous black hair. 'Gorgeous. I'm really taken with you.' Tiffany felt her heart speed. 'I'm going to give you a present.' It raced even more. 'You're the sexiest bird I've had in ages. But. There's just one thing missing?' Tiffany tilted her head to look at Crawford. 'A tattoo,' he said. 'That's what you need. A top-class tattoo. An I'll pay for it.'

Pricey went crazy when Kieran told him about Nathan being a bestialist. Threw an absolute stormer. 'Blokes like that should be shot,' he declared. 'No. That's too good for them. Gassed. Blokes like that should be gassed.' But even that wasn't sufficient. He paced frantically up and down trying to devise an appropriate form of execution. 'I'm an animal lover,' he cried. 'We always had dogs when I was a kid. Whippets.' He came to a sudden standstill. Looked at Kieran with horror. 'Animals carry diseases. It's a well-known fact. He must be rotten with half the diseases known to man. And he's stickin a fucking needle in people's skin. He could infect the whole bleeding city.'

Roberts had been sitting bolt upright for hours while Nathan used what felt like a flame-thrower on his back. He tried to make conversation to take his mind off it. 'Have you noticed how kids never collect pennies for the guy any more, Nathe? Bonfire night tomorrow and I haven't seen a single kid with a guy. It's the same in

76

London, ain't it? I haven't seen one for years, have you?' But Nathan was too intent on his work to reply, just kept telling Roberts not to move, keep still, don't slouch. Like a fucking sergeant major.

Now, at last, he was free to rise from the chair, move about. His back still burned like fuck but the pain was nothing now he had the ecstasy of movement – to walk about, bend, stretch.

Nathan brought a mirror from another cubicle and held it behind Roberts as he stood in front of the one fixed to the wall. Roberts smiled at Nathan reflected in the glass. Nathan was grinning, exposing his bejewelled teeth. They both knew he had done good work.

'Perfect, mate. Fucking perfect.' The upright Kalashnikov occupied the length of Roberts' back, from the level of his hips to the bulge of his cervical vertebra. When Roberts stood still and straight the gun was in perfect proportion. When he bent his back or swung his arm it elongated or broadened elegantly. It really was a class piece of work. The swelling had started of course, podgy pink protuberances breaking out, the biggest beneath the trigger. But these would go. 'Fucking excellent.' Roberts muttered his delight.

When his shirt and jacket were back on Roberts fetched out his wallet. 'Right, let's settle up. How much do I owe you?'

'For the gun, nothing,' Nathan told him. Roberts looked at the tattooist quizzically. And waited. 'It's on the house. But. I was hoping you could do me a favour. A spot of trouble I'm having with the shop you might be able to help me with.'

Roberts kept his wallet in his hand. 'Go on,' he said.

Kieran didn't like November. A grey old month his Auntie Bridie called it. Nothing good ever happens in November.

And she was right, he thought. Pricey looked at him as if he were talking in another language when he told him this. They were driving towards Kent Street. Beyond the car window the city was dissolving in grey mist. Pricey had shaved his head, not that there was ever much more than a black stubble up there. Kieran had noticed he did this before jobs like this, shaved everything off, sort of the opposite of Sampson, he thought.

Pricey's overcoat lay on the backseat, the pick-axe hoisted on a sling beneath it. 'Kennedy!' he shouted suddenly. 'He got shot in November.'

'Oh, yeh.'

Kieran had rung Tattoo City that morning, told the kid they would be in later. It was simple: an envelope with a grand inside. Then he wouldn't see them for a month. And it was sensible. It made business sense. Any security problems he had, and they were bound to come in an area like that, all he had to do was call. They would give him the number when they picked up the readies. He had expected to hear the kid growl 'Fuck off' in his ear. But there was nothing, just 'See you later then'. Perhaps he had seen sense; you can't beat blokes like Crawford.

'There's that Tiffany,' Pricey said, pointing at the corner of Bromsgrove Street. 'The Welsh bird from the Hippo.' He banged the horn but Tiffany didn't recognize them. She turned, lifted two fingers and went on her way.

Tiffany was in a bad mood. That painted ponce with more metal in his face than Newport Docks had told her she would have to make an appointment. Who did he think he was? Even when she flashed the wad of twenties Crawford had given her, all he did was tap his desk diary and say Monday week was the best he could do for her. She had gone all disappointed, told him this was a special present for her birthday, then smiled coyly, something she was good at, and suggested there would be more than cash in it for him if he could squeeze her in. He'd looked straight at her and said he'd prefer sex with a giraffe. Tosser. Well, there were plenty other tattooists round here, cheaper too. She'd go to one of them. She crossed the street to avoid an old boy with a beret and a tray of poppies she could see on the next corner. All she wanted was a gecko, about six inches, climbing up her thigh – on the inside. If Crawford was into tattoos she might have something else too. Barbed wire round her ankle. Chinese writing down her back. She wasn't going to miss her opportunity.

'You two look like undertakers,' Nathan sneered when Kieran and Pricey marched into the shop. He was referring to the black overcoats both men wore.

'It's cold out there,' Kieran said in explanation, then felt stupid.

'You know what we're here for,' Pricey snarled. 'No more fucking about. Where's the money?'

'I told you. I'm not interested. Now fuck off. I'll take care of my own security.'

Pricey was unbuttoning his overcoat. 'I don't think so.'

Kieran's eyes were on Nathan. He saw him watching as the coat fell open. He had seen the axe, there was no doubt about that, but he seemed completely unperturbed. Just grinned, in fact, showing off those unsettling teeth. From the corner of his eye Kieran saw Pricey reaching in for the axe. He could do this in one movement: take the axe from inside his coat up in a curved swing to land wherever he chose. Kieran had seen it before.

'You're a stupid bastard, you know that?' Pricey was saying. 'You have to have it the hard way, don't you?'

The axe was up. Kieran tensed for its downward crash. Nathan's eyes followed it. He stepped back. Then Kieran blinked. He couldn't believe it. His stomach lurched. Shit! The axe stopped in mid-air.

The curtains to the corridor of cubicles had parted. It was like something from Belfast. On either side of Nathan stood a man in a balaclava. Dressed in black from head to foot. Fucking great black boots, army ones. And each man held a rifle: one trained on Pricey, one on him. When Kieran heard the click of the safety catch he thought he was going to shit himself. How the fuck had this happened? This shouldn't happen. He jumped at the sound of the axe tumbling uselessly to the floor.

'Which one?' the man on Nathan's right asked him.

Nathan looked from Kieran to Pricey, then back again. Choosing. Kieran could feel hot beads of sweat bursting out of him; a rivulet trickling down his spine. Nathan was staring at him now. Hard. Kieran wanted to look at Pricey. He needed some sort of sign. Nathan grinned. Those fucking teeth again.

'The one with the chopper.'

Before the words were out of his mouth, the guy closest to Pricey had hold of him and was dragging him into the back. The other gunman followed. Nathan came towards Kieran. The fist moved too quickly for Kieran to see it coming. His head hit the door.

Nathan stood above him. 'Think yourself lucky I didn't choose you. Now get up and piss off. If I ever see you again you're a dead man.'

Kieran had never seen so many people in Crawford's office. He'd got everyone there, some blokes Kieran hadn't even seen before. Kieran noticed that he was the only man in the room without a poppy in his lapel. He had just gone through the story again although he had told it to Crawford half a dozen times already.

'Execution,' Crawford said dramatically. Everyone waited. 'One of my men, one of *us*, has been executed by this tattooist creature, or at least by those behind him. I knew all along he wasn't the one-man outfit he claimed to be. It didn't make sense. We shall have to have a full enquiry about this. Why all the facts about this creature . . .' He stopped, looked around the room. 'Creature,' he repeated, rolling the R. 'I use that word deliberately. Kieran, tell them what this tattooist is.'

All eyes turned to Kieran. 'He's a bestialist,' he announced.

There was silence in the room. A narrowing of eyebrows. Some men looked at each other, others looked down.

'A bestialist,' Crawford repeated. 'That, gentlemen, means he fucks animals.' A shocked murmur travelled through the room. 'Apparently penguins and giraffes are his favourite.' Now there were groans of disgust. 'But I shouldn't think any animal is safe with him around.'

'What we going to do about it, Andy?' It was Carlton who asked the question. He was new to the team but a mate of Crawford's since schooldays. He had just finished a couple of life sentences and seemed to have become one of the inner-circle since his release.

'For the moment, we wait,' Crawford told them. 'We have to show respect for Pricey. Take care of our dead. It's the civilized thing to do. I shouldn't think this mob will want the law involved any more than I do, so they'll probably dump him somewhere we'll find him.'

'And after we've got Pricey back?' Carlton again.

'That's what I intend to apply my mind to now, Carlton. We've obviously got to nail this gang. The thing is how? I want you all back here, Sunday afternoon. We'll plan our strategy then.'

Fat Alex was uneasy. He sometimes got *tourists* down here, people who didn't know the bar's reputation. In the summer people off the narrow boats from the canal outside sometimes strayed down. 'We don't do food,' he would tell them, stick a pound on a pint. 'No soft drinks.' It usually did the trick.

Tonight, however, two young soldiers were propped against the bar supping their pints of Bass like they were in the NAAFI. Soldiers in the Little Moscow. Alex was confused. There was a war on. He'd already heard them talking about being in Iraq. You had to respect the lads on the front line. And it was Remembrance Sunday tomorrow. They were probably involved in one of them parades they have in the city centre. He regretted now he didn't have a poppy. They were both wearing one. The trouble was Saturday night the place was full and he knew their presence was having an unsettling effect on his regulars. Still, they seemed friendly enough. At least the one was, said his name was Kirk, the other just said he was called Roberts. But they were minding their own business, not looking round at all.

Then something happened that was very disquieting for Alex. His instincts were good, always had been. It was how he kept this place going; he knew when something wasn't right. The soldier called Roberts was getting his round in and asked Alex if he sold a lager called Prague Blonde. There was only one bloke with a deal on that: Crawford. It was in all his places. That set alarm bells ringing for Alex. There were plenty of innocent explanations, of course: these lads had been to one of the clubs, the Hippo, Pinks, the Candy Strip, and liked what they drank. But. There was something about the way this Roberts lad asked. Alex didn't like it. Of course, he said nothing. Just told them he didn't do much in the way of bottles. They settled for two more pints of Bass. Quite a few of Crawford's boys were in right now for a quick one before heading off to the clubs. If anything else dodgy came up Alex would have a word with one of them.

Alex knew his instinct was right as soon as he saw him coming down the stairs. That tattooed pervert. Both soldiers left the bar and shot towards him. They moved so fast a whole lot of drinkers looked up. They saw this tattooed lad, face full of rings and studs and bolts, standing between the two soldiers. Everyone went quiet. Just Mud on the jukebox.

At first Alex thinks it's an old sack the lad's got over his shoulder. Well it is, but when, with his military escort, he marches towards the counter, Alex can see there is something under it. Not something – someone. The kid drops Pricey, gagged and trussed double, wearing only his Y-fronts, on to the floor. He nicks the rope with a knife and Pricey unfurls. Then the three of them about turn and leave. Everyone's so gobsmacked they just watch them go. Then people start to move towards Pricey. Alex can't quite stretch far enough over the bar to see, so he trundles round. Others have reached Pricey first but everyone is just standing looking at him, staring down. Alex sees why: CRAWFORD: FUCK OFF! is tattooed in letters that reach from the top of Pricey's swollen red chest down to the edge of his underpants. Someone removes the gag from his mouth, releasing a torrent of effin and bleedin.

'And the cunt's gone and put a kangaroo on my arse.'

Shouldn't it be FUCK OFF CRAWFORD? Kieran thought as he looked at the lettering on Pricey's chest. But of course, the longest word had to go at the top where there's more room. Pricey's a pretty trim chap. There are some in here whose bellies are big enough for him to have done it the right way round.

Everyone was in Crawford's office again, Pricey seated on a chair in the middle, his shirt open so that all could see what had been done to him. Everyone knew, of course. Word got round. Some had joked about it, especially the kangaroo, but now every face was stony as they listened to Crawford.

He made it clear that this was war. Our man hadn't actually been killed as at first feared but what had been done to him was inhuman, an attempt to humiliate us all and undermine the organization and therefore a threat to the livelihood of every man in the room. Our response would be decisive. He pointed out that several people had suggested ideas and he would like everyone to hear them. Carlton thought that we should lift this kid Nathan; we didn't know for sure his importance in the gang but he had been their front-man, their method of communication. Once we had got him we should treat this pervert appropriately: take him to Dudley Zoo if he liked animals so much and drop him in the bear pit. There were some grunts of approval at this but also some scepticism. Red Biz pointed out that he didn't think they had bears in Dudley Zoo any more, just a few small animals, and certainly no bear pits. Each suggestion was listened to by the assembly. Pricey himself said that he too thought Nathan should be lifted. That first all his teeth should be knocked out. It was when he was advocating that the metal in Nathan's face should in some way be electrically wired and increasing voltages applied that Crawford stopped him. Everyone could see he was getting impatient.

'This is a war,' he repeated. 'Like the War on Terror. We don't know who the enemy is. Only that the tattooist is right at the front. We have to destroy him and that shop of his; wipe both from the face of the earth.' The silence in the room was heavy when Crawford paused. Each man was tensed for what he would say next. But he was taking his time. He walked round the room looking at the men he had assembled around him.

'You are my most important men,' he said at last. 'This has got to be done right. I've given it a lot of thought. I want him blown up. Him and his shop. So's everyone knows they can't take liberties like this.' He paused. Then:

84

'A car bomb,' he said purposefully. 'Like in Israel and Iraq. A suicide bombing.' Crawford glared at his men. No one met his stare.

Nathan had won. He knew they would be back, but only to save face. There would probably be some offer to join up with them in some way – if you can't beat em, make em part of you; that was the usual philosophy. But he was having none of that. He had in his desk the small handgun Roberts' mate Kirk had provided for him – they had been brilliant those two. He'd give that bird Roberts had been knocking off, Carle, a freebie when she came in this morning. He looked for her name in the appointments diary – eleven o'clock. Yes, Roberts and Kirk had helped him pull off a coup, but now they were gone. He had to manage the victory himself. That was okay. His intelligence, his fitness, his toughness: these would see him through.

He had tongued her gecko. He had licked round the chain of rosebuds on her ankle. Four nights in a row he had screwed her. She was in. She knew it. She'd got him. She'd always fancied black blokes. And she liked him too. Big, strong, good-looking, powerful, rich. The list made her laugh out loud in delight. It might not last for ever but she knew she could make it last some time. The best thing she ever did, leaving Cardiff to come here. And when, lying in his arms, he told her he had a special job for her, told her the money he was going to give her for doing it, she knew her days on the game were over. She was moving into the big time. Forget the Hippo, he told her, I'd like you to move in with me.

The job was no problem. Too easy in fact, but she wouldn't let herself think about that. She was a good driver and she was pleased to be getting one over on that bastard in the tattoo parlour. The Range Rover had been nicked, of course. Carlton drove her to Whitworth Street where Pricey was waiting with the keys. Tiffany listened to the instructions again. It was eleven o'clock now. She was to give it twenty minutes. Time for a couple of the boys to get in and tie the tattooist up out the back so he didn't get hurt. She'd to drive the Double R up Bromsgrove Street into Gooch Street North and, taking a little veer to the left at the corner with Kent Street, go full blast into Tattoo City. No danger. Crawford had promised her. 'I wouldn't risk anything happening to you.'

'No danger at all,' Carlton repeated as she climbed into the vehicle. 'Like tanks, these things.'

The boys will get her out the wagon and they'll all leave through the back. A car already waiting. Then it's back to the office for a glass of champagne and her wages. She hoped Crawford would be there.

Tiffany watched Pricey and Carlton leave. Okay, she knew it *was* dangerous, despite what they said, had to be, a bit, but she didn't care. This was her chance. It was like working with the SAS with these boys. They'd look after her. She was Crawford's girl. She glowed with excitement. She had dreamed of an opportunity like this.

Pricey and Carlton were parked up at the far end of Gooch Street North. Kieran in the back. Carlton had his mobile rammed into his ear talking Crawford through. Yes, he told him, the kid was definitely in there, he'd got a customer with him. Pity about that, but it couldn't be helped. Kieran could tell Crawford was worked up. Carlton was calming him down. Reassuring him that everything was done. 'The wagon, boss? Beautifully fused.' Then he stopped talking for the Range Rover had turned into the street and was picking up speed rapidly. 'Shit, man!'

Carlton whistled. 'Look at that baby go. Formula Fucking One.'

The Range Rover continued to accelerate, whizzing towards Tattoo City. They heard the impact – the sound of breaking glass, the scream of tearing metal – but only for a second. Pricey prodded the other mobile. All was consumed in an exploding roar. Smoke. Flame. And for a moment it seemed to Kieran as if they too might be engulfed. 'Done,' he heard Carlton say to Crawford. Pricey had his foot down and was roaring away before the sound of the explosion subsided.

The Night
of the Great Wind

*In Chinese mythology the wind is Xian, the stealer of souls,
who resides in the Black Valley beyond the great oceans.
He is the greatest fear of sailors, for they are easily taken.
There are times when he rages ashore scouring the land
for souls. The old, the sick and infants are easy prey.
Those he takes have no hope of resurrection or peace, they
will toss for ever in turmoil among the waves of the Black
Valley. He is the bringer of fear. No one can be easy when
he is abroad.*

*In some stories he assumes the form of the dragon and
travels inland, breathing hot winds and fire.*

The seventh of January 2005 was the night of the big
storm. It was at its worst in the North of England. By mid-
afternoon of the following day the streets of Carlisle were
under eight feet of water: nine died, three thousand people
were evacuated from their homes and the whole town was
without electricity.

In Birmingham – which is without a major river, so only
the drains and sewers ever flood – there was not much rain,
but the wind was ferocious.

In her flat on the sixteenth floor on the Druids Heath

Estate, Jean Boyce was in bed dying. Two floors below, in an empty flat he had just broken in to, Jimmy Slim sat hunched in the darkness, waiting to die too. Both heard the wind as it raged between the tower blocks, hurtling the debris of the estate high into the air, smacking it against walls and windows, bouncing it off car roofs. Satellite dishes broke off balcony rails and flags of St George, intact since last summer's European Championship, sailed away.

Dot Scudamore sat beside the bed of her sister Jean, listening to the rasp of air moving in and out of her diseased lungs. Eric, Dot's husband, was away for a few days in Rotterdam on business. She was used to his trips away – usually to Holland. *Trips away*. Dot smiled at the phrase; in the old days there had been stretches in prison but he hadn't done time for years now. Too shrewd.

Dot had turned off the television at the end of the bed half an hour ago and now sat beside her sister in the darkness, listening to the wind outside and the ghastly shunt of air within Jean's chest that preceded each gasp for breath. Dot wondered if this was a gale, officially. She wasn't sure of the difference between high winds and gales, the two terms they used on the forecasts, but this, tonight, was strong enough to frighten her. For a fortnight now she had watched pictures on television of the devastation caused in Thailand, India, Indonesia, by the Boxing Day tsunami and comforted herself that here in England we are safe from the vicious whims of nature. Now she was doubtful: perhaps it is true; you're not safe anywhere.

When she had called round this afternoon she had wanted to fetch an ambulance, but Jean had begged her not to. She didn't want to go to hospital; she wanted to stay here, in her own home. The district nurse would be round in the morning. She would be all right till then.

So Dot had persuaded Jean to go to bed, where she had

made her comfortable. 'I'll stay the night with you,' she told her sister. 'Eric's away. It makes no difference.'

To the Chinese, wind has a special significance. They distinguish between types of wind: cold, damp, hot, dry. But all are destructive forces, malign influences. In Chinese medicine, wind is regarded as one of the external causes of disease. Therefore, the execution squad, on its way to Druids Heath to seek out Jimmy Slim, was naturally uneasy.

Dot switched on the lamp beside Jean's bed. The pink light was useless for checking her sister's colour, yet there was no point using the overhead that filled the room with sickly yellow. She switched the lamp off, returning the room to darkness. Beyond the window, bundles of clouds the colour of the worst kind of bruising scudded through the sky.

They both married villains, she and Jean. But there the similarity ended. Eric did all right. He concentrated on jewellery. He joked that he was a more accurate valuer than any la-di-dah who worked for expensive jewellers or antique dealers. And he was right. He traded in the raw materials too: gold, silver, uncut diamonds.

Jean, on the other hand, had landed herself with Ray. He looked like a film star in the early days, could have had any woman he wanted – and he didn't turn many down. A good talker. Full of plans and dreams; a charmer.

But it all went down the pan. He was small-time. Robberies, mostly on teams, along with a bit of solo work. Mostly commercial, but a spot of housebreaking. One prison stretch after another. Eric wouldn't have anything to do with him work-wise, said he was a loser, that he was bad luck, and he was probably right.

Ray's looks didn't last long. His health went. He died at fifty-four, without two pennies to rub together, of the same cancer that was now finishing off his wife.

Yes, Dot reflected, it was she who had got the better deal. A beautiful house, cars, holidays abroad three or four times a year, jewellery minor members of the royal family wouldn't turn their noses up at. While for Jean it was this shabby council flat stuck up in a hole through the ozone layer, barmaiding until her coughing got so bad they sacked her, then cleaning for a year until she couldn't go on. She's got bottle all right, Dot thought.

She looked at the luminous face of her gold wristwatch. Nearly midnight. She was going to miss Jean; she was a good sort, always cheerful and optimistic, though God knows she had no reason to be.

In the big red room above the casino Hsinshu sat alone, his phone on the table before him. He was deaf to the sounds of the gambling below, which drowned the noise of the wind attacking the city. His ears would only awaken when the phone rang. This was his first test.

In this room, just a few hours before, the trial of Jimmy Slim had taken place. Hsinshu was still in his first year as Emperor of the Seventh Dragon. All twelve Barons assembled round the table, six each side, should see him for the man he was. His element was Metal. They must see and understand this. Hsinshu had sat at the head of the table listening carefully to all that had to be said about Jimmy Slim. Then he had risen, turned his back on the table and paced a little with his chin cupped in his hand, deep in thought. Considering. Coming to a judgement. All waited. He took his time. Then, when he was ready, he moved back to the top of the table, looked Jimmy Slim in the eyes, called him by his rightful name, Hsiaohai, and pronounced his death sentence.

Now in the empty room he was worried. He hadn't put a foot wrong since his take-over. He had run the Seventh with martial efficiency, adhered to and upheld the rightful codes, imbued his men with pride again and with ambition. Their domain had enlarged – considerably: their interests increased, their profits soared.

Jimmy Slim's treachery had given Hsinshu the opportunity to consolidate his reputation – to prove his mettle. He heard again the silence, loud as a collective intake of breath, when he pronounced the sentence. Jimmy Slim held his head high, sullen and defiant, but Hsinshu saw the fear trickling in his black eyes.

They had stood over Jimmy Slim while Yangku went to alert the squad on stand-by downstairs. When they arrived, Jimmy Slim jumped to his feet and marched away with them as if eager to have this over with. As if he were ready to meet his end honourably. Hsinshu had been pleased. It was as it should be in the Seventh. Now the little bastard had escaped and he had three squads running round looking for him. This was wrong. It was not as it should be. It showed the rottenness that had been allowed to set in. The word of the Emperor should never be questioned, even by one for whom that word meant death; it was part of the Code.

Tonight the world around Dot had compressed into layers of sound like geological strata. The wind, louder and more powerful than anything else, formed the thickest layer; the noise of the objects it flung around formed a separate layer of discordant, erratic syncopation; Jean's breathing, harsh now and not unlike the barking of a dog, a further layer; and other sounds were squeezed, trapped almost, between these layers: the screech of car brakes from far below; alarms; the lift squeaking and clunking its way up and down the spine of the building; snatches of music from here and there.

She stretched out her hand and touched the turned sheet beneath Jean's chin. It was slimy with phlegm. She withdrew quickly, pulled a tissue from the box beside the bed and wiped her fingers. With another tissue she wiped Jean's mouth. Perhaps she should change the sheet. But it seemed cruel to disturb her. Not that her sleep was peaceful: the breathing was becoming louder, more desperate, her mouth gaping wide in its quest for air.

This was dreadful. She couldn't let her carry on like this all night. But what could the hospital do? Stick her on a trolley with a mask over her face pumping oxygen into her. For what? To extend her life by a few more hours, a day or two. Then through the raucous gasps there was a cry, near enough a scream. The body spasmed.

Dot reached out for her sister's hand. 'It's all right, love. I'm here with you. Dot.' The body settled; the gasping continued as before. Gently Dot laid her hand on her sister's forehead. It was wet with cold sweat.

His name was Shuko, which means bonebinder, and he had no fear of the wind for his element was Wood, which is supple and can bend and sway with the vicissitudes of the wind. Shuko knew that Metal controls Wood, which was why he had become a loyal and true servant to Hsinshu. We should know the powers of our energies but also their limits.

Shuko stood beneath a swaying fir tree, listening with pleasure to its struggle with the wind. The needles of the fir branches whipped his face, but he would not move. He was like the tigress that for a thousand years stood guard at the South Gate. An opposing army fired a hundred arrows into her hide yet still she stood, her eyes blazing black and gold. If we cannot kill the tigress, cannot even make her fall, the army concluded, what hope have we of defeating her master, the Emperor? And so they retreated. Other forces, disbelieving the story, came as far as the South Gate, but seeing the tigress standing patiently,

94

hearing the hundred old arrows clicking together in the breeze, they took not one step further.

Shuko's eyes were fixed on the brightly lit doorway of the tower block a hundred yards away. Jimmy Slim was somewhere in that building. Shuko had followed him here. You are not the only Dragon with a powerful bike, Jimmy Slim. If you come through that door Shuko's gun is ready. Despite the words in his head, Shuko hoped Jimmy Slim would not come through the doors. To use the gun, especially tonight in such a wind, would be unlucky. Water controls fire. Far better he stayed there. When the squads arrive we will find him.

When Jimmy Slim had gone into the tower block Shuko had disabled his bike with the emblem of a blue wave emblazoned on it. He had done this carefully without causing the beautiful bike any damage. It would be within the Code for Hsinshu to award this spoil to Shuko. If he did, Shuko would change the colour from blue to green as was right for one whose element was Wood.

Shuko had phoned the squads with Jimmy Slim's location. Then he had phoned Hsinshu. One ring and he answered. His ears were waiting. Shuko had detected relief in Hsinshu's voice. It would not be right for the Emperor to express gratitude, for he has the right to expect service from Dragons, but Shuko heard, despite the roar of the wind around him, the sound of a relief so great that he knew it was gratitude Hsinshu was feeling towards him. Great things would follow this night's work, Shuko knew.

Dot was in the kitchen having a cigarette and making herself a cup of tea. There was no drink in the flat. She wished now she had slipped a bottle of vodka into her bag before leaving home, but she had not known then she would be away so long.

Looking out from the kitchen window, it seemed the wind itself was visible. The stripped winter trees twisted and contorted as if under torture, bent this way and in a second the other in the wind's force. Suddenly she laughed out loud, for the story of the Three Little Pigs had entered her mind. *I'll huff and I'll puff and I'll blow your house down.* She saw pictures that must have come from childhood books – or had there been a film, Disney perhaps? – of the wolf forcing clouds of breath from his mouth. Then the pictures were superseded by those of tornadoes, 'twisters' they called them, didn't they? In America. On television programmes about disasters. They destroyed everything in their wake. She had seen cars lifted and flung around. Then, beneath the roar of her own English wind, she heard the steam from the kettle, the switch click off, the mad scratch against the kitchen window of the little conifers in Jean's window-box, like the fingernail clawing of someone trying to get in. She popped a tea bag into a cup. Perhaps she should give Jean something to drink, but the task seemed impossible. She poured boiling water into the cup.

Crouched in a corner of an empty flat on the fourteenth floor, Jimmy Slim could hear the wind too, but it was consumed for him by a greater noise, the repeating echo in his ear of Hsinshu telling him that the Code of the Dragons demanded the death of traitors.

But he had got away, defeating not only the squad but also this evil wind that had fought him continuously as he rode his motorbike south from the centre of the city. It had taken all his strength and concentration to keep the bike stable, but he had done it. If he could defeat the wind then he could defeat Hsinshu. He repeated this to himself several times as if trying to engrave it on his consciousness so that it would become incontrovertible fact, a belief he could hold on to.

He knew they were out there looking for him. They had followed him as far as this estate but then he had woven in and out of the labyrinth of short streets and cul-de-sacs, whizzed like the wind itself round the tower block. His element was Water. Water is controlled by wind. He must not forget that. He must use this water energy tonight of all nights, then he might save himself. Now he said to himself: *My energy is the power of Water. It can move round, over, under objects. It can absorb, wear away. It is the awesome strength of the great wave.* On Jimmy Slim's chest was a blue tattoo of a standing wave. His fingers reached in through his shirt and he touched it as he repeated the words. He thought about the white man with the blue arm who did this tattoo: he died by fire. As a rule Jimmy Slim did not like white people, although he would fuck white girls if he wanted, but he did like the strange young white man who made his tattoo. He did the small flame on his wrist too: the flame, sign of the Dragon. All members carried this sign. Jimmy Slim did like black people, which was where his current problems arose. He got talking to Strombo last year at the dog track. It wasn't long before he knew most of the Doberman Crew. He liked those guys, the way they looked, the way they talked: very free spirits. It wasn't long before they were offering him little jobs, paying well and then offering even more for information about the Dragon's drug runs. It was how he got his bike. But also how he got here.

Jimmy Slim remembered his first kill. The skinhead. The Code said the Dragon killed by fire and in Jimmy Slim's time that had always meant guns. Since Hsinshu became Emperor he had allowed knives and machetes because his energy was Metal. As he recalled his first kill, Jimmy Slim thought that perhaps his present predicament was inevitable. The power of his own energy was an irresistible force. Once the skinhead was unconscious he had taken him to the canal and dropped him in. Stood on the bank in the dawn light and watched the water do his work. He saw again the white face of the skinhead bobbing gently beneath the surface of the oily water.

A gust of wind struck the window of the flat on the fourteenth floor with such force that Jimmy Slim jumped and felt sweat rise across the surface of his body. He did not like wind. This night was unlucky. Then he checked himself. *You are the power of Water. You can work with the wind. Go with it. Don't fight it. Wind and Water. Against each of these Fire, which is the energy of the Dragon, is defenceless. In combination you will have the power to survive.*

Hsinshu rose and, leaving his phone waiting on the table, turned to face the dartboard which hung on the wall at the back of the red room. He focused on it. Meditated on his target. When he was ready he strode to collect three arrows. Standing before the target he placed his left hand inside his shirt to rest on the Chinese character for power that was tattooed in black in the lower *jia*, just beneath his umbilicus. He took his energy to his right hand. He breathed deeply, then threw the arrows. All three reached the House of Twenty simultaneously and stood together in the board as close as Siamese brothers. Hsinshu smiled to himself; he was a true leader. It was no surprise to him that at that moment his phone began to tone.

Dot wished she knew more about the pulse. She had her index finger pressed against the radial artery of Jean's left hand. The pulse seemed very fast. She knew from television dramas that you should count the number of beats in a minute. She glanced at her watch, but what was the point? She didn't know how many there should be.

Jean took another gasp. Her chest cracked, as if somewhere inside her a drawer was being banged shut. Then she lifted her head, was suddenly clearly awake. She grabbed Dot's arm and raised herself a little. 'Why?' she gasped into Dot's face. 'Why did you make me do it?' The effort was too much for her and her head flopped back onto the pillow, but she wasn't finished. 'Twice,' she managed to moan before closing her eyes and turning her head away from her sister.

Dot used a tissue to clean from her face the flecks of mucus that had flown out with her sister's words and discovered that she was wiping tears away too. She knew exactly what Jean was talking about. The 'twice' left no room for doubt. She wiped her hands, rubbed another tissue over the face of her watch.

After all these years. Out of the sediment of their past. And these may have been her last words. Dot's own pulse was racing now and she recognized the urge to shake Jean, make her talk to her – about anything but that. Those should not be the last words Dot would have to remember.

It was the abortions. Of course it was. When Ray was inside, Jean used to have the occasional fling. She tried to keep them quiet but Dot was always able to wheedle it out of her. They were nothing serious until she met Derek Wilkes, a foreman at Longbridge. That went on for years. Twice Jean became pregnant and both times she had wanted to pass the child off as Ray's. But Dot wouldn't let her. She wasn't going to have Ray treated like that, left to bring up somebody else's kid, think it was his own, love it as his own. So she threatened to tell Ray everything she knew if Jean tried that one. Derek was married with a family and he wasn't going to chuck that over. So Jean got rid of them.

'I think you'd have left Ray for Derek if he'd've had you.' Dot found she was speaking out loud to her sister. She expected no reaction to her words and she got none. Just the gasping. 'Another good-looking bloke, Derek. You always got the good-looking ones.' Often when Dot saw Gary Lineker on television she was reminded of Derek Wilkes. It was the smile. But there had been something special about Ray when he was young.

After all this time, and now right at the end, it was the abortions. *You made me.* It was true, she had. And perhaps it was wrong. But – she tried not to continue the thought, but it was too late – if it was wrong, I've been punished, haven't I? Well and truly. Horribly. You never knew your children, well, they weren't children at all. But Lee, he was nineteen. Nineteen. Dot was sobbing. Reaching for another tissue. To lose your only child at nineteen. God, if she'd done wrong, she'd been well and truly punished and so had he. She could not control her sobs and their noise deafened her to the sound of her sister's struggle for breath and the terrible wind beyond the window.

When Hsinshu had pronounced the sentence of death upon him Jimmy Slim was prepared. He knew the Code. The sentence was inevitable. Only a weak leader would have delivered a lesser penalty. He had felt no fear, was sure he would meet his end honourably. When the squad came for him he did not hesitate, but rose to meet them. He noticed the crimson blindfold trailing from Feiyang's pocket. It meant nothing. Jimmy Slim was ready to play his part in what was about to be enacted.

Then the great wave rose up in him. He jumped them at the car and made for his motorbike. He saw Shuko, the bonebinder, step from the shadows. He heard the shots he fired die in the wind. Jimmy Slim ran like the wind and he ran with the wind and when he reached his bike he rode in the same way, like a surfer.

Now though, sitting crouched in the darkness of the empty flat, he had become stagnant. He must resurrect his energy. Mental level. He must think before he acted. They had taken his phone, his gun, his knife. He had only himself. It was a phone he needed now. He had friends in the Doberman Crew, he had done good work for them. They could save him. Time was tight but they were clever. The black men could save him. They would like to wound the Dragon, destroy it if they could, take over the spoils. This could be their moment. That is how he should present it. If he had a phone he could call Strombo. Those Rastas were clever; they could be here in minutes.

There must be a thousand phones in this building. He looked out of the window. When he had arrived here the sky was black; now it was blue, a fierce, proud blue reflecting the light of the city. Below, he saw the squad's car crawling slowly towards the building. He saw Shuko, the bonebinder, step from beneath the swaying trees into the street light. The car stopped by him. The squad got out and Jimmy Slim saw there was a back-up squad coming to a halt behind them. Arched against the wind, their feet planted apart, their heads bent in close, they talked with Shuko. Then they straightened, turned to look at the tower. Moved towards it.

Dot couldn't get Lee out of her mind. Eric seemed to have coped much better. Father and son were quite close when Lee was a boy but as he grew and became a bit wild there was a tension between them; Eric was always too quick to criticize and Lee wouldn't stand for it.

The coroner had given a verdict of Death by Misadventure. But she knew it wasn't that. They said he must have got into a fight, or hit his head on something and then fallen into the canal. No. Someone had put him in that water, she knew it. And she had lost count of the times she had prayed that whoever it was would pay for it, meet a terrible end. Eric had used his contacts, even in the police, to try and find out what had really happened, but nothing came of it. Sometimes she thought she had learned to live with it, but she never would. Every so often something would happen to bring it all back, and the pain and the desire for revenge were as powerful as ever.

She tried to get her mind back on Ray, tried to see him handsome and smiling as he was when she first met him. She hadn't told Jean about him when she took her to the dance at the Unicorn all those years ago, this chap she'd seen, so well-dressed, so good-looking, who smiled so nicely. If she had, would it have stopped Jean? Of course not. As soon as she saw him, she went after him. Though to be fair, it was Jean and not her who Ray was interested in, right from the start. Still, as things turned out . . . But perhaps with her he would have been different.

Poor Jean. This terrible gasping was doing Dot's head in. She couldn't let it carry on like this. She must do something. The pillow, perhaps. It would only take a minute. The trouble is they might do an autopsy. Then she could be the one doing time – probably longer than Eric ever did. But surely they wouldn't. The doctors knew Jean had cancer. She was only here because she wouldn't stay in hospital, wouldn't go to the hospice. Kept telling them she'd manage with the district nurses. Poor Jean.

'You never did know when you were beaten, did you, love?' Dot told her sister.

It was moments like these that Shuko lived for. He would never be a leader, but as a loyal and true servant to Hsinshu there were times when he was able to assume his master's authority. This was such a moment. He stepped out from the cover of the fir tree and raised his arm. The wind thrashed at him but he stood firm as any tree or tiger and raised his arm in the headlights.

Shouting against the wind, Shuko assigned tasks. He placed three men on the door. Three more would take the lift and work down from the top floor. Three would use the stairs in an upward sweep. They should take Jimmy Slim alive. Hsinshu did not want bullets left in the building. The two drivers should remain in their cars. If Jimmy Slim escaped the building they should use the cars to kill him. Then Naokung, whose element was Fire, shivered in the wind and, stepping back, looked up at the tower block. He laughed suddenly and loudly as those whose predominant energy is Fire are prone to do when taken by surprise, for he had seen the silhouette of a figure in a window two floors from the top.

It is the nature of Water under pressure to rise, then spread and fall. Jimmy Slim sprinted the steps to the top floor, booted the first door he saw. It shook against his force. Booted again, it flew open and sagged against the wall. Jimmy Slim surged through.

Dot thought it was the wind. Perhaps the whole building was coming down. Recent television images of hotels and beach homes being washed away swept through her mind. She jumped to her feet. She must escape. She rushed to the bedroom door. Jimmy Slim saw the black corridor open into blue like a channel of clear water. He made for it. Instead of a sea creature, it was a fat old woman he met in the doorway. He saw yellow hair, grey painted lips. Dot screamed when the male shape surfaced from the darkness. Jimmy Slim took her by the throat and walked her backwards into the bedroom. In the lesser dark he could see the glint of rings on the hands that tugged at his. He could feel her panting into his face.

He flung her down on to the bed. Released from the collar of the man's fist, Dot opened her mouth to scream again but only a stifled gurgle made it out into the room. She felt Jean's head beneath her back. Above her stood the young man. Thin. Not very tall. But his anger and strength were greater and more dangerous than the howling wind outside.

'Where's the phone?'

Dot heard his words, or heard words, but they made no sense. She was swamped by his presence. His violence. This man was going to kill her, she had no doubt. Would he rape her first? She hadn't the strength to resist.

He reached out and pulled her up towards him. 'The phone,' he bawled in to her face. 'Where's the phone?'

'In the other room. Through there.' He flung her back and as he did so a new darkness instantly descended.

The lift stopped between the tenth and eleventh floor. The three men inside, poised and ready for action, were consumed by a shocking still blackness. Everything had stopped.

In the stairwell Shuko cursed as the darkness fell. He cursed in Chinese. His curse was echoed by the other men. He would not be defeated by this. Naokung had seen Jimmy Slim on the fourteenth. They were now between the third and the fourth. Jimmy Slim could not use the lift. They merely had to continue to rise. He held on to the metal banister for guidance and, calling to the others to follow, kept climbing.

For the three men suspended in the dark at the centre of the tower block this was an impotent agony. They tapped the sides of the lift, located and pressed the useless buttons. There was confusion. This building was bad luck. Where was the emergency power? This building was useless. A shit-heap. Then anger and fear as they simply had to wait, hanging in the dark.

Jimmy Slim looked out from the window on the sixteenth floor. All the tower blocks were in darkness. A few headlights snailed in the underworld below, but the sky was black and empty, occupied now by nothing but the wind. It was pointless searching for the phone. Behind him the woman on the bed seemed to be crying. He smiled to himself. This wind might yet prove to be his saviour.

The greed that was one of the flaws in Jimmy Slim's character asserted itself. He had seen the rings on the woman's fingers, the gold wristwatch, the pearls around her neck. Spoils you don't turn your back on. They might not be as valuable as they looked. What would they be doing in a place like this? But Jimmy Slim would trust his instinct. Old women were funny: they often held on to valuable items despite the circumstances in which they lived.

He has started to undress me, Dot thought, as Jimmy Slim pulled up her head and unclasped the pearls. Then he slid the rings from her fingers, removed the gold watch from her wrist. The room was full of her gulping breaths. It was not until he said, 'Where's your money?' that she realized she was being robbed, not raped, and found her strength. 'I haven't got any money. I'm just visiting . . .' Jimmy Slim hit her. 'In my bag. In the kitchen.'

There was no point stumbling around trying to find the kitchen, then the bag, just for a few pounds. He had the jewellery. Now he must get out of here. Back out into the wind.

He found the stairwell door easily enough. He tugged it open, felt for the banister rail and started to descend. He could hear the rings tinkle in his pocket, a louder sound, it seemed to Jimmy Slim then, than the whip of the wind beyond.

When Shuko heard the door open he stopped dead and listened to the descending footsteps. The men behind him did the same. Silent. Motionless. Hardly breathing. The Dragons stood listening to Jimmy Slim coming towards them in the dark. He stepped straight into Shuko's arms and gasped his shock. The lights came on. A dim blue light showered the stairwell, illuminating for Jimmy Slim his fate. Distantly he heard the chug of the lift resuming its ascent.

They took Jimmy Slim back into the empty flat on the fourteenth floor. An hour ago it had been Jimmy Slim's dark haven; now it was full of the shadows of men. Shuko was on the landing, on the phone to Hsinshu. When he came into the flat he took the crimson blindfold from Feiyang, but he did not tie it round Jimmy Slim's head as he expected. Winding it round his fist, he made a mitten of it and used it to protect the window lever from finger-prints as he thrust it upward. Jimmy Slim understood.

The wind roared in and filled the room. It might have knocked Jimmy Slim from his feet had his legs not been grasped by Yihsi and Naokung. Feiyang and Shuko took him by the arms and all four men lifted Jimmy Slim up and hauled him through the open window out into the waiting wind.

Hsinshu was downstairs in the casino. He had just lost money on number 14. Shuko's call had distracted him; he had changed his mind at the last minute. Then he smiled. It was not such a bad thing for him to be seen by the punters losing money on the roulette wheel with good grace. It showed that we are all subject to fortune.

Looking for Starkweather

The police officer presses Play again. The grainy image fills the screen. Like life creeping into very old pictures. A post office. Small. Local. The door opens. Pause frame. The police officer peers in to the man held in the doorway. Young. Nineteen or twenty. Black spiky hair. Jeans. Footwear out of frame. Hawaiian shirt over white T-shirt under leather jacket. There is something familiar about him. The officer is sure of it. The shirt, maybe. Yes, the shirt.

I was living with Nana Beryl and Nana Coral. I didn't go to school much the last couple of years. Nana Beryl worked afternoons so I used to look after Nana Coral. Her mind had gone by then.

Most of the time Nana Coral dozed in her chair. Having a snooze. *Nana Coral is having a snooze.* I used to watch videos. Before she got really bad, gunfire would wake her up. Or shouting. She'd wake up and shout back at the telly, not making any sense. All sorts of bits of words flying out.

Some days were better than others. On good ones she would watch for a bit. She even clapped sometimes when someone got shot or jumped from one building to another. Excited. Like a little kid.

On the ninth floor we didn't need curtains. On sunny days I had to keep shifting the telly about because of the glare. Nana Coral didn't like that at all. 'No, Minna,' she would cry. Minna was her sister. Dead for years. 'It's not Minna. I'm Lucy. Your Lucy.' She looked hard at me, trying to work it out. When she got upset she'd reach into her pants and pull her incontinence pad out and wave it around, like she was signalling for help. I'd turn the telly off when she got really distressed. Cover the screen with a towel because of her reflection: 'Who's she? Looking at me. In my clothes. Look. Who is she?' Sometimes I'd look out onto the estate, at all the other tower blocks, and wish I could jump from roof to roof.

With a lot of films, I'd be half watching them and half keeping an eye on Nana Coral. Or I'd fast forward through the boring bits. That could make her smile. In winter, on cold, dull afternoons, I'd make bowls of Coco Pops for us. For a time she managed them herself, but in the end I had to feed her, though she didn't like it. 'You bloody fool,' she'd say, if something on the screen caught my attention and I missed her mouth. 'You bloody fool.' Other times she'd spit a mouthful out. Or lean her head back and let them ooze out, like lava.

The police officer presses Play. The man in the Hawaiian shirt moves to the counter. Still can't see his feet. The hand moves up. Reaching. Grasping the hair of the woman at the grille. Pulling the head back. Now the other hand. A streak. But the officer can distinguish the knife.

True Romance. It feels like the first film I ever watched. Except it was more than watching it. Like coming home. Like getting out. Like falling in love. Like meeting people you know will be friends for life.

Falling in love. I didn't know it then but that's what was

happening to me. Fifteen years old and I was falling in love with a man I didn't know existed. A man who had been dead for thirty-five years. Starkweather. Charles Starkweather. Chuck. That's what Caril called him: Chuck.

The police officer reaches for the tape machine. Presses Play. She keeps her eyes on the screen – the held image of the knife in mid-air – as she listens to the witness. 'She wanted stamps, the woman. She'd been waiting for a while. I apologized. I'd had three pensioners, one after the other. Collecting their pensions, paying bills. You can't rush them. So she's been waiting. I was just putting the stamps into the tray, two books of six, when I saw something behind her. Just a blur really.' The police officer releases the held image. Watches the knife rise. 'It all happened so quick. I thought it might be a drunk or a druggie. Stumbling. You get them. But. So quick it was. Her throat was right back. The knife. "I'll cut her throat right out. Throw it at you." He growled. Low. Harsh and horrible, like an animal. Horrible. I couldn't see her face. Just the throat. The knife. She groaned. Gasped sort of. "Please," she said. Then again: "Please."

'"All the notes you've got. In there." He nodded to the deposit tray. I reached into the drawer and got a couple of bundles. Then a couple more. Dropped them in the tray. He made her pick them up. Then he eased her backwards towards the door. He was shouting: "Keep back, or I'll carve her." I was sure he would do it. Everybody was. Then they were away. She just changed as they got to the door. Stood up. He let her go. And they were gone.'

It seems now like it was all one long winter's afternoon instead of hundreds of them. One long winter's afternoon with Nana Coral dozing in her chair and me watching *True Romance* over and over so I knew most of the words.

Others, too. *Wild at Heart, Drugstore Cowboy, Natural Born Killers*. There was something about those films. Love is one thing. A girl just gives herself to a guy who's kinda wild and restless, a rebel, doesn't give a shit. You see what's happening? I'm talking like an American. That's what happens. I just loved listening to those girls. And they were all so pretty, but not showy with it, just ordinary girls, except that once they'd met their guy they'd met their destiny and they followed it. And the guys were all wild – wild at heart – killers, natural born killers. In parking lots and motel rooms, in clubs and on lonely country roads they left a trail of death wherever they went.

In *Drugstore Cowboy*, when Nadine dies of an overdose and she's lying there on the floor beside the bed and Bobby and Dianne and Rick are all looking down on her wondering what to do, I always paused it there. Every time. And I always wanted to do something. Break the screen. Climb in. Say, 'I'll be your girl now, Rick. Take me with you. I'm one of the crew.'

It was while I was watching *Natural Born Killers* that Nana Coral died. She hadn't been well all day. She was hot and I couldn't get her to drink anything. She just wanted to sleep and it was really deep. Big sighs from her sometimes. I don't know which bit she died at. I hope it was the bit where Mallory throws her white veil over the bridge and it sails away in the air floating slowly down to the river. I love that bit. I was sitting on the floor when the film started, resting my back against Nana Coral's legs. But, like always, I got closer to the television when it got exciting. When it finished I just sat in the dark room thinking about it. Then I realized how quiet it was. Even in the gloom I could see her head had fallen onto the arm of the chair. I knew she was gone.

So then there was just Nana Beryl and me. And that wasn't easy for either of us. It had been different when

Nana Coral was there; everything was about looking after her. I had to go back to school. Not regular. 'Just show your face,' Nana Beryl said. 'Just till the end of term.'

It was fate. Media Studies. I want you to prepare a talk about your favourite film, the teacher said. Five minutes. But not just the story. We're going to the computer room. I want you to do some research on the Internet. See what you can find out. Background. That's what I'll be looking for.

I put in *True Romance*. And there he was. Or at least his name: Charles Starkweather. That's where I saw it for the first time. True Romance *is one of a number of successful films Hollywood produced in the nineties loosely based on the case of Charles Starkweather, the nineteen-year-old from Nebraska who, with his fourteen-year-old sweetheart Caril Fugate, embarked on a murder spree that horrified the nation. Together, in the space of three weeks, they took eleven lives including those of Fugate's parents and little sister. Starkweather was executed in Nebraska's electric chair on 25 June 1959. He was twenty years old.*

I put *Natural Born Killers* in. The same thing. *The story of Mickey and Mallory Knox, written by Quentin Tarantino, though fictional, is inspired by the case of Charles Starkweather and Caril Fugate who, in December 1957 and January 1958, went on a robbery and murder spree in which they were to take eleven lives.* It was fate. Weird. All four films that I put into the search engine mentioned Charles and Caril. The films I watched all the time. I had been watching them. Him. I had never heard of *Badlands*, but all of the sites mentioned it. I left school at break and went into town. HMV. I wanted to nick it. It felt right. But it was just the empty case. So I bought it, but I went into River Island and nicked a couple of tops to make up for it.

*

It was the best. *Badlands*. I watched it over and over. And that's when I sort of knew. The next time I was at Media Studies I put Charles Starkweather into the search engine. There were tons of sites. If he was so famous, how come I'd never heard of him? There were pictures. He was beautiful. Better than any of those who played him. I wanted to talk to him. I wanted to go with him. Be Caril. I couldn't get my head round the fact that he didn't exist any more.

It was fate. Nana Beryl was watching a programme about reincarnation. About how the spirit floats around in the ether before being reborn. This woman was saying that if someone has done really bad things, like Hitler, say, then they might come straight back so they can try again, make things right, or sometimes they have to stay in the ether a long time waiting for the right circumstances. And the right place. She said she'd been a Roman slave and a Red Indian. You can end up anywhere.

I never did drugs but I liked boys who did. It was the eyes. I loved those eyes. When they really needed a fix. Like sex. Wanting so bad. And it's all there in the eyes. Trembling as well. Then you can get them to do anything.

Tango was a real junkie. I used to see him at the Cottrells' picking stuff up. I knew all the Cottrells from when I was fostered. I knew their sister, Stacey, so I'd hang around there sometimes.

Tango used to do a bit of housebreaking or stuff from cars. Some outfits on the estate would take stuff if it was good – laptops, things like that – but the Cottrells were cash only. He fenced through Easy Ted Nicholls.

'He's cheap,' I told Tango. 'You'll never get anything off him.'

'No.'

'I can help you get some cash.'

That's how it started. Hairdressers. Small ones in back streets where they only use cash. If you go in the afternoon, about four, you can pick up a hundred easy, two if it's Friday. Straight through the door. The smell gets you first. Horrible. Warm and cloying. The warm stench of chemical: shampoo, setting lotion, lacquer. Then the startled eyes, all looking at you. Old women mostly in those places. Captured under their driers, like space helmets. We'd just stand there. Looking. Let it sink in: danger. Just watching the eyes. Understanding, slowly. That was always good.

The police officer is going through paperwork. All the written statements. She finds what she is looking for. Checks the date. Yes. It's possible. That's what a police officer must always remember: anything is possible. A lot can happen in five years. 'I didn't know at first. I didn't realize. You just don't expect. Then I noticed Pauline had stopped rolling. I looked in the mirror. She was pale. It was then the lady under the drier next to me screamed. I turned. The girl had pushed the drier down on her. Oh my God! I still feel sick when I think of it. You could smell the hair burning straight away. I never saw much of the chap; it was the girl that was with him. She starts screaming like an animal. Terrifying. A mad cat. Pushing the point of the scissors into the lady's throat. You know every time I tried to get off to sleep last night I saw that. The scissors. So close against her throat I thought they were in. And that girl, baying away. Then, they're just about to leave. They're at the door. She stops. Everything is quiet. She looks around. Then comes back to the lady with the burnt head. I really thought she was going to kill her. But she just looks down at her. Sneers and says, "As Bobby Hughes says, That's just the way it is, sweet."'

*

If there was more than one hairdresser, Tango would go for the one nearest the door. Drag her to the desk where they kept the cash. The places we chose, there was never more than three hairdressers. Tango used a knife. I had scissors. I started. Marched to some old bird under the drier and pulled it down on her. Before she starts off, I'm screaming for her. Then it's scissors pushed against the neck. 'Shut the fuck up,' I'm yelling, 'or I'll put these through your throat.' The screamer couldn't hear but everyone else could. Worked like a dream. We were in and out of those places in five minutes flat.

It was all right with Tango. Good at first. But as soon as he got his drugs that was it.

'Let's nick a car and go to London,' I'd say.

'Nah. We're all right here.' Boring.

I dreamed of riding cars from town to town, maybe with another couple like in *Drugstore Cowboy* and *Another Day in Paradise*. 'Let's nick a car and go to Glasgow. See your dad.'

'What'd I want to see that bastard for?'

'Can you get a gun? Ask the Cottrells. They'd get us one. Let's try it with a gun.'

'You're fuckin barkin. A gun. We're doing all right with the blades.'

The police officer slotted another cartridge. She should have left an hour ago. Perched on the edge of the desk, she pressed Play. The image appeared. A building society. The cartridge held the segued tapes. Made a little film. Woman enters building society. Now the camera shows her at the counter. Another piece of tape, from behind the cashier's head. The woman through security glass. Not a woman, a girl really. She can't be much more than sixteen. Her lips are moving. The police officer knows from the witness statement that she is asking how to open a savings account.

Now the door again. The man in the Hawaiian shirt. Camera change to behind the cashier. The knife is held to the side of the girl's head. The assailant's mouth opens wide, closes, opens again, like gasping. But the police officer knows that he is yelling that he will cut this girl's face off. From ear to nose. That he will sling it at the security glass. A hand comes into frame dropping a bundle of cash into the deposit tray. Then another. The police officer presses Replay. Then Hold. The girl's head is bent forward. You can't see the knife. It looks as if his fist is in her ear. But you can see the man in the Hawaiian shirt. The police officer stares, hard. At the fist. The man's neck. The chin. But the eyes are blurred.

I first saw Ben in a fight outside the Social Security. He was beautiful. Blond. Like Starkweather. And a knife scar on his ear. No lobe. When he got on a bus I followed him. Sat beside him. 'What you doin ridin buses? You should nick a car. Take me for a ride.'

He had a great smile. 'Just what I was thinking myself.' He said it really slow. Smiling the words out. Bad. I knew I'd found him.

'What you calling me starkers for?'

'Not starkers, Starky.'

'What for?'

'That's my secret.' And I never told him.

Nana Beryl said no. 'He's not moving in here, Lucy.'

'Chelmsley. He's not moving in here, Chelmsley.'

'I'm not calling you that.'

'It's my name now. Chelmsley Wood. It's where I'm from. It sounds good. It sounds American. It's what I'm called now.'

'Oh, Lucy.'

'No, don't try to get round me. Take your hand away. It won't work. I want Ben to come here. And his sister.'

'She's too young, Lucy. You know she is. Twelve? Thirteen? She should be in care.'

'She was. I told you. She ran away. They don't know where she is. They don't know Ben's got her. He'll not let her go back into care. If they can't stay here, he'll go somewhere else. Wolverhampton, he says. And I'll go with him.'

The Hawaiian shirt. Always there's a Hawaiian shirt. The police officer watches the assailant in his Hawaiian shirt lean in with his knife towards what appears to be his victim but is his accomplice. Has to be. Stop. Back. She watches again. Stop. Play. Stop. Yes. The fall of the shirt. Could it be? It's possible. Anything is possible.

'D'you think she's beautiful?'

'Alabama? Yes.'

'How old d'you think she is?'

'I dunno. Twenty-four? You've asked me that a hundred times. What do you keep watching those films for?'

'Because I want us to be like them.'

'We do okay.'

'We haven't killed anyone yet.'

'You're a fuckin nutter.'

'Yes. Yes, I am. And I want you to be one too.'

Ben was right. We did okay. He was a criminal through and through. He wanted money. He wasn't into drugs. He took me to the Little Moscow. I was the only girl in there.

'Is this where you'd come if you wanted a gun?'

'Maybe.' He had a look sometimes, when he went close. Secretive.

I looked around. Most of the blokes were old. There were some young ones playing snooker. An Asian kid with a shaved head waved his cue. 'I was in youth DT with him. Bal. Dunno what it's short for.'

When three lads came down the steps he gave me a tenner. 'Get this changed and play the machine. I need a word with them.' He followed them into an alcove and they talked.

I did all right at first, went as high as twenty-two quid. But I was down to four when he came over to me.

'Go home now.'

'I wanna come with you.'

'Don't be daft. Go home. I'll see you later.'

'You gonna do a job.'

'Yeh.'

'Without me.'

'Yeh, without you. This is a proper job. Now fuck off home. You know Ami don't like being on her own with Beryl.'

'But.'

'If I have to hit you. I fuckin will. Now git.'

I never saw him again. They wouldn't let me. Said I wasn't a relative. I had no right. Ami could have, I suppose, but they didn't know about her. We kept her quiet. She didn't cry much and I didn't cry at all. Nana Beryl bawled her eyes out for an hour. The law had chased them all the way to Spaghetti. They'd done a jewellery job. One of the workshops in Deritend. Hell of a chase: three miles. Sirens wailing. The van tumbled off the M6 ramp. Thirty-five foot: high as a house. Ben was in the back. That night I dreamed there had been just the two of us in it. And it was an open-top, not a van. And I thought about the bit where Mallory talks about her and Mickey becoming angels. Up in the stars. American girls can talk like that and it doesn't sound daft.

A really weird thing happened at Ben's funeral. Fate again. 'It's fate, Mallory.' That's what Mickey Knox used to say. We were at the crematorium, waiting for the coffin to arrive, and there's a list on the door of all the funerals for that day. His name was there, at the top of the list: the first one. Charles Starkweather. My heart stopped. I couldn't believe it. Then when I looked closer it said Charles Fairweather, 87 years. But even so. It'd got to be a sign.

I knew then that I wasn't going to find him. Not in the way I thought. But I started to realize that there was another way.

The police officer comes in early. She watches all the tapes again. And again. Last night she felt she was getting close. Now she is not so sure. She is missing something. She knows she is. One small thing. If she can recognize this, all will be revealed. She smiles to herself. You watch too many films. It isn't as simple as that.

She goes through the written statements again, then listens to those on tape. Then something, on a tape: 'I didn't know what was happening. I just heard someone shouting. And these two running round the corner. I thought it was two girls running at first. Then they turned . . .'

The police officer goes back to the screen. The man in the Hawaiian shirt holding the girl. Her head is back. The blade. If only she could see more of the blade. She looks at the young man's face. Mouth open. She looks at the chin. She wonders.

We looked after Ami, Nana Beryl and me. Well, me. Nana Beryl didn't like having her there really. She wanted it to be just her and me. Like before. But she was okay. Ami didn't go to school so we used to watch films together. Lots of films, but mostly my favourites. It was like I was waiting for her to grow up. Watching her grow up. Helping. Training. We played games. Hold-ups. Attacks. Raids. Once we took Nana Beryl hostage in her bedroom. Tied her up. Waved the blades at her. Scared the living shit out of her.

I carried on going down the Moscow for a bit. I talked to Bal and a couple of others, but I knew I wasn't going to find my Starkweather there. People talked to me more when I changed my hair: dyed it black, cut it spiky. More when I wore a leather jacket, jeans. Then I got the offer of a couple of jobs. But no one would sell me a gun.

'You're changing, Chelms,' Fat Alex said to me. 'You're changing into a boy.'

'You can call me Chuck then,' I told him.

On Ami's fifteenth birthday I took her into town. I knew she was ready. Designer shops. I bought her some nice dresses. Dresses that turned her into a woman. A red one, like Alabama's. And some shades like the ones Dianne wears in *Drugstore*. After, we went to the markets.

'Look,' she said, pointing. 'Like Clarence in *True Romance*.'

Hawaiian shirts. Loads of them, hanging round a van. A fiver a go. I bought six.

'Goin on yer olidays?' Alex said.

It was the first night I wore one of my Hawaiians. There's a grotty old mirror outside the toilets. I caught my reflection. It stopped me. The bloke that looked back at me. I'd found him. I went into the Gents. And it was in there, a week later, that I bought my gun. A Webley. American.

'You're lucky to get that, Chuck,' Nechells told me. 'American guns. Very rare now. All fuckin Russian gear. Chechnya. Kosovo. Feels good, doesn't it? And you look the part. So, a undred and fifty to you, Chuck.'

'Deal.'

'When we goin to use it?' Ami kept asking.

'I dunno. We do all right with blades. We'll just keep it in reserve.'

'Boring.' And she pouts, sulks a bit. Then I tickle her and she laughs. She puts her arm round my neck. 'I love you, Charles Starkweather. I love you.'

If Nana Beryl's around when we do this she swears. Waves her fag at us. Gives us abuse. Foul stuff. But she knows I've got a gun now. So she quietens down. Sticks a video in. Watches that.

Dream of the Stunt

The man who walked above cities had come home and there wasn't a copper in Birmingham who wouldn't be on duty today. The local breakfast show DJs were already babbling on about how the eyes of the world were upon us.

The dawn arrived with full sun. As the forecasters had predicted it was going to be a good day – hot. From his room on the sixteenth floor of the Hyatt Dowd could see three of the seven orange cranes that stood atop the city centre's highest buildings. The black line of wire linking them scored the pale blue sky. It was along this wire at eleven o'clock this morning that Chad Hallam would make his record-breaking walk high above the city of his birth.

Con knew you could never escape the past. Not one like his anyway. He should be happy, but he knew that at some point the storm would come – without warning, probably – and so he was always waiting. Like the lone yachtsman he had been reading about: calm weather for days, just enough wind to do the job, keep the sails full, and then . . .

Con had always supposed it would be a phone call. Sometimes when the phone rang he was sure it would be one of them. He had never bought an answer machine. When the fear was upon him he just let the phone ring.

But it wasn't like that. He was mowing the lawn after tea. Thinking about bedding plants. He looked up and there was Danny Rivers' face above the hedge. He hadn't seen it for thirty years but he recognized it instantly.

'Moynihan, you old devil. So this is where you've been hiding away.' Rivers opened the gate and came in to the garden. 'Lovely,' he said, looking around. 'You've got green fingers and no mistake. Now put that thing away and let me take you for a pint. For old times' sake.'

'This city's changed all right,' Rivers said cheerfully as they drove. 'A fair bit of redevelopment,' he chuckled. 'You'd hardly know the place. Very American now. All these tall glass buildings.'

The car curved past the Bull Ring towards Digbeth. Con thought they were heading for the Irish Club there. He tensed as the car continued past it, heading towards Tyseley. Oh no, he thought. Not there. He had been trying to forget that place for over thirty years.

'Well, this place hasn't changed,' Rivers said when they were settled in the Little Moscow with their pints and Bushmills chasers.

'No,' Con agreed, and it was true, everything in here was still the same. He looked across to the jukebox. He remembered the songs playing that night: 'Rock Your Baby' by George McCrae, 'Long Tall Glasses' by Leo Sayer. If he ever heard those songs now he went cold. The barman was still the same. Older but still fat. Fatter if anything. Con remembered the dirty white pumps the barman had been wearing that night, his soiled grey trousers. Another image that remained with him. He and Rivers had been sitting in that alcove, the one nearest the steps.

'Well, there's great excitement about and no mistake.'

It took Con a moment to understand. The bar was half empty. 'Oh, the high-wire walk. Yes, everyone's looking forward to it. Local lad makes good. That sort of thing.

And the walk itself will be spectacular. A real festival for the city.'

Rivers drained his Bushmills. 'I was over at St Catherine's on Sunday. Father Ray tells me your lad's got great prospects too.'

'Lonnie, yes.'

'Father Ray says he's a fierce left foot on him. Birmingham City youth team, is it now? Not that I'm surprised. You were a fine sportsman yourself in your youth, Con. A great man for the hurling.' He drank from his pint. 'I ran into Mary in Dublin a few months back, Con. She's still a fine woman. Yes, indeed. But you left her very bitter. "Men," she said to me. "One should be taken out and shot every Monday morning."' He laughed heartily. 'She has the daughter over there with her, she told me.'

'Katie, yes. She went with her mother, Lonnie stayed with me. It was the football. There were already scouts showing an interest.' This rupturing of his family was something Con was usually reluctant to talk about, but now, well, where was the harm in a chat? So long as it didn't stray to the old times, the history that bound him and Dan.

'You never married yourself, Dan?'

'Me, no. Still one of the Mallow Road bachelor boys.'

The Mallow Road, where they had all started out. Country boys really. They grew up on a small estate of civic housing planted in the countryside a few miles from Cork City. On a clear day you could see Blarney Castle from his bedroom window. Country boys raised on myths of patriotism and injustice, stories of the rebels and their glorious fight. '*Tiocfaidh ár lá*', they had called to each other and thrust their fists into the country air, intoxicated by the history they had inherited. 'Our day will come.' He shuddered as he thought about it. All those stories. And with their teenage years, the hurling and the fishing and dancing with the girls to showbands down on the quay was not enough. There was a war to be fought, glory to be had. They were such easy meat.

As Dowd pulled on his shirt he thought of all the other coppers in this city getting up now, showering and shaving. In an hour they would all be in briefing rooms, looking at charts and maps, listening to orders. Like a military operation.

A week ago Dowd had been really pissed off at the thought of today. He hoped some loony with a chainsaw would do his thing so he could get on with his real job. Then he was assigned to Personal Protection – hence this nice little number of a night in an expensive room in the Hyatt. The subject was in the penthouse, two floors above, and hopefully sleeping like a baby.

Dowd lifted his mobile from the bedside table and pressed 4. It rang only once.

'Morning, sir.'

'Just checking you're up, Jack.'

'Yep. Up and ready to go. Looks like a nice day.'

Dowd took the lift to the penthouse. The uniformed officer standing outside nodded. 'There's not been a peep all night, sir.'

So everything was on schedule. Hallam's parents should arrive here at eight-thirty. The family would leave at nine for St Chad's Cathedral where they were to hear mass together. From the cathedral Hallam would be taken to the Radisson, where, after what was described on the schedule as a toilet stop, he would take the lift to the roof and begin his ascent of the crane-ladder to the starting point of his walk. I'd need a toilet stop, Dowd smiled to himself, if I was going to walk a tight-rope across the city.

124

Dowd breakfasted with Jack. 'Is that all you're having?' He indicated a bowl of muesli. Dowd had ordered a full English.

'It's enough,' Jack told him.

Dowd shook his head. 'I don't know how you keep going. So, Jack, d'you think our friend Hallam is going to make it? Will he be on the open-top bus with the mayor for his triumphant ride to the Council House – or will we be scraping him up and trying to control a hysterical crowd, their fiesta turned into a Diana?'

'He's done them before.'

'Not as long as this.'

'That's the clever part,' Jack explained. 'He's got five staging-posts, in fact, one at each crane. So it's only the longest stretch, between the Orion and the top of the Pallasades, that will break the record. Not the whole city-walk. It wouldn't qualify.'

'Why do you think he does it?'

'The money, I suppose. It's made him a rich man.'

Dowd's breakfast arrived. 'There must be more than that.'

'Fame. And he's obviously driven by the challenge. Or was at the start.'

'So why is he bringing God into the act all of a sudden?' Dowd cut into his bacon. 'Mass at the cathedral. He's never done that before.'

'He says he has, only privately. Today, well, it all adds to the drama. The performance. His last show.'

'Go out with a bang, eh?' Dowd grinned. He forked a mushroom into his mouth. 'The archbishop's loving it. Blessing the bloody cranes, for Christ sake.'

'Whatever you think, sir, it's still a magnificent achievement.'

'Heights have never worried me much, Jack. When I was a kid, about fourteen or fifteen, you know how groups of lads play dares, or used to? Just sit in front of bloody computers now, hacking into the Pentagon. Well, ours was to edge along this narrow little parapet on a railway bridge near us and stand there until a train came. That was stage one. Stage two: when the train came you had to piss on it.' Dowd laughed. 'Twice I did that.'

'Not quite the same as Hallam's walk.'

'No. I guess not.'

Inside St Chad's Cathedral, Chad Hallam knelt and prayed to God for safety and success. He prayed too for forgiveness of the sin of vanity. He knew he was no longer driven only by the dream of walking through the air above cities, his ambition since boyhood. In the circus they called it *The Dream of the Stunt*. But with success had come the need for more attention. Once it was enough that people threw their heads back, opened their mouths and stared up at him in awe. Now he wanted attention on the ground as well. And he had certainly achieved that. He had turned stunts into shows, international spectaculars. He knew that while people admired what he did and rooted for him, what they really wanted, despite themselves, was to see him stumble, slip, miss his footing and sail defenceless to destruction below, carrying their own worst fears with him. That was what drew them to the events. And what he now felt might drive him too. He was glad today would be the last time.

Last year, high above Vancouver, his concentration abandoned him for a moment. A seemingly irresistible urge to let go, swoop down like a bird. A message from God, he was sure of it. It was then he decided to return to his home town for his longest and final walk. To complete the story. The fact that Birmingham was not a world-class city – not New York or Rio de Janeiro, not Bangkok or St Petersburg, all cities he had walked above – was important, for it seemed that by walking here he was in a way blessing Birmingham, bringing the world's eye to it and conferring upon his city an enchanted status.

As he received the communion host, Chad placed himself in God's hands. Turning away from the archbishop, he caught sight of his father waiting in line behind him. He prayed that today could bring about some form of healing between himself and his father. Not that there had ever been any row or rift. Just that from as far back as he could remember, this man, who had always done his duty, in many ways the perfect father, was a mystery to him. No closeness. Whenever they spoke, it seemed to Chad that his father had something else on his mind, was never fully with him.

It had been agreed with the television companies that his parents would be on the roof of the Rotunda, the first to greet him when he came down. They had been instructed to hug each other for the cameras. Chad hoped that in that moment there could at last be a real closeness.

His father had received communion and was now kneeling in the pew beside him. And what, Chad wondered, would his father feel if something went wrong? His mother, he knew, would be distraught and he felt guilt for the pain he might cause her. But his father? He had given him no encouragement. Shown no pleasure at his success or fame. He had agreed to play a part today only because it was the last time. Chad returned to his prayers – for safety and success.

Con was at the bar getting the glasses refilled. He didn't like the look he was getting from the barman. He couldn't recognize him, surely. Not after all these years. Con looked down. Long tall glasses. The barman said nothing.

'Health to you and yours.' Rivers downed his Bushmills in a single gulp. 'Ah.' The back of his hand skimmed his mouth. He lifted his pint and drank. Wiped his mouth again. 'Well. Down to business.' The words broke Con's heart. 'I'm sure you'll be wondering why I'm here, Con. Why Danny Rivers has suddenly turned up like some wee leprechaun at the bottom of your garden.' He laughed so loudly that the barman turned to look. An Asian hoodie at the pool table glanced across. 'The truth is, Con, we have a small job for you.'

Rivers' eyes glittered black fire. Powerful, cruel eyes. Words ignited in Con's head, stupid words. He was held by Rivers' eyes. *That old black fire has me in its spell, that old black fire I know so well.* The hardness was back in Rivers' face. Nothing had changed, Con realized. Time was powerless against men like Rivers.

It came out so pathetically: 'The war's over, Dan.'

'Never.' The word like a jumping fish from his mouth. 'Never. *Tiocfaidh ár lá.*'

Rivers leaned in towards Con. 'We brought chaos to this city once, Con,' he hissed. 'You and me, Vincent, the others. And for years we had the upper hand for it. British cabinet ministers turning up in Dublin bars disguised in caps and scarves like dock workers. We had the upper hand then,' he gasped, rested for a second before continuing. 'Now. There's been a shakedown. Power has changed hands again. This is the time and place to strike again. Write a new agenda. While the Brits are busy fretting about the Muslims.'

'The place?'

'The Irish made this city, Con. Irish labourers built it, and a grand place it is now, I'll give you that.'

'Then why blow it up?'

Another roar of laughter. 'We're not going to blow anything up. Just light a fuse – and stand back.' The laughter led to a coughing fit. Rivers' shoulders shook, flecks of phlegm shot from his mouth. He leaned back in his chair, eyeing Con coldly as he recovered. 'You've always been a powerful man with a gun, Con. I remember you with the rabbits on the Mallow Meadows. You filled many a family's pot before you left school.'

Almost to himself, Con said, 'I thought you had finished with me.'

'Will you listen to the man? Finished? Listen, boy, you're with us. Always have been, always will be. That's the way it works, Con. You know that. There was never a fiercer man than yourself for the cause. You were passionate with words, so you were. Eloquent, I would say. You inspired me and many more with your talk of injustice, fight to the death. And you backed your words up with actions. Many a time.'

Con felt hollow, like an empty boat, bobbing on the water. He wanted to say, *I am old, tired. That was another man entirely; I never see him now.* Injustice? What was more unjust than six innocent men receiving life-sentences? A most bitter wrong. He remembered the day he had signed a petition. His hand shook for an hour afterwards.

Con told Rivers he'd make his own way home. He'd given him what he wanted. He stood outside the bar, glad of the darkness. But May darkness isn't really dark at all. Not like November. That was a dark night, all right, 21 November 1974. He and Rivers sitting in the Little Moscow. Drinking. Waiting. Rivers telling stories and laughing. Aching with tension. But without doubt. Then, as arranged, Vincent came down the steps, ordered a whisky, drank it, went to the toilet and left. Silently, they watched him climb the steps. A minute later they followed. The narrowboat was near the bridge. They boarded it and by the time it had passed under the bridge they had their plastic bags and were away, each about his business. The boat chugged slowly on into the darkness.

An hour later they were back in the Moscow. Drinking fiercely. They could hear the sirens. The barman looked hard at them. Or so Con thought.

Con himself went into the darkness that night – a darkness from which he had never been able to return. And what right did he have to do so? Once in, there's no way out. Never. He had said these words many times to many men and they were still true. He had said them once, a long time ago, to Finbar Doherty.

Once in, there is no way out. It seems that applied to the city too. As the man *in situ* he need only have remained a few weeks beyond the hit – wind up the cell, cover the ground, slip away. But he could not walk away. So he stayed. Walking the line of a quiet life. Head down. Then he met Mary and family life took over. But the shadow was always waiting. In the heart of the city. Lurking.

Now Con walked to the Maltese chip shop. Just to look at the pretty brown-skinned girl who worked there. Mediterranean sunshine smiled out of her. Outside, looking in at her, he shovelled chips into his mouth, knowing that he would throw them back up into some gutter before he made it home.

Dowd didn't often feel the power of the collective and he was enjoying it. Standing on the cathedral steps with Jack and the others, he scanned through dark glasses the crowd standing behind the photographers on the closed-off ring road. The descending ramp provided a good view. Both to the crowd and to those observing them. There were a number of young women in the crowd, some with banners reading WE LOVE YOU, CHAD and WALK MY WIRE, CHAD.

Beyond the crowd a scaffolding tower held international television crews, their cameras focused on the cathedral. Dowd felt like an actor on a film set. From here he would report to the Rapid Response Incident Room set up in the

Rotunda. This was a pity for there were a few women he'd noticed in the crowd he wouldn't mind chatting to. One in particular, in a spotted dress.

Standing now above the city on the first staging ramp, Chad Hallam took up his wand. Weighed it. Grasped it. Ready. There was no breeze. Perfect. He scanned the city. So many trees. He swallowed. There was a comforting tension in his belly, but he knew his concentration wasn't what it should be. In every other walk his mind had been numb with concentration. He knew the cause of the problem. As he had left his parents on the steps of St Chad's, his father had taken his hand and grasped his shoulder. 'Good luck, son,' he said. 'I'm proud of you.' The power of it had drained him. He tried to force it from his mind. He looked out at the wire, saw the filigree metal cross, like an ink sketch in the sky atop St Martin's Church, the silver wings of the cockerel from which it emerged caught by the sun. Long deep breaths. That was the key. Long and steady. Let everything leave the mind. He counted the breaths. On the fifth exhalation he lifted his right foot out onto the wire high, high above Birmingham. A murmur rose from below. Only the breathing. The feet moved with the breaths. Step followed step. Breath followed breath. He did not hear the applause. His mind was numb.

When Rivers arrived with the gun Con said nothing. He had rehearsed tirelessly how he would tell Rivers. He wouldn't do it. He had done enough. Enough for the cause. Enough to damn himself, of that he was sure. He could do no more. But he said nothing. Too long a sacrifice can make a stone of the heart. He took the gun. Handled it. Examined it. All the time Rivers' black eyes shone on him. Con listened as Rivers gave him his instructions, followed the man's stubby finger across the map.

'We'll have a pint now.' Rivers folded the map and returned it to the brown envelope. He dropped it on Con's kitchen table.

'No, Dan. I don't think so.'

'Come on, man,' Rivers laughed. 'You'll not see me again.'

'Till the next time.'

Rivers roared. 'Fair play to you, Con boy. Fair play to you.'

In the bar Rivers read Con's mind. 'It's a job that must be done,' he said sternly. 'And you're the man to do it. You've lain low all these years. Had time to raise the family. There's many never saw their children grow. You have what it takes. Always did. Quick and clean and make yourself disappear. You have done it before.'

'I have that.' Con had been thinking all day about how he could disappear.

'And it's the perfect moment. Doherty is an informer. Remember that. Remember what it means. It doesn't matter how many years have passed. Many good men went down because of him. He was one of us and he turned to save his skin and collect the Brits' money. A new identity. A nice little life here. Harry Hallam, indeed.' Rivers was warming to his subject. His mouth twisted. 'Well, now the bastard will get what he deserves. And doing it this way we re-emerge with maximum publicity.' He smacked his lips. 'It'll be as good as Brighton.'

'The lad might fall and he –'

'He won't fall. It's a stunt. I don't know how he does it, but he won't fall. He never has before.' Rivers drew breath. 'And if he did, well, it's an even bigger stunt.'

Rivers was angry. Con wasn't there. He should be on Waterstone's steps opposite the Rotunda. The Hallams' car was due any minute. He scanned the crowd again. No.

Not a sign of the man. He checked his mobile. If there was a problem Con should have rung. He tapped the gun inside his jacket. Contingency. At least he had planned for this possibility. He thought for a moment of the suicide bombers he'd read about. They kept their nerve, didn't back out.

Applause from across the city echoed between the buildings. The walk had started. Rivers moved through the crowd. 'Stupid bastard,' he muttered. 'To think he could pull a stunt like this.' There were plain-clothesers dotted among the crowd. Rivers could spot them a mile away. Useless, so they were. There was one who hadn't even removed his dark glasses, like something from a Tarantino film, talking to a girl in a spotted dress. As he edged past, the car carrying Chad Hallam's parents pulled up.

At six minutes past eleven, when he heard the sound of the gun, Chad Hallam was silhouetted against the clock face of the museum tower. It was a distant echo – a click or pop. But it entered his consciousness. He gasped. His eyes flickered. He swayed. Noise from below. A gasp echoing his own. He went with the swaying rope. Let the pole hold his balance. He was sure there were screams. But. As he swayed high above the city he regained the rhythm of his breath and control of his feet and with them the steel wire. Step followed step. It was all right. Nothing serious had happened.

*

Dowd had been disappointed when he had not got the Doherty killing. It was what his career needed, a case with an international profile, and it came as a blow to realize that he was not, as he would have thought, the obvious choice. Six months later, learning that the investigation was being scaled down, he was pleased. Poor old Fellows would have to face the media this morning and admit, in effect, that they had nothing. That wouldn't do his career much good.

When the phone rang it was Trevor, the desk sergeant. 'Dowd, there's been a shooting. Outside the Blues training ground. One confirmed dead so far. Unofficially, an apprentice. Lonnie Moynihan. Heard of him? The super wants you to look after it.'

Gangland, probably, Dowd thought. Who knows what these players get involved in? Pity it wasn't first team. Much more high profile. Still, you never know. 'Come on, Jack. We've got a job.'

Electric Pink

Martin stood in an archway on Essex Street, outside the Norway Room, smoking a spliff. The distant rhythms of the Norway imbued the moment with melancholy; he liked it. The rain had stopped. The glazed black street reflected the lights: the yellow streetlight; the triangular blue lamp above the Norway; the white headlights of a car passing through. Smears. Like a painting.

On the adjacent corner the long pink neon panels of the Rosebud Club glowed softly. Too far back to be more than ochre shadows on the tarmac canvas. A black rosebud engraved the length of each panel. Dulled in daylight, the place was sometimes mistaken as something to do with the Labour Party. Two burly shaven-headed doormen in black bomber jackets in the doorway, though Martin knew they weren't men at all, technically.

He inhaled deeply. The dope and the cold wet air were clearing his head. It was what he needed. Too much was happening too quickly.

He looked again at the luminous panels. The door opened and the burlies stepped aside. A girl stood for a moment silhouetted against the pink. She looked out into the night, turned her head this way and that, peering up and down the street. Her blond hair swayed. She stepped into the streetlight and something inside Martin tightened. She was beautiful. Beautifully curved in her tight, shimmering pink dress. Pink against pink. Her blond hair long, lustrous. She lit a cigarette, let the pack fall and moved into shadow. Scanning the street again. Waiting. For a lift, or a cab? Then she buttoned her fur jacket and started to walk. From his alcove on the other side of the street Martin heard her stilettos clicking towards him.

As she drew level he pulled hard on the spliff. Her head turned sharply towards its glow. Martin stepped out of the darkness. She hesitated, then walked on. Martin followed. Stopped under the Norway's blue lamp. She turned. Saw him standing there. Her footsteps slowed. She turned again. Martin inhaled down to the roach. Chucked it. And followed.

He took her to Carbon Dioxide. They sat in the chiller, shared a couch. She asked for vodka. He had the same. She had run out of cigarettes. He bought her a pack. They were playing old jazz records. It was nice. The dance music from the floor below pulsed through their feet, but stopped there.

He stroked her hair and she smiled. Leaned back to him. Immaculate make-up. Beautiful teeth. 'You've got a lovely smile,' he told her.

'Thanks.'

She told him her name was Veronica. There were no other questions. Martin knew that would not be right. Not now. And it was just the now. That was all that mattered. So. He kept her amused. Joked. Showed her a trick with coasters. Paid her compliments. The colour of her lips, her nails: it was the electric pink of the Rosebud panel, Martin was sure of it. And he knew the colour. It was familiar, safe. But he couldn't remember from where.

She let his hand play in her silky hair. He took hold of her head, turned her to face him. 'You're so beautiful. You're making me horny. I want you so much.' He pushed his knee against hers. Brought his head closer.

She moved her head away. His fingers let it go, drifted onto her shoulder. She looked down. Lifted her glass. Finished the vodka. Reached for the cigarette pack. The lighter.

He put his hand back in through her hair, cupped her neck. She turned. He was grinning. 'It's okay. You don't have to tell me. I know.'

SUNDAY 5 P.M.

Martin woke. It was dark again. Dappled dark from the Venetian blind. He turned in his bed. Empty.

In the lounge the man was sleeping stretched naked across the couch. Martin switched on a lamp. The room glowed soft and comfortable. The man stirred but didn't wake up. Like a painting, an old oil, Martin thought. An Old Master possibly. But his mind was too disturbed to pin down what it reminded him of. Like the pink.

He sat in an armchair facing the sleeping man. Breasts. Small and pert, perfect, in fact. Hormones obviously. But still a man. There was no body hair. The make-up was mostly gone, a little pink still around the lips. The wig on the floor deflated gold. He had been looking through the CDs. Three or four were scattered beneath his hairless legs. All Mozart.

What the fuck are you doing, Martin? he asked himself. Fucking men. You're in enough shit without this. In the Norway last night he'd used coke, dope, the pulsating rhythms of the room, the feel of the crowd to dissolve his worries and it had worked. Or at least it had worked when he met Veronica.

He had screwed up with both the Dobermans and the jewellery boys, the Panyatskis. Shit. He looked round this flat he was so pleased with, his original paintings, his collection of classical music, the designer furniture. Was it worth it? Perhaps he should start flogging everything off, pay at least part of his debts. Come on, he told himself, this isn't like you. Where's the old confidence? You can see this through. Blag it out. You always do. Something will turn up.

The man opened his eyes. Looked across at Martin. 'What time is it?'

Martin turned his wrist. 'A little after five.'

'Sorry, I should have gone, but it was pissing down.' He sat up. Took a cushion to place in his lap. 'I'm Ron, by the way.' He looked awkward. 'I'll just get my things together and go.'

His things. That meant the dress, the knickers, tights, all scattered over the bedroom floor. Ten pink fingernails rested in an ashtray under the lamp.

'I'd like to see Veronica again.'

MONDAY 3 P.M.

Martin knew Strombo wasn't convinced. But he was wearing his red bandana today, which was a good sign.

'Look, give me a bit more time. Please. Five grand isn't that much. Not to you, mate. And you know you'll get it. I've always come up before. With interest if you like. I've got some silver coming in, for delivery. I can delay that a bit. Flog it on and give you a down payment. A couple of grand.'

'When?'

'Should be within the week.'

Strombo sighed. A long, long sigh. 'You takin the piss, Martin?'

'No.'

'Yes, you are. You ave got too cheeky, boy. You show no respect. The only reason you walkin, breathin even, is cause you bin a good man for me in the past. But this is the end. You ear me, man?'

'Yes.'

'You too fancy, you know that? Wiv your clothes and your paintins. I give you till Wednesday. You got that? Last word. Wednesday.'

MONDAY 9 P.M.

'Have you brought Veronica with you?' Martin asked when this lad in jeans and a leather jacket, just a regular guy with a rucksack, turned up on the bridge.

'She's in the bag.'

'Come on, I'll buy you a pint first.'

Martin took Ron to the Little Moscow. He knew none of the Panyatskis would be there. But Big Eric might be and he could have a quick word with him, see if he could do anything about the silver. Eric had always been good to him.

They sat in an alcove. Easier to see than be seen. Ron was surprised by the bar, not the sort of place he thought Martin would drink in. The last place in fact.

Martin found that he was buzzing – and he hadn't even taken anything yet. All sorts of tension inside, but the biggest thrill was that in an hour or so he would be with Veronica again, made even more pleasurable by the fact that he was sitting here drinking pints of lager with Ron. Two regular blokes having a drink together. There was no evidence of breasts under the rugby shirt. How did he do that? And he was a good bloke; Martin liked him. I like both of them, he thought. Like having a mate and shagging his sister.

Ron was impressed when Martin told him he was a jeweller, had his own little workshop in the Quarter, did one-offs. He told him no more than that, though curiously he would have liked to. When Ron said he was a customs officer at the airport Martin was very interested. That could be useful. And he listened carefully as Ron answered all his questions about his work, explaining how he issued International Customs Certificates that gave automatic clearance to baggage and freight, told him about Black Bags and Diplomatic Immunity. Martin was glad his head was clear; there were very definitely possibilities here that might solve his problems. Stuff in and out of Amsterdam. Or any of the other places you could fly to from Birmingham.

It was like saying it to a mate. 'Come on, let's grab a bottle of vodka from somewhere and go back to mine.' *And meet up with your sister.* He said that only to himself. But as they climbed the steps from the Moscow he could feel himself getting horny. Well horny.

TUESDAY 7 A.M.

'I'd like Veronica to come round on Wednesday – no, Thursday, let's make it Thursday,' he told Ron as he sat waiting for a cab. 'I want to have a romantic evening in with her. Cook her a meal.'

Ron beamed. He had never thought he would find this. 'She's a vegetarian.'

'Fine. Does she like fish?'

Ron thought this was very funny. 'She's very partial to a bit of salmon.'

TUESDAY 2 P.M.

Martin was in his studio. He had just finished machine polishing. Rings, brooches. Art deco style. He was pleased with his work. The brooches especially. Like something Tamara de Lempicka would have worn. Shields of silver, each with a semi-precious stone. Yes, he was pleased. But even working he'd not been able to lose himself. It had prompted the familiar voice he lived with when things were tight: *Why don't you concentrate on this? You're good. You could build a nice little business here. Others do it. Why get involved with all the other stuff? Trying to be a top trader. You're no match for the big boys. Sure, you blag your way through. But why?*

He thought about Veronica. His stomach lurched. As exhilarating as any deal and in a different kind of way. This was a more interesting conversation to have with himself. He boxed the rings ready for the safe.

He had never fancied a man in his life. No changing-room messings about at school. So why, suddenly? The first time he took Veronica home he was wrecked. An excuse? It was the external woman he wanted. But it was the man he fucked. And he knew what he was doing. The arched curve of the spine. The shape of the buttocks. The cries and gasps that had been so stimulating, driven him on. They were a man's. That first time the cock and bollocks were just an impediment, they got in the way a few times, but he ignored them. Like an unfortunate birthmark or blemish. Take no notice. The second time. As he slipped the silky pink knickers away the cock bounced up, and he had held it, rubbed it. So? What did that make him? Gay? It couldn't. When he was with Ron there was no desire. None. He became Veronica and the lust was stronger than anything he had ever known.

He traced the brooches with his fingers. Couldn't resist stroking the silver curves. Good work. It's the stress of all this shit, he told himself. Once it's sorted I'll ditch her. But he knew he was looking forward to Thursday night.

With the jewellery in the safe he locked up. There was

an old Jag parked outside. Big Eric. The passenger door opened. Martin walked round and got inside.

Eric was puffing on a cigar, filling the car with smoke. 'You knock off early.' Martin said nothing, waiting. Eric turned towards him. 'For a bright lad you're a right cunt, aren't you?'

There was still nothing to say. If a bollocking from Eric was going to buy him a few more days he'd just sit tight and play the reprimanded schoolboy. He'd had plenty of practice at that. The thought almost brought a smirk to his face, but he killed it. No point in antagonizing the man. Eric had got him off the hook more than once. He had lost his son a while back and Martin thought that might be the reason he helped him out.

Eric lowered the window on his side, threw his butt out into the road. 'Look, Martin. I've had the Panyatskis on to me all week about you. They even came round the house. You're in serious trouble, son. I hope you realize that. They're making threats that put the wind up me, I tell you.' Martin didn't like the sound of this. And there was something in Eric's voice. No. He didn't like this at all. 'I take it you haven't got the money?'

'No.'

'Shit, Martin, where's it all gone?' Martin shrugged. 'Up your nose, half of it, I bet.' He sighed. 'Look. I'm going to try and help you out. Again. Though fuck knows why.'

'Thanks, Eric.'

'Hold on. It won't be so easy this time. Cash flow's dead at the moment. You still got that Rotterdam pile of mine, I hope?'

'Course I ave,' Martin lied. When he talked to Eric his accent broadened.

'Good. And how much of your own gear have you got? Constructions. Silver, gold, stones. The lot.'

Martin considered. 'Coupla grand, I guess.'

'That's what I thought. Now listen, Martin. This is the deal. I've talked very nicely to the Panyatskis. You put my stuff together with your own. Bring it to me. Tomorrow. Eleven o'clock. At me lock-up. You got that?' Martin nodded. 'I'm meeting the Yatskis at twelve. And for your sake I can't be late. It'll buy you a month. Settle the debt in time and I get mine back. You lose yours. Interest.' Eric turned full face to Martin. 'Now listen carefully. I don't care how you do it, but settle and on time. They're not fucking about, believe me. Sell that place if necessary.' He punched his thumb towards the studio. 'Or those fancy paintings of yours. D'you hear me?'

'Yeh. Sure. Thanks, Eric.'

'Don't thank me. Just do the business. Or I'll strangle you meself. And for fuck sake sort yourself out and grow up.'

WEDNESDAY 3 P.M.

Ron had done the early shift at the airport, four till ten, and was in bed but awake when Martin phoned in the middle of the afternoon.

'Hello, mate. I wondered if you fancied a drink tonight.'

It was good to hear from him. But he tried to be cool. 'Who is it you're asking out? Ron or Veronica?'

'Veronica's for tomorrow night. A romantic meal for two. Salmon. Soft lights. Good wine. A little Mozart in the background.'

Ron giggled. 'She'll love that. Turn into quite a naughty girl I should think.'

'That's what I'm hoping.'

'And tonight?'

'You, mate. If you've nothing else on.'

This struck Ron as funny. 'Where?'

'Same place as before.'

It was working out okay. He shouldn't get so worried. Martin did a couple of lines and lay back on the couch. His favourite Mozart piece was playing, the Clarinet Concerto. He looked around the room. He loved this place. Loved his pictures. And, yes, there it was. He knew he'd seen it before. Electric pink, exactly the colour of Veronica's lips, her nails. Streaks of it tucked between daubs of brown and fawn and orange in the Turnbull. An omen. Had to be.

Yes, it was all working out. He felt in control again now. Tomorrow he would buy a ticket to Amsterdam. Take his own stuff with him. Head for Rotterdam. He had some contacts there, could get a decent price. Lie low for a while, let things settle down. He'd come up with something. Could even go on the game, he laughed to himself, now I've had the practice. He shut down the thought. He'd sort something out. Give Ron a key to the flat tonight, get him to look after it. He could trust him. The studio would have to take care of itself. He was excited by his plans. I'm at my best like this, living on my wits. He was sure he could make some money in Holland, or come up with something to bring back. It was instinct with him. Or porn. They made movies over there. He could do that, that would bring in a few bob. And tonight he would talk to Ron about one of those certificates, 'International Clearance' he called them. That should cover any problems getting his stuff out of Birmingham and into Holland. And maybe getting stuff back. A girlfriend whose brother was a customs officer. That was a stroke of luck.

THURSDAY 2 P.M.

Martin put the air ticket to Amsterdam inside the safe beside his bagged up gear. Everything was ready to go. He would pick it up later. It was best to get out of here now.

He had stood Eric up and he was sure to be round. He reckoned he had another day before the Panyatskis started anything. He should have taken a flight today, he knew that, but he wanted one more night with Veronica.

A blue BMW pulled up outside. Panyatski's boys. The one with the question mark tattooed on his cheek was on the phone. Getting instructions. Reporting in. They walked towards the studio. Easy. No hurry. Big blokes.

Martin went through the back. He ought to have a gun. Everyone else had them. That was something he must sort out. He kept a bike in a shed out there for moments like this. He was on it and away. Heading towards the rows of crumbling streets awaiting demolition just beyond the Jewellery Quarter. He knew this place well. Stored stuff here sometimes. No one went in these boarded up houses. Too scared they'd fall on top of them. He could lose himself here for a while. But.

The BMW pulled round the corner into his path. He turned a wheelie. A four-by-four pulled up behind him. Fuck! More of them. He dropped the bike and shot off towards some garages. He ran like shit but he was unafraid. Exhilarated, more like. This was his game, after all. He was in his own territory. He knew this place. Out of the garages and down onto the road. And there they were. The BMW. Question Mark already out. A length of rope in his hand.

THURSDAY 2 P.M.

Strombo's fingernail tapped his gold tooth. No bandana today. His dreads piled back, held in place by a gold clip. Four gold rings on his fingers. Two gold chains, one around his neck, the other on his right wrist. His left wore a gold watch. His black eyes glittered stronger than all the gold – a frightening sight.

Gilly knew it so he sat waiting, his own eyes directed at the floor, for the man to speak. He could wait all day if necessary.

A sigh. Long. High. Sibilant. Like a snake disturbed. Gilly sat up in his chair, looked towards the man. The tension had left Strombo's face with the sigh. The decision. His jowls hung sadly. 'There's no alternative,' he said quietly, but Gilly knew the words were meant for him. He nodded. 'Shooters. Take Raza wiv you. In the night. Tonight. Take im sleepin.'

'Sure, man. Respect.'

THURSDAY 8 P.M.

Veronica let herself into the flat. She had called Martin but got only his answer machine. He had given Ron a key last night, so he wouldn't mind her going in, waiting for him. For their date. It was dark. In the lounge she flicked a switch. A man rising from the couch. She froze. Not Martin, another man. 'What?' A foreigner. Brown-skinned. Bearded.

'Who are you? Where's Martin?'

THURSDAY 11 P.M.

The sex was over. Veronica lay beside the sleeping man, this stranger who had little English. If she had understood, he had found Martin hanging from a lamppost. Or at least a man wearing Martin's clothes, with his wallet and credit cards. She didn't believe him. Such things didn't happen round here, not in Birmingham. You had to go to other countries, dark, troubled lands, to find people hanging from lampposts and trees.

It was still raining outside. Veronica could hear it now. Heavy. Torrential. The man beside her slept a troubled sleep. His muscles spasmed. His head turned. A fear took her. Perhaps he had killed Martin. No, it was a wind-up; had to be. The sex had been okay, but not like with Martin. *He* took her like a woman. Was hungry for her. This man was clumsy and unsure. His leg twitched now. It was the roles that had excited her. This man had turned into Martin just as Ron turned into Veronica. She thought of their clothes, Veronica's and Martin's, piled together on the floor.

What if this was some sort of test and Martin turned up to find her sleeping with his friend? Somehow she didn't think he would be surprised. He must know that Veronica was a slag. Perhaps that was one of the things he liked about her.

There was so much about Martin she didn't know, that she wanted to know. She wished he were here. She did like him. She loved this flat. The furnishings, the music. Mozart. The paintings. Abstract. Without shape or meaning. Wonderful.

The foreigner stirred and moaned. She had enjoyed the violence – the knife. It had aroused a rough aggressive side of Veronica she hadn't known before. She looked forward to exploring it.

The fear again, of something terrible. As strong now as earlier when she thought she might die at the hands of the man snoring beside her. Where was Martin? They had a date. Martin and Veronica. The last one before he went to Holland. A meal. He wouldn't not turn up: this was his home.

She nudged the sleeping man. Poked him hard. He turned, snoring. It was useless, nothing was going to wake him.

FRIDAY I A.M.

Raza inserted the sliver of metal into the door lock of St Nicholas Tower. Gilly waited as the man did his work. A thrust with the shoulder. A flick of the wrist. Raza's knee came up, but it wasn't necessary. A click and the door yielded.

They took the stairs. The sleeping building was silent. Moonlight through an oblong window on each floor. Raza repeated his work on the door to Martin's flat, which opened with conspiratorial ease. The men took their guns from their jackets. Peered in. Stepped in. Raza stretched out both hands, frisking the wall. His left hand hit the switch. Light. They stopped. Listened. Then moved. Lounge: empty. Bathroom, likewise. At the bedroom door they paused. Snoring. The men looked at each other. Raised their guns. Raza nodded. Gilly booted the door. It flew open. A figure rising in the darkness. 'Mar–'

Both guns arced the bed with silenced fire. Ten seconds of clicking and grunts. Then silence. They waited. Only their own breaths. Silence. Everywhere.

FRIDAY I A.M.

Dot was in curlers and dressing gown when the doorbell rang. Ready for bed but distracted by the late film. Cary Grant. A nostalgic weakness as good as chocolates. She knew immediately something was wrong. Eric had his key.

She let the police officers into the hallway. She could hear the music from the film she hadn't turned off. She looked at the young officers, their troubled faces. She had been through this before.

'We've come about your husband, Eric Scudamore.'

The other officer put his hand on her arm, alarmed by the look on her face.

'Shall we go in here? Where you can sit down. I'm afraid there has been an accident.'

Restoration

Although the gym can be as dangerous to the individual as any other part of the prison, there often exists there a spirit of camaraderie that is found nowhere else. Remand prisoners use the facility at specified times, separate from those serving sentences.

Today they form three distinct groups. And there is a man alone, isolated from the others, doing stomach crunches on a mat not far from the door. The instructor and a prison officer stand nearby chatting, keeping an eye on him. Soon the officer will accompany this prisoner to the shower. Then escort him back to isolation. It is for his own safety.

'That's him,' a housebreaker called Walsh tells his training partner, Tapper. Tapper turns his head. 'He looks younger than he does in the papers,' he comments.

'One sick fucker, if you ask me,' Walsh says. Tapper screws his mouth and agrees.

Fat Alex didn't get many Chinese in the Little Moscow, so when one made his way cautiously down the steps one night everyone noticed. Alex knew immediately this lad wasn't one of those pissy sweet and sours that called themselves Dragons and were throwing their weight around all over Brum right now. They dressed like Mormons in sharp black suits. This one was wearing an anorak and trainers, had glasses. Alex would say that good eyesight was Req. 1 for Dragons, the amount of shooting they did. This lad was pretty nervous, anyone could see that. He ordered half a pint then sipped at it like he thought it was spiked. Alex didn't like that.

'We close at eleven, pal.' The young man's eyes narrowed. He didn't understand. 'The rate you're drinkin, mate,' Alex clarified. 'Sommat wrong wiv it?'

'No. It's fine. Thank you.' He spoke with an educated accent.

Alex always thought that was funny, foreigners with our accents. There was a bloke called Tariq came down the Moscow regular before he got banged up. Drank Guinness, wore a turban and spoke with a broad Wigan accent. Alex could never get over that accent coming out of an Indian face. He could listen to Tariq talk for hours.

'You waiting for someone?' Alex asked.

'Not exactly. Did you ever know a man called Laurence Pell?'

'Lol. You won't bump into im down here, pal. Not tonight, nor any uvver. E's dead, Lol is.'

'Yes, I know. I would like to find out some things about him.'

Alex looked at the lad. Perhaps he wasn't Chinese after all. Something about the features. Japanese perhaps. Well, he certainly couldn't be enquiring about Lol because he thought he was his long-lost father. Nechells came to the bar, an empty pint glass hanging from each of his outstretched fingers. 'Hold on a minute,' Alex told the lad as he went to pull the round.

I found myself arriving very early in the morning, before the cleaning staff had finished, before some of them had arrived. I took to having a cup of tea in the café down the road. At that time in the morning it is mostly full of lorry drivers eating unhealthy breakfasts. I sat in the window looking out into the early morning street. There is a hairdresser's shop opposite called the Cutting Room. The first time I noticed that it amused me, the irony of it, but later I felt sad when I looked at it and thought of the day ahead. I changed my seat so that I was facing the lorry drivers, watching them eating and smoking, so very much alive for now.

One morning a couple carrying plastic bags came in and ordered toast. The woman was younger than the man and smartly dressed. He wore jeans and a leather jacket. I could hear them talking. The man was in a bad way, disturbed. Very jumpy. The woman was trying to be helpful, talking to him about the future. She didn't touch him though, didn't touch his hand when she was trying to be reassuring. At last she said, 'The important thing is, you're out now. You've done your time. All those years are over. It's time for a fresh start. Look to the future. Make something of your life.' The man lowered his head, put his hand across his eyes, trying to hide the fact that he was weeping. He didn't look like George, but the connection was made in my mind. It felt as if I was being allowed to witness a moment from his past. I didn't really understand until then how fascinated I had become by him.

When I went in that morning, I was first as usual, so there was just George and me. I had taken to having a few words with him when we were alone. I looked closely into his face – it was still intact at that time – and I just, well, tried to learn from it. Understand. Know, I suppose. A fatal curiosity.

It wasn't very difficult. Administration is still very old-fashioned. I knew paper records were kept – name, age, etcetera. All the cleaners knew me, they called me the early bird. No one thought anything of it when I went into the *office. I had a file in my hand that I looked through until the women there had finished vacuuming. Then I merely found the keys to the filing cabinets in a desk drawer and went through the records until I found what I was looking for. There was not a lot of information: name, home city, date of birth; but it was enough for then. I discovered that George was Laurence James Pell, born in Dublin on 3 January 1955, resident in Birmingham when he died of a neurological embolism on 16 March 2002.*

The flesh is brown now of course, and soggy in places with formaldehyde. The muscles were strong in life and the torso, shoulders, arms all well defined. A man who had either trained rigorously or done hard physical work for a number of years.

I remember that day well. I was working on the upper arm. Using the scalpel to cut through to the long heads of the biceps to expose and remove the cephalic vein from the deltopectoral groove. It is a bleak kaleidoscope of colours that is revealed as you cut through a cadaver. Tones of brown and grey mostly, some pink and yellow. The tendons and ligaments often retain a milky creaminess, almost white at the insertion into the joint, but this quickly fades, turning to yellow once they have been exposed. The textures of fibre change continuously, so that at times you stab with or press down hard on the scalpel; at other times, like an archaeologist, you carefully etch your way round bones and between tendons. I discovered that day as I cut away layers of tissue exposing a length of George's humerus that it had been broken in two places. I used my fingertips to palpate the edge of the scapula, the acromion. There was evidence of fractures in these too. A car accident? A fight? The brain had been removed weeks before but I remember putting down my scalpel at one point that day and just peering into that bony cavity, like a tiny cave, where it had once lain. The man himself, I suppose. That is where he was.

I see now that an obsession was developing. I needed to know more about him. Know him, really. The process of dissecting a cadaver is for me, though not for many of my fellow students, a very personal process. There is an intimacy. You take apart the physical man. Every part of him. Cut away. Open up. Stretch out. Then cut more. Sections of tubing, slices of tissue. Except it is not him. It is impossible, for me at least, not to want to know about the life that was lived in this body. And often, as I considered George's life, I remembered the man with his plastic bags in the café. I became convinced that George must have spent time in prison. I hear that some men spend all day in the gymnasium there.

It didn't take long to go through court records. I enjoyed that. Searching for him. When I found the dates of his court appearances I read the reports in the local papers. George was, as I suspected, a petty criminal. He served many short sentences of a year or two in prison.

The half-pint glass was empty when Alex returned. 'That was quick.'

'You told me I was drinking too slowly.'

There was a naïve quality about this lad. He smiled at Alex as if hoping for approval. There was something lonely about him. Still, Alex knew you had to be careful. 'Same again?'

'Very well. Yes, please.'

Alex refilled the glass. The boy was less nervous now. He looked around the bar not feeling so out of place, though of course he was. 'What part of China you from then?' Alex placed the glass of cold lager on the counter.

The lad drew a channel with his finger in the coat of condensation and smiled at Alex. 'I am English,' he told him. 'I was born in Slough. But my parents are Malaysian.'

'Oh. Right.' Alex watched his customer empty a third of a glass of lager into his mouth. His shoulders came up as he swallowed. Alex had seen hundreds of mouths drink thousands of pints. This lad wasn't a drinker by any means. His face tensed, the eyes compressing into lines. Like a child taking medicine. A curve of foam clung to his lip. He wiped it away with a handkerchief. That surprised Alex.

'So you knew Mr Pell, sir?' The boy returned to his subject.

Alex didn't like the 'sir'. It was only the police who called him sir, or people on the phone trying to sell him something he didn't want. Mobile phones usually. 'Call me Alex,' he instructed. 'What's your name then?'

'Bahari. Bahari Sonsang.' He held out his hand and Alex shook it while repeating the name slowly.

'Bit of a tongue twister that,' Alex said. 'Mind if I call you Barry?'

Bahari smiled and shrugged his shoulders. 'That's fine.'

'Well, Barry, I did know Lol. Not well, e was just a customer. Not even a regular. E might come in every night for a few weeks, then you wouldn't see im for months.'

'Perhaps he was in jail. I know he was a petty criminal.' Alex winced. 'I would like to know what he was like as a man. Was he married? Does he have children?'

He seemed harmless enough, but Alex pushed his belly into the counter and leaned across. 'Why you so interested in im? E's dead. What's e to you?'

Alex saw caution in the man's eyes. Perhaps he wasn't so young as he looked. 'I would rather not say.' He lifted his glass and took another hefty swig. The handkerchief came out again.

'Then the same goes for me,' Alex told him tersely and moved away.

My bed-sitting-room is very close to the college, within walking distance. It is not very tidy, I'm afraid, piled high with medical books. I am not a particularly social person. Throughout my course I have been happy to return in the evenings and spend my time studying. The same is true of weekends.

But things have changed recently. My concentration often fails me. I may be reading about the hepatic flexure and it is myself and other students reaching into the pit of George's abdomen that I see. Pulling him apart. Walking down the street, I find I am thinking about George and his life, hoping – though I recognize the stupidity of it – that I will turn the corner and bump into him. I know him so well, in some ways. He has even entered my dreams.

While I was working on his hand I was continually troubled by thoughts of those hands in life. Had they built things? Given pleasure to women? I bent the right hand that was still intact into a fist one morning and sat for a while looking at it, wondering if he had ever fought with it, used it to inflict damage. Had that hand ever fired a gun? Killed?

When I was alone with George in the early mornings I asked him these questions and with the repetition something like an answer came. I could never find out about the real man while I allowed him to be cut up and broken down into components. He was dead. The life force gone. Deconstruction into small pieces leads to nothing but the knowledge of those pieces, not the whole mechanism. With living things there is something more.

I dreamed of healing him. Resurrecting him in a way. I had a dream one night where he sat up and together we put back the side of his head I had spent that month removing. In another we shared a cell. He was whole except for his hands and feet, which were as skeletal as those I had seen on the gurney that day. And he laughed at their ridiculousness. It was a nice laugh.

*

Big Eric Scudamore was in tonight, sitting in an alcove with a few cronies from the old days. A couple of Crawford's crew were with them, picking up tips presumably. Eric wasn't much of a regular any more. Getting old, Alex supposed. When he came to the bar Alex had a word with him.

'See that Chink kid over there.' Eric twisted his neck. 'E's askin questions about Lol Pell.'

'Lol's dead.'

'E knows that. Wants to know what kind of bloke e was. Did e ave a family?'

Eric twisted his neck again and took a closer look. 'What you tellin me for?'

'Well you knew im. Better'n most. E did a few jobs for you.'

'No. I bought the odd bit off im when he freelanced, that's all.'

'But you knew im. Ad a pint with im.'

A sound that was closer to a laugh than anything else rumbled in Eric's chest. His shoulders shook a time or two and his jowls lifted. 'Oh, yeh. We've shared a few barrels in our time, Lol and me.' He looked along the bar again. 'So what's he want to know for?'

'Won't say.'

Eric's eyebrows lifted. He took another look. 'He's no copper. Journalist?'

'Don't think so. Talks posh though.'

'What is he? A Jap?'

'Says e's English.' Alex smirked. 'Born in Slough. But is family's Malaysia.'

Eric lifted a glass of bitter and drank. He slicked away with the back of his hand the foam that clung to his lip. While Alex was at the till Eric pushed the four full glasses he had ordered together. Once he had pocketed his change, he wrapped his large hands round all four and heaved them up. 'Give us a few minutes,' he said over his shoulder to Alex. 'Then you can send im over if you like.'

I started coming to Birmingham on my days off to do research in the Central Library, reading through crime reports in local newspapers going back many years. I found a number of reports of cases involving George. And accompanying one on his sentencing for theft and hand-ling stolen goods, a photograph of him. It was wonderful to find. He is staring at the camera, unabashed, and there is just a hint of a smile on his lips. He looks strong. I have spent a long time looking at that picture. There is no trace of fear in the eyes. I used the picture as a screen saver and put a copy on my notice board. Another copy I had lami-nated and kept with my books in my rucksack. Sometimes I would rest it on the remains of his head. Try to see him whole. One night I woke with an overwhelming desire to go into college and dress him. But in what? What sort of clothes did he wear?

Later I discovered a newspaper account that mentioned the Little Moscow. The prosecutor claimed that George and his two co-defendants had planned their robbery in there. George's counsel conceded that while his client and the other defendants drank together in there regularly . . . I didn't need to read further. I had a sort of home for him, an address.

Eric was in the mood to talk about Lol. For the past hour he had been reminiscing with Pully and Mick the Skip. When Crawford's lads, Kieran and Toaster, joined them, they had amused the younger men with stories of their escapades. Pully had told of the time he had scarpered from the old Victoria Courts when some prat of a copper hadn't locked the holding cell. Eric had talked of business trips to Amsterdam and Rotterdam selling hot jewellery, and recalled the time he had three chunks of uncut diamond buried in one of his missus's tulip pots out in the garden. The law had done a warrant search of the whole house, tipped everything up, even checked the cistern in the lav, but it was February and they weren't going outside. He bought a timeshare in Majorca with that.

When Alex brought the young man over, introducing him as Baz, he settled himself on a stool and called to Imran to look after the bar for a few minutes. Alex wasn't going to miss anything if he could help it.

Eric answered a few questions, said Lol was a good bloke, reliable, not much initiative though, liked to be part of a team, told what to do. He was married a couple of times, no kids as far as Eric knew, both marriages had ended a long time ago. There used to be a bit of a story that his first missus used to knock him about, beat him up rotten. Or so it was said. Eric couldn't swear to it.

Bahari took everything in. He didn't make any notes and there was no sign of any tape-recorder, not that Eric was giving anything away, only what everybody knew, and anyway, Lol was dead, couldn't do him any harm now.

Alex was coming to the conclusion that this wasn't going to turn into anything interesting and he might as well get back to the bar when things changed.

'What about the tattoos?' Bahari asked. 'The three intertwined circles at the top of his back.'

Alarm bells rang for Eric. Bloody loud ones. He had known Lol for years, he had seen the tattoos on his arms and the L-O-L on each of the three middle fingers of the left hand, but he knew nothing about intertwined circles at the top of his back. How the fuck did this little Jap know Lol had tattoos on his back?

Everyone round the table recognized the change in atmosphere. Eric leaned forward and exhaled cigarette smoke. 'Look,' he said firmly, holding the man's eyes. 'I'm not sure I like this. I've answered your questions, now you answer mine.'

Bahari was aware of the sudden tension. The other men were leaning towards him now too, creating a curtain of cigarette smoke that veiled them from him.

'Why all these questions about Lol? How come you know about tattoos on his back?'

'I have been working on him,' he told them calmly. 'He is known as George to us. Real names are never used.' Pully looked at Mick the Skip and saw that he didn't understand either. 'I have been working on him for months now and I just wanted to know more about him.'

Eric, like the other men, was trying to make sense of what he heard. 'What d'you mean, working on im? You a writer of some sort?'

'Or a private investigator?' Pully put in, pleased by the idea that had suddenly occurred to him.

Eric knew that he had been complacent, too trusting. The pleasure of his reminiscing earlier in the evening had led him, uncharacteristically, to lower his guard. He regretted that now. 'Come on,' he commanded. 'What's the game?'

'I'm not a writer, or an investigator. I am a medical student at Liverpool University School of Medicine. As part of our anatomy course we dissect a cadaver.' Bahari saw that he needed to explain. 'A dead body. George – sorry, Lol – is the cadaver I have been dissecting and studying.'

I couldn't take him back to the Little Moscow in the way I would have liked. In one dream I had we walked in together. But I could return something of him.

Last week we had to cut the lips away. I couldn't go on. The scalpel wouldn't move in my hand. To gain the knowledge I thought I needed I had to break apart every piece of the man. That's not right, is it? So I decided to

restore him, or at least his head, and take it back. First to
the Little Moscow. Then possibly to his family.

All the men sitting round the table in the alcove were suck-
ing on their cigarettes. They exhaled as one, enshrouding
Bahari in an ectoplasmic mist of blue and grey smoke, so
that as he continued, his words came to them like those of
an Edwardian medium.

'As you cut away a body, take out and examine the
heart, the liver, the lungs, as you remove the skin and
muscle and tendons, right down to the naked bone, as you
look down the microscope at slivers of the man's brain, his
kidneys, the pancreas, you want to know about the life
they sustained, or at least I did. What happened when all
these things were living and functioning.'

Alex had a stomach as strong as an oak cask but he
could feel it turning. Eric was trying to figure out if this
bloke was a loon or for real. Or even a set-up on Alex's
part. But one look at Alex's pale face told him he could
forget that one. Eric couldn't remember any funeral for
Lol and he always attended funerals when he could. And
there was no family as far as he knew. 'How did you get
hold of him? Lol's body, that is.'

'Bodies have to be the donation of the individual.
Families or executors cannot donate them. George – Lol
must have donated his body at some time in his life.
Signed all the legal papers.'

'How much would he have got for it?' Alex asked.

'Donated, you prat.' Eric turned on him. 'Donated. That
means you give it for nothing. Like stuff at the charity
shops.'

Kieran had turned green. He was remembering a news
bulletin he had heard on the radio at lunchtime. He
looked down at the rucksack leaning against Bahari's
chair and took a large gulp of Guinness before asking his

question. 'What's in there?' The others heard the agitation in his voice. 'What have you got in your rucksack?'

'George's head. Sorry. Lol's head.' And he lifted the bag to his lap and loosened the toggle.

There were jerks and jumps from the men around the table. Alex rocked on his stool. But no words made it out of the gaping mouths, before cigarettes went back in. Hands twitched, but unable to stop this freakshow, were left to fidget, tap knees, hold on to seats, grab cigarettes, curl and uncurl nervously, as the unpacking of the rucksack took place in front of them.

Bahari knew how to do it. He had attended lectures where the removal of a body section from a bag or container took place. He plunged his hands into the bag and, taking the head by the ears, lifted it slowly, letting the bag fall away. He placed the head on the table. 'I have managed to get some of his brain and have put it back in position. But much of it has been distributed among various laboratories and colleges around the country.' He placed the cap of the skull on top of the head, restoring it to its original form.

To Toaster the head of the man he had never known looked like a Toby jug, like those on his nan's mantelpiece, sitting lopsidedly amongst the beer glasses and ashtrays. Eric's own face hurt as he stared at the face before him. He tried to superimpose his memory of the man he had known in life, sat with at this very table, upon this ghastly brown object before him. Kieran blessed himself. Mick the Skip felt the need to make a joke. 'Look's like he's been on holiday.'

'Formaldehyde changes the skin colour,' Bahari explained. 'I have tried to repair the face as well as possible.' He paused in case any of his audience wanted to compliment him on the job he had done. When no one said anything, he laid a finger against Lol's left cheek. 'I have had to pad most of this side of the face.' His finger traced a criss-cross black line, like the indicator for railway tracks on a map, that travelled from beneath the chin, up to the ear and across to the bridge of the nose. 'I have sutured the incision as well as I could,' he said proudly, although he could see that the skill he had employed and the care he had taken were not appreciated by the wide-eyed men he addressed. But the enthusiasm in his voice was undiminished as he continued to explain his efforts. 'I have repaired the face as accurately as I can, using only a newspaper photograph for guidance. I have tried to match up the creases and folds and return as much definition as possible to the face.'

Kieran was on his feet. Lol's head wobbled as Kieran's leg caught the table. Everyone held their breath. A full glass slopped beer. Kieran pushed his way round the table, pulling the ashen-faced Alex to his feet. The two men, standing in the mouth of the alcove, formed a blind to its interior.

'Ring the police,' Kieran hissed into Alex's ear.

It took a moment for Alex to recover from the shock of being hauled so quickly to a standing position. 'The police. I can't do that. You know we never . . .'

'He's been on the news,' Kieran insisted. 'National. They're searching for him. Stolen body parts was all they said, but it's Lol's fucking head, for Christ's sake.'

'But we don't shop people in here, Kieran. You know that.' Alex considered. 'Look, we'll send im on is way. Tell im the police are after im. I'll say I'll keep Lol in the stock cupboard for im. Till e's sorted out. I'll say it was a place Lol liked. E's a nutter, e'll swallow that. Then when e's gone I'll sling it in the canal.'

'Alex. It's a man's head you're talking about.'

'There are others in there. Blokes e knew probably.'

*

There was a brief whirr as the tape rewound. Dowd pressed Stop. Then Play. *I couldn't go on. The scalpel wouldn't move in my hand. To gain the knowledge I thought I needed I had to break apart every piece of the man. That's not right, is it? So I decided to restore him, or at least his head, and take it back.* Dowd hit Stop again and looked across the desk at his assistant. 'Good work, Jack. You've got everything. That last bit alone will close the job.'

Jack was uneasy about it. 'But he hasn't done any real harm, sir. It's treatment he needs.'

'Jack, he nicked a fucking head. He's been wandering round with it in his rucksack for two days. In two cities. He's taken it onto trains, buses, into pubs. He's probably sat with it in some bloody café. How would you like to think that the bloke across the table from your egg and chips had a head in his bag under the table?'

'But it's a dead head.'

'Jack. Any head in a bag's likely to be dead.'

'But it doesn't belong to anyone.'

'Yes, it does. It's the property of Liverpool Medical School. So at least we've got theft on the charge sheet.'

'He's just some poor bloke who's cracked up. Give him a break, sir.'

'You're right. He has just cracked up. But he's been all over the front pages of every tabloid in the country for the past three days. Stolen body parts was grisly enough, but look at these.' Dowd dragged the pile of newspapers stacked at the side of his desk into the middle and turned them to face Jack.

'MISSING MEDIC: IT'S THE HEAD.' He lifted the paper from the top of the pile to expose the next. 'Look at this one. DOCTOR FRANKENSTEIN – STOLEN HEAD HORROR.'

'But he's not a monster, sir.'

'He is. Look at the papers. If the *Sun* says he's a monster – a fucking monster he is. It's the way we decide things,

Jack. We've got to throw as much at him as we can. Let the judge decide what happens next.'

'So you're going for custodial remand.'

'Too bloody right I am. We've got no choice. Anyway, it's for his own good. We accept a bail application and his picture is on the front page of all the nationals tomorrow. The telly too. The bloke who saws the head off a dead body and clears off with it. Who's to say some other nutter out there won't have a pop at him? Anyway, I'm not risking the stick we'll take if we don't push as hard as we can for custody. If it's refused, at least the magistrate will carry the can.' Dowd could see that Jack still wasn't convinced. 'Come on, mate, be sensible. We can't have someone like that walking round.'

'But haven't we got to get the head back before we can think about charges?'

'Jack. What's wrong with you today? You know we haven't. He's admitted it. You got the statement.'

Jack knew Dowd was right. But he was still uneasy. He felt sorry for the poor bastard. He'd done the interview for Dowd. Interview? Sonsang had just opened up. There weren't more than a dozen words of Jack's on the tape. He recalled the slight figure, newly discharged from hospital, so anxious that he should be understood. Jack had been impressed by some naïve but basically decent quality about him; 'moved' was the word he would use if it didn't sound so bloody soft. He didn't doubt that every word Sonsang spoke was the truth, and there weren't many times he felt like that at the end of a statement.

'So, it's prison for the poor little bastard.'

'Probably end up in Broadmoor.'

'Great.'

'We just have to do the job.'

'And he won't even say who chucked the head in the cut.'

*

Tapper had been thinking about the Chink all night. Thought about him in the gym doing his stomach curls. Alone. Protected. He saw him in the breakfast queue. He was disgusting. When Tapper got the chance to talk to Walsh later in the day he told him what was on his mind. 'He shouldn't be allowed to get away with that.'

'You're right.'

'A total sicko.'

'You're right.'

'Cutting a bloke's head off. A bloke who's dead. Someone should do that to him.'

'Dead right.'

'Brain dead,' Dowd said to Jack as he put the phone down. 'They're turning the machine off this afternoon. Got to sort out some organ transplants first.'

Jack said nothing. He continued to work away at the computer. Then he rose suddenly, walked across to the window and opened it. 'To let a little air in,' he explained to Dowd.

The Causes of Crime

The Causes of Crime

Gary Lanahan was in shock. That's how it felt – screwed. He stared at Tony Blair. A slick of sweat coated the prime minister's upper lip, a gooey moustache indicating strain; this was the last thing he needed at the start of a general election campaign. Gary's gaze shifted to his wife, Amanda, standing in the doorway between kitchen and living room. Strain showed in her face too. Pale. Tired. Creases around the eyes. The mouth frail.

'Obviously, our sympathies are with the workforce who have lost their jobs.' Amanda grunted. Her hands fidgeted. 'The first thing we have to do is ensure that if, as I'm afraid looks increasingly likely' – the prime minister fiddled with his fingers too – 'negotiations with Shanghai Automotive have broken down irretrievably, then we must put together a package to ensure that those affected are either retrained or quickly back in employment. I don't underestimate how devastating today's news is for those families.' Amanda returned to the kitchen.

Now the MG Rover logo filled the screen. The camera panned back to reveal a reporter standing outside the gates Gary had passed through barely an hour before. She was talking to a group of workers. Gary didn't recognize any of them.

'Sixteen years I've worked here. And my dad before me.'

Gary killed the sound. Let the man mouth silently. Through the window beyond the television his five-year-old, Josh, was demonstrating a wheelie for his little brother, Alfie. Gary watched his sons playing. He heard the sizzle of fat from the kitchen as Amanda dropped burgers into the pan; the aroma of teatime filled the room. He knew what she was thinking about. Mortgage. Food bills. The boys. Credit card accounts. The holiday they had booked. This house, the car, their way of life slipping away. His stomach churned. He rose to his feet. Poked his head round the kitchen door. Found a smile. Amanda looked up.

'It'll be all right, love.'

She tried to respond with a smile. 'Will it?'

'Course it will.' A clown's grin. 'Leave it to me.'

Next day, going to work was like entering a film set – cameras everywhere. 'It's like being famous,' Charlie Roberts told him as they entered A Block. 'I had two reporters round the car when I was parking.' Later in the morning word went round that if you wanted to be on the telly you should go to the Black Horse at the end of the afternoon shift. Channel 4 were doing their entire news programme from there tonight. The beer was on the television company. An hour later you could choose between the Black Horse and the Longbridge Tavern. ITV were going from there. Union reps marched up and down the floor, paper and clipboards in their hands. 'They're auditioning,' Charlie explained. 'Working out who's going to have their say on the box.' By lunchtime BBC cameras were inside the factory, filming the track.

Gary went straight home. Trade secretary on the news announcing a £150 million package. It wouldn't save any jobs but at least they'd get paid until the election. The camera closed in on the sympathy in Patricia Hewitt's eyes; Gary listened to the sadness in her voice. If she didn't talk so posh you'd think she was one of us.

Once the boys were in bed Amanda produced a pad on which she had listed all their outgoings. It was tough enough as it was; they were usually in the red by the end of the month, but they got through. Now? Who could say? When she cried and all the fears of the day poured out of her, it ripped Gary apart. He put his arms around her, drew her head on to his chest. Gently he stroked the sobs out of her.

'It'll be all right,' he told her. 'It'll be all right. I promise it will.'

Amanda looked up from her ironing. 'Finished?'

'It's going to start raining soon.'

She chewed her lip. Glanced out of the window. 'Charlie's still up his ladder.'

'He'll be down in a minute. Look how dark it's getting.'

'It's pointless anyway.'

She went back to her ironing and her hair fell over her face. Gary turned and went outside. Across the road Charlie was descending his ladder. 'Just in time,' he called to Gary. 'It's gonna piss down.'

'Any minute now.' Gary put the paint and the ladders away. He'd wait till she'd finished the ironing before washing his brushes. He stood at his front door. Waited for the rain to start. Wished for a cigarette, but he'd stopped now. He looked around. The garden was a picture. He should have the painting finished in a week. Get an agent in then. *Pointless*. Amanda's word echoed in his head. And Charlie had used it a couple of hours back. 'You know who'll get the benefit of this?' He raised his paintbrush towards his house. 'Building society, when they repossess.'

'Don't be like that, Charlie.'

'It's true, Gaz. Look. There's four houses already up for sale in this grove. Neil's is going up Monday. Then there'll be yours and mine. Seven. And there's only fifteen houses in the bloody place. And half the roads round here are the same. We're not all going to sell. All this graft we're putting in – pointless.'

It was hard trying to keep cheerful. Hopeful. Last night he and Amanda had considered what they could sell. She made a list. CD player. Couple of radios. DVD player. They wanted to hold on to the car for as long as they could. Get this month's mortgage out of the way. That was the important thing. Amanda did her calculations. It wasn't going to happen. Then he made the mistake of suggesting they put Josh's bike on the list. That sent her up the wall. Yelling and screaming. She'd hardly talked to him since.

He walked to the end of the path and through the gate. He'd just go to the end of the road and back. When he got tense like this he needed to move. His gym subscription had been the first thing to go. He would have liked to go for a run despite the impending rain. But he knew if he changed into his kit now Amanda would have something to say: *Running in the middle of the day; you're not on holiday, you know.*

Brenda was a good woman. She pulled up in her blue Ka and carried two bags of groceries into the house. 'It's just the basics.'

'You don't have to do this, Mom.'

'I can do this for you, Manda, till things pick up.'

Gary took the bags from his mother-in-law and heaved them on to the kitchen counter. 'It's very good of you, Bren.'

'No. That's what family's about, Gary. Sticking together. Helping each other through the bad times.'

Gary had always got on well with his mother-in-law. From the day she had met him she had treated him as one of her own, and now, when Amanda's fear got the better of her, it was Brenda who could soothe her and settle things.

'Here, now, I'm not doing this very often' – she slapped a twenty-pound note down on top of the washing machine – 'you two have a night out. And no arguments, my girl.' She wagged a finger at Amanda. 'I'll baby-sit.'

Amanda was cleaning, something she never seemed to stop doing now, wiping down the window ledge. 'Charlie's got viewers. Couple in a Golf. Must be all right. A little girl.'

'They'll probably look at this too. They're all the same.'

'They haven't booked an appointment.' Tension in her voice. Irritation, something like that. 'They'd see both at the same time. Across the street.'

She moved away from the window. Josh came tearing into the room, chased by Alfie, and collided with his mother. She grabbed his arm. Tugged. 'Will you stop running around inside.' The boy pulled away, overbalanced, fell against the table, hit his head, started to cry. Amanda dragged him up. 'See what you've done now. How many times . . . ' She raised a hand.

'Mand!' Gary rose from his chair.

'Sorry!' Josh wailed.

Amanda stopped herself, pushed the child away and went into the kitchen. Gary comforted his son, then led him by the hand into the kitchen to say sorry to Mommy. Nothing had happened. Her face was stoned into a smile. What was all the fuss about? Nothing to be sorry for.

There was time left. They could get through this month. But what was the point? Nothing was going to change unless he made it happen. Even if they survived this month, they wouldn't the next. And they couldn't keep relying on help from Brenda; life was no easier for her. He threw down the *Evening Mail*. Even as his eyes had scanned the columns of vacancies, just like they had last Thursday and the Thursday before, he knew the point had been reached. For days he had struggled – longer if the truth be told; the thought had been there for a long time. Blood will out.

Gary hadn't been on the estate for years. He passed the tower blocks, grey and looming despite the sunny evening, each named for some rural paradise a long way from here. Bluebell House. Primrose House. A kid was taunting his younger brother to hysterical screams by threatening to drop his bike from the balcony of Foxglove. On the ground below, two hooded youths shouted up encouragement. 'Drop the fucker. Go on.'

Beneath the blocks, tight rows of small houses. Paxton Road was the second in the grid. Gary heard the sounds of kids and television from inside. Teresa opened the door in a dressing gown. Rollers in. Fag in mouth. The smell of curry.

'Gaz! Haven't seen you for a long time. No one dead, is there?'

'No, nothing like that, Treese. I just wanted a word with our Steve. Is he in?'

'Nah, love. And I'm not expecting him back till late. He's got something on. But if it's urgent I can call his mobi. You can come in if you like, but we're having our baths.'

A microwave pinged. 'Catch it, Mom.' A tabby cat shot out from behind Teresa, chased by one of the kids.

'Leave her, Tyler. She'll come back when she's hungry.'

'No, not urgent. Just wanted a chat.'

'Well, he'll be in the Moscow later.'

Steve wasn't there when Gary arrived a little after nine. He ordered a lager and absently watched some blokes playing snooker. He'd only ever been down here a couple of times before, years ago, with his dad and brothers. He'd put all that behind him when he married Amanda. He was the one that was going to be different. When his dad died that was it – break the ties. And look at him now, in the Moscow drinking a pint he couldn't afford, waiting for the only one of his brothers that wasn't inside. And it didn't look as if he was coming in tonight. But he did. Arriving with two other blokes, Steve broke into a broad grin when he saw Gary.

'Watcha, bruv. Long time no see.' Steve clapped his brother on the back. 'Knew you'd be here. Treese phoned.' Steve introduced his companions, Nechells and Linton, got the beers in, then to Gary: 'Let's go over here for a bit.' He indicated an alcove. 'Won't be long, lads.'

'So what is it you're after, Gaz?' It was fairly brutal the way he said it, but the smile was still there and there was no point Gary pretending he had come to see how Steve was, a brotherly chat: how's the family; how're the kids getting on at school. He had put far too much distance between himself and his brothers for that.

Gary leaned towards Steve, spoke quietly and confidentially, although he wasn't sure why, it just seemed form in here. He explained about the redundancy, about how tight things were, a bit about it all causing problems with Amanda.

'So you want a loan?'

Gary thought about the state of Steve's house. 'No, not a loan. Some work.'

Steve laughed. 'You mean a job? Like a career?'

Gary looked hard into the smiling face of his brother. 'You know what I mean, Steve. Work. A payday. But something worthwhile. Something worth the risk.'

Steve looked across to his mates. They had started a game of darts. The two brothers were silent for a moment, then Steve's grin was back. 'But Gaz. You ain't never done nothing wrong. Not since school. You'd be better off down the job centre, mate.'

'You think I haven't done that? Courses, that's all they talk about. Retrain. Refresh your skills. Relocate. Re this and re fucking that. That's all they talk about.' It was good letting it all out.

Steve listened, let him get it off his chest. It would be wrong to say there was closeness between the brothers but, as they downed another pint then played pool with Nechells and Linton, something nearer to it than they had known for a long time emerged.

Towards the end of the evening Steve followed Gary into the Gents. Stood at the next urinal. 'It's been good tonight, bruv. Good seeing you again. Honest. I'll see what I can do for you. There are a few things coming up. One of them big money. But . . . for big money . . . Look, give me a ring on the mobi if you want to know more about it.'

'I do.'

'No. Not now. Think about it. Think about Dad. Think about Jez and Terry. The time they're doing. You ain't like the rest of us. You've done well. Kept your nose clean. Yer own house. Think about it. Then ring me.'

Johnny Lupisano stood on the bridge and exhaled cigarette smoke. It smelt good to Gary. He would have loved a fag right now. Johnny tapped the cigarette and ash dropped to the water below. It was a fine summer evening. Nearly ten, with only a hint of dusk in the sky. The door of the Little Moscow could still be clearly seen further down the towpath. Gary hadn't seen Johnny for years, not since he was at school with Jez, when he'd watched the two older boys play football sometimes. Johnny's grandad had been a prisoner of war in the city and Johnny had inherited the dark, Latin good looks to match his name.

'Steve's explained the situation,' Johnny drawled, 'and

I'd like to help you, Gary, cause of the ties. Our dads were mates and Jez has been my mate since we were at school. My best mate you could say Jez is. Went to visit him a month or two back. He's hanging on in there. You should go and see him, Gaz: he's yer brother.'

Gary said nothing.

'Look, Gary, I'd like to help, but I've got to be sure. What I'm putting together is big-time. Out-work; I'm just the agent. But it's real pro. It could put ten grand in your pocket just for labour. But you ain't done nuthin like this before, Gaz. So I have to be sure that if you say you're in, then you're in. No getting cold feet and crying off at the last minute. We don't work like that.'

'Ten grand. For a night's driving.'

'That's right. But don't fool yourself, Gary. That sort of money. It's a big job. You go down, you go down good.'

Ten grand – that was nearly six months' take-home. That'd take the pressure off for a while.

Johnny took a final pull on his cigarette and let it fall into the canal below. 'I know you don't have any form, Gary. That you're considering this cause times is hard for you. And listen. I'm not trying to talk you in or out. But don't get in if you can't take the heat. If it's going to keep you awake nights. But what I can tell you is that it's a highly professional job. Very well organized. A big team. A corporation behind it. So. Have a think. I'm putting the team together this week for a brief Thursday. I'll phone you Sunday. See what you think then.'

As Gary stood in the doorway of their bedroom watching his sons sleeping, he knew this was the moment he would make his decision. For two days it had been going round and round in his head: first he was in, then he wasn't. First the money was too big to turn down, then the risk was too high. And today Amanda had picked up a little job wiping geriatric arses in the care home where her mom worked: only five quid an hour because she wasn't trained, but she could have as many hours as she wanted. It would tide them over, or at least help a bit – and what did that mean? They'd still be scrimping, still getting further and further into the red every time the mortgage was paid – *if* it was paid – still buying the cheapest of everything, still saying no to the kids. And when he got a job he knew he wouldn't earn Rover money. Charlie had applied for the post, up at four every morning, then pounding the streets for less than half their Rover money.

Above each of his sons' beds hung a mobile of planes. Both boys loved planes; sometimes he took them to the airport as a treat just to watch them. The poor little buggers still thought they were going on holiday in a few weeks. Alfie's mobile stirred for a moment as the boy grunted in his sleep; the one above Josh was motionless. Gary could stand here for ever just looking at his boys. How many blokes must there be tonight, he wondered, banged up for Christ knows how long, who were wishing they could do just what he was doing now?

But ten grand. Over a year's mortgage taken care of in one night. That would really take the pressure off. And – he couldn't escape the thought – three or four nights' work like that a year and you'd be laughing. The kids could certainly have a holiday.

He went into the bathroom. Turned on the tap. And rang Johnny Lupisano.

The smell of bacon and eggs frying wafted up. They were in a room above Tina's Tasty, one of Johnny Lupisano's cafés. Below, truckers and road workers were tucking into their dinner.

Gary couldn't eat a thing right now. In fact he wanted to throw up. It was the single word: 'bullion'. As poisonous to him as botulism. A bullion raid. Jesus! What had he got himself into? Bullion. That meant real time.

There were six of them with Johnny; all seated round two Formica-topped tables pushed together. Each man had a number. Gary was Number Four – only Johnny knew their names. They had come in through the back and would leave the same way. Each had been provided with a cup of tea, and cake if he wanted.

Johnny stuffed a Rothmans into his mouth, lit it with a gold lighter. A blue flame. The whiff of petrol. 'I'll run you through it again. Remember, you're Team B. You will each be picked up from your designated spots at the times you have been told.'

Johnny had had a brief word with each man individually as they arrived. Gary was being picked up at ten-thirty on Stoker's Bridge.

'At eleven-thirty we assemble at Whittaker's Yard. The gates will be open and the vans we are using will have been selected and prepared.' Gary noticed the heavy gold watch on Johnny's wrist – it took more than a few greasies to make that weight of bling standard. 'You will each be allocated your van and a mobile. At five-minute intervals you will proceed across the city to Birmingham Bullion. I have already told each of you the individual route you should follow. You also know your waiting points. Each within a minute or so of the yard. Team A go in fifteen minutes after midnight. As soon as they have the place secure and the goods ready for dispersal you will get the call. Drive straight to the gates. Give your number. You will be directed from there. You open the back. You assist the load. You leave and take the route I have given you to your individual destination. You each know what type of vehicle you will be met by. The goods will be transferred; you will be given an envelope containing eight thousand.' He nubbed his half-smoked cigarette. 'I will personally deliver the balance within the next week.' He smiled, knowing he didn't really need to say this. 'Obviously, this is to ensure that each of you drops off your van exactly where I told you earlier.'

Gary lifted his mug and sipped at the tea. It was going cold. He glanced at the black lad opposite him, Number Two, about twenty-six or twenty-seven, who looked as if he hadn't a care in the world. It all seemed well organized. None of these other blokes seemed like losers. And he liked all this security stuff, no names, individual routes: yes, it had been well planned; professional. It should be all right.

'No, Gary! No. You're not doing it.'

'Ten grand. One night.'

'One night. What about the ten years you'll get?'

'I won't. It's professional. Well organized.'

'Gary, I told you when I married you, before that, when we got together – I told you, put your family behind you, forget them. I told you, I'm not marrying a criminal, and that still stands.'

Is this what he wanted to hear? Or had he wanted permission? After all, he didn't have to tell her. On the surface she had pushed him into it, two days of nagging: *You're different. What's going on, Gary? What are you up to? It's not the fags. You're planning something. Tell me. Yes you are. Something's going on. Yes, it is. You're not thinking of doing something, are you? To get money. Gary. Tell me.* On and on. But he could have stopped it. He wasn't so dim he couldn't have come up with an answer that would have stopped the questioning, satisfied his wife, instead of always allowing some doubt to remain.

Yes, he knew now that he had wanted to tell her, but what he also realized now was that he had wanted her to say yes: *Yes, go on. Yes, do it. Ten grand, yes!* And: *Ten grand for a night's work, Gary. Five or six nights like that a year and we're made.*

But after twenty-four hours of tears and pleading, after a second day of sulking and refusing to speak to him, Amanda had finally seen sense. He had carefully explained everything to her, taken her step by step through the plan to reassure her that this was a professional organization he was with, everything taken care of, checked to the last detail. Then he had reminded her of the security the money would provide: 'Ten thousand, kid. That buys us over a year on the mortgage.' In the end, if she hadn't actually given him her blessing, at least she had got off his back, accepted the situation, and today there had been an ease between them that hadn't existed for months.

Steve was already in the Moscow when Gary arrived. He moved away from the crowd he was with and joined his brother at the bar. 'Glad you could make it.'

Steve had phoned Gary earlier. He knew better than to call round the house. 'Can you talk, Gaz?' he'd asked.

'Yeh. Mand's at work.'

'How you feeling about tomorrow?'

'Nervous.' He heard his brother laugh. 'Shit scared if the truth be told.'

'Thought you might be. Look, come up the Moscow tonight if you can get out. I'll buy you a drink.'

The brothers took their pints over to a pillar. Steve chalked their names up for a game of pool.

'So you're a bit jumpy?'

'More than a bit. Been on the bog all day.'

Steve put his hand on his brother's shoulder. It was a long time since Gary had received a gesture like that from any of his brothers. 'You'll be all right, mate. I promise you. This is tip-top professional class, grade one. You couldn't be in a safer team.' He leaned close in. 'I shouldn't be telling you this, but. I'm on Team A. On the inside. Opening the place up.'

So it had happened. Blood will out, as his dad used to say. The last of the Lanahan lads had rejoined the family. And as he drank and laughed with his brother, enjoying a closeness he hadn't known he was missing, his fears subsided. He wished now he hadn't told Amanda. He wished too that he could tell Steve what he had done – but that was impossible, as impossible as backing out.

Gary reached his pick-up point at ten-fifteen, a quarter of an hour early. He leaned over the bridge to look down on the railway track and canal that lay side by side below. In the distance the solid outline of the city centre, above it a silver film of moon, not much more than an outline, just a pretty bit of debris in the darkening sky. And now the moment of waiting. He could do with a cigarette.

Gary turned and rested his back against the bridge. He had expected to be nervous, but he wasn't. Not leaving the house, nor waiting here. He heard a motorbike, then saw it as it reached the brow of the hill and pulled in beside him. Now there was a moment of uncertainty.

The rider lifted his visor. An Asian lad. 'Number?'

It took Gary a moment to realize. 'Four.'

The rider handed him a helmet, gloves. 'Here. Jump on.'

'I wasn't expecting a bike.'

'That's the point.'

Breedon Street. A piece of waste ground just round the corner from Whittaker's. The sky's darker now. Clouds busy arriving. Black and blue shapes, like animal silhouettes hanging on a kid's mobile. Lights in the distance from Hockley Station. All six bikes arrive within a couple of minutes of each other. Beautiful. More waiting, but no one speaks. Gary's still not nervous – tense, yes, keyed-up, he can hear himself breathing – but not nervous. A phone rings and they're off again.

At Whittaker's the gate is already open. Rammed. The

lorry pulled over to one side. A blindfolded security guard held against it by a man with a gun. They dismount from the bikes. 'This way,' a voice barks. 'Keep yer elmets. Put em back on when yer get to the job. Got that?' They follow the dark figure to the vans – a yard with at least twenty of them.

'Number One.'

'Me, mate.'

'This is yours. Keys. Ere's ya phone. Number Two.'

'Me.'

Gary is overwhelmed by the precision of the operation. To be part of this. How many blokes all told? Inside his van he turns the ignition. They move forward in number order. Meticulous. Like a parade. He's excited, enjoying this. The van in front stops. Suddenly. Gary hits the brake. Noise. Shouting. Then there's light from the front. Bright as fuck, silhouetting the driver in front of him. And the one in front of him. Sirens. Now he's nervous. A van roars through the gate and stops. Blocking everything. Fuck! He sees a uniform. More light. More uniforms. The drivers in front of him are piling out of their vans. Dogs are barking. Gary thinks he is going to shit himself. His bollocks are in his mouth. He can taste them, wrap his tongue round them. A copper has the driver in front in a headlock. Another joins him. The door of his van flies open. Same trick. Gary's head is wrenched down, then up; feels like it's coming off; feels like it's flying through the sky, all the way to Villa Park. Then his head is jerked to a standstill face to face with a copper. His neck hurts.

'Number?'

'What?'

'Number?'

'Number. Four. Number Four.'

'Name?'

'Lanahan. Gary La–'

His head is yanked close to the copper's face. He's been smoking; Gary can smell it on his breath. 'I'm going to trip. Then it's on yer bike. Understand?'

Understand? Of course he doesn't fucking understand. He doesn't know what he is talking about.

'Follow the wire fencing round the back to the wall. You can get over that. Make it quick.' With that he pulled Gary further towards him, toppled and, as he went down, loosed his grasp. Gary turned and ran.

He could hear shouting behind him. Dogs. He could hear the steam engine shunt of his heart as it pounded him forward. Round the corner into the yard of vans. But it was all wire fencing, ten feet at least. He stopped. Should he turn back? No, he didn't know what was happening, but he'd carry on. Shit, what choice did he have? Of course he'd carry on. Just pound away. Then he saw the wall. A loading bay. As good as steps. He was up and over. Dropping ten feet into the empty street below. He would head for the back of the railway station. Nip across the tracks. Cut through the gardens on the other side. That would be safest. His stomach wanted to empty itself. But his brain was working: issuing commands, simple and clear, like a survival manual. *Keep going – cross here – turn right at the end.*

He rounded a corner. A car parked at the far end of the street. The lights come on. Fuck! Probably nothing. A coincidence. What the fuck, he can't turn back. It's coming for him, the car. He can't see what sort it is, small, but it's coming towards him. Lights on full beam. He can't see inside. It stops beside him. Shit, what's happening? He bends, opens the door. 'Get in quick, Gary.' It's Brenda. She taps the dash. 'There's some fags in there. You probably need one.'

He was plainclothes, but he was still obviously a copper. Whitehouse. He shouldn't be here. Not a copper. In his house.

'You're small fry, son.'

Gary snorted. 'Small fry,' he repeated Whitehouse's words. 'To you, or them?'

'Both.' There was a copper's sneer beneath the affable tone. 'Don't fret. No one's going to suspect anything. You got a chance and you did a runner. Any of them would've done the same.' Whitehouse nodded towards Brenda sitting opposite him. 'She stopped you doing a long stretch, mate. Be grateful.'

Gary wanted to say, No, she didn't. If she hadn't interfered it would have worked. Like clockwork. I'd have ten grand in my pocket now. But he didn't say those things. Just sat there, letting the copper go on praising Brenda.

'She's one tough lady. Super says she made it clear you were the price.'

'Small fry.'

'Sure,' he smirked. 'And no problem to let you slip through the net to get our hands on that lot. And there'll no doubt be a sizeable reward for Mrs Clayton, here. Eventually.'

For the first time the mask that had been Brenda's face eased; her lips lost their tension. For days Gary had listened to his wife and mother-in-law justifying Brenda's action. How it had saved him. And with talk of a reward it was like they had had a lottery win. Amanda smiling more than she had done since the closure notice, even coming on to him in bed last night. He knew Bren was only doing what she thought right, yes she was trying to save him, but it was still grassing, something he had been brought up to consider only marginally better than paedophilia. And. There was that feeling. Sitting in the car. Part of something. Easy money. This is good.

Whitehouse was talking to him. He had gone all serious. 'I'm here today, Gary, to make it absolutely clear to you that although nothing has been officially recorded –'

he looked across to Brenda '– we know about you now; you're not the squeaky-clean Lanahan we had you down for. You'll be in our minds if anything else crops up. On our list. So, keep out of trouble. Keep away from people who might get you into trouble. You hear me?' Gary nodded. Brenda looked pleased. 'So, Gary, keep clean.' He made to rise.

'And you definitely can't do anything for my brother?'

Whitehouse returned to sitting, but leaned forwards towards Gary. 'I'm fucking sure we can't do anything for him,' he hissed. 'Sorry for swearing, Brenda.'

'Don't worry about me, love. I've heard it all before. Used it about that family too.'

'Gary, have you been listening to me? Do you realize how lucky you are? Thanks to your mother-in-law. Your brother had a gun. He was part of their attack team. Went in first. If there had been any resistance he would have used that gun. Killed some poor sod. Of course I can't do anything for him. He's off for a long stretch.'

'And good riddance.'

The copper smiled at Brenda's words.

'What I want to know, Gaz, is how you got away with it.'

'I wasn't the only one.'

'No, but there weren't many.' Teresa sat tense and upright on her settee. She wore a blue tracksuit and her blond hair was pushed into an Aston Villa baseball cap. An ashtray rested in her lap, a cigarette in her hand. Her gaze never wavered from Gary sitting at the table. Her face Botox stiff. 'Somebody grassed, Gaz.' He could feel the anger in her. Could see she was trying to keep a lid on it. 'That job was watertight. All top professionals. Except you. You only got in because of Steve.'

'What are you saying, Treese? You're not saying I'm the grass?'

'Somebody grassed,' she snapped. 'They were waiting for them. At Whittaker's, and at Birmingham Bullion. It was perfectly organized. It was so tight even the boys who opened up the bullion sheds didn't know where the vans were coming from. Didn't know about Whittaker's. It was only Johnny and you drivers who knew that part.' She stubbed out her cigarette viciously.

'There were six drivers, Treese, and the gang inside.'

'And only one outsider.' She spat the words contemptuously. She wanted to fly at him, he could see that. 'Only one amateur, one new boy. Steve tried to help you, Gaz. You came to him for help. But this wasn't allotment stuff. This was big-time. It could have got us out of this place.' She waved a hand at the room. 'Changed our lives for ever. Now Steve's looking at ten years min.'

She lifted the cigarette pack that lay beside her on the settee. Took one. Threw one to Gary. Lit her own. Chucked him the lighter. Each drew on their cigarettes.

Teresa spotted ash on the knee of her tracksuit, brushed it away, licked her thumb and rubbed at the mark it had left. 'Whoever grassed – they'll find em out. Whoever did it, they'll get their heads blown off.' Gary gasped on his fag. Teresa saw the shock in her brother-in-law's face and relished it. 'Their families too.' The nearest thing to a smile Gary had seen since he entered her house. 'Welcome to our world, Gaz. Or welcome back.'

'Treese, why would I grass? My own brother. I needed the money too. You know that. You know I'm not a grass.'

There was so much anger in Teresa she couldn't stay still any longer. She lifted the ashtray and carried it across to join Gary sitting at the table.

'No, maybe not.' She pointed at him with her cigarette. 'But shall I tell you what I reckon? I reckon that wife of yours is. I told Steve it was trouble involving you. But he went on about how you was his brother, how blood's thicker than water, your mortgage, your kids, marriage problems, all that stuff. I reckon you let it all out to that wife of yours. She's always had you where she wants you. I reckon you told her. And she's our grass.' She drew her cigarette back between her lips, but her eyes never left Gary's.

'No. Definitely not.' He was surprised to hear the absolute certainty in his own voice. 'Not Manda. Definitely not. Neither of us would do that. My word on it. On Mom's grave. We wanted the money. Needed it. I was hoping for more work after this.'

Teresa tutted, or ticked; some scoffing noise escaped.

Gary was on the patio trying to coax Josh to put his bike away when he heard raised voices. The front door slamming. He went inside to the kitchen. 'What was that?'

Amanda was dropping chips into the pan. They sizzled in the hot oil. A pack of frozen burgers and two tins of beans stood on the kitchen counter. 'That effin Teresa.'

'What did she want?'

'She said she wanted to talk to me. I told her I didn't –'

The kitchen door flew open and Teresa raged in. 'Don't you ever shut the fucking door in my face, you stuck-up bitch.'

Amanda was too shocked to speak. Josh came in behind Teresa and stood huddled in a corner watching the roaring woman.

'I came round here to find out why. Why after your husband comes snivelling to mine for help, and gets it, why you, you stuck-up cow –' she poked her finger towards Amanda '– why did you go and grass them all up?'

Alfie, drawn by the noise, had left the TV to come and stand in the doorway. Frightened by the shouting, he started to grizzle. Gary picked him up. 'It's all right, son. Teresa, I told you. Manda didn't grass. Nor did I. We don't know who it was.'

'I don't believe you, Gary.'

'Gary. Will you get this mad woman out of my kitchen?'

'His own brother. Family.'

'Not my family, thank God. Nor yours. And you're rougher than the lot of them.' Gary had never seen his wife like this before. Teresa's fury must be infectious. 'Why don't you tell Teresa what your dad used to say about her, Gary?' Teresa swung round to Gary. 'The only honest words that ever came out of that man's mouth.'

'Okay, Mand. Leave it now. That's enough.'

'No, leave her, Gary.' Teresa turned back to Amanda, a dangerous calm in her voice. 'Come on then, love, tell me what the old man said.'

'"I've got four daughters-in-law," he used to say. "And each of their names begins with A. There's Allison, Andrea, Amanda and Arsehole."'

Teresa made for Amanda, who side-stepped her.

'Just get out,' Amanda shouted. 'Gary, get rid of her.'

Teresa seized the pan of sizzling oil. Lifted it from the stove. Held it. Looked around. There was silence.

Teresa's gaze scanned the kitchen. As if she didn't know where she was. Confused. She wailed, then she hurled the steaming pan, sending a wave of golden oil leaping across the kitchen to Amanda.

Performance

Of all the drugs of my life performance has been the most potent and the only one I miss. To take an audience on a journey; to feel it travelling. And the climax – that delicious roar from the darkness. It was this addiction that drove me to tour again. Europe. North America. South America. Australia. They would not let me into Russia. I had an audience there, but those fat men in fur hats said no. It made me laugh.

In all the places I visited the young made up more than half the audience. Mop-heads in fairytale clothes; it was a joy to me. They put down their Rolling Stones records, switched Bob Dylan off for the evening and came to travel with Dietrich. There were older people too, of course, devoted fans of decades' standing, but it was to the young I was singing.

In the spring of 1966 we were in the United Kingdom. A week in the largest theatre of each of the major cities: London, Liverpool, Glasgow, and so on. Eight in all. I played ten nights in the Royal Albert Hall in London and every house was full.

As important to me as ticket sales is the size of the crowd outside the stage door. They wait hours for a glimpse of the star; an autograph if possible. It is part of the performance: there must always be an hour's wait, two is better. The car arrives. The crowd become excited: *She is coming.* Each time the stage door opens they jostle forward; but no, it is just a musician, or a technician. They 'ooh' and they 'aah' as bouquets are carried out. The longer they wait, the more precious the moment.

I have been told that actresses today leave theatres in jeans and duffel coats. No make-up, no jewellery. Bah, I say, it is a nonsense. They have taken Brecht too seriously. Yes, it is he I blame. They do not understand what an audience needs. The sparkle of stardust. Illusion should be respected. Why else are we artists?

The act of departure must be brief. Accept the flowers, the gifts. The chauffeur comes forward to relieve me of them. It is better if he has to make two journeys, but no more. One cannot accept everything; some must be disappointed. It is the nature of things. If it is not raining I will sign some autographs. Three or four. No more. They are trophies; not easily won. Then they will be cherished. We must never devalue the currency of what we are.

It was the opening night in Birmingham, a large industrial city in the middle of England; a third of the way through the British tour. As usual the performances had gone well: a standing ovation; two encores; seven minutes of cheering and calling for me before I instructed the house lights.

Two hours had passed since the performance concluded when Beatrice, my maid, gave instructions to the backstage manager that I was ready to leave. A mirror and my stole were in position at the stage door. I always check the image is perfect before leaving the theatre; walking through the stage door is making another entrance. One has to work constantly at being a star.

It was as I stood before the mirror, Beatrice arranging my stole, that the night turned bad. A doorman had been posted outside to assist my passage through the crowd. 'Is she still in there?' one of them shouted at him. 'We've been here over two hours now.'

'No,' I heard him reply. 'You're all right, she's still in there. You have to remember, she's very old. They have to carry the old girl off the stage. Can't manage it herself.'

'Are you serious?' an incredulous fan asked.

'Crippled with arthritis she is. Like any other old lady. Can't walk more than a few steps. Carry her on and off stage they do. That's why she's standing there at the beginning when the lights come up.'

I was frozen. He was talking to my audience. Making me sound like poor Piaf. Pity was not a component of the image I worked to create. Arthritis and glamour are not bedfellows.

But this man was still not finished. He was enjoying himself. 'Then there's the oxygen in the dressing room. Prising the feet out of those heels and soaking them in a bucket of nice warm water to get the circulation back.' People were actually laughing. This merely gave him encouragement. 'Then the doctor has to check the pulse. Make sure she's still alive.'

'*Halt ihn,*' I hissed. An instruction given first in a language not understood gives power to the command. 'Stop him! Immediately!' I leaned close in to the manager's pale face. 'Fire him. Or I shall not be back tomorrow.' I headed back to the dressing room at a speed that would have astonished my misled admirers, shouting, 'Instant dismissal! Or I will never set foot in this theatre again.'

Within fifteen minutes there was a timid knock on the door. 'I apologize most sincerely, Miss Dietrich. I will defend the man no more than to tell you he was very distressed to learn that he has upset you. He has been dismissed and has left the premises.'

When I emerged they had been waiting two and a half hours. I regarded them smiling – gave six autographs, stretching nimbly across for books from those further back, moved around, marched firmly to the open door of my car.

As the car pulled away a young man appeared out of the darkness across the street, a piece of paper and a pen in his waving hand. It is a common thing. Rather than stand with the crowd, some isolate themselves and then rush to the car, hoping I will instruct the driver to wind down the window. It is a practice I do not encourage. Also, he was holding just a piece of paper. Autograph books, photographs or programmes only. I do not sign any bit of paper snatched from anywhere in a hurry.

The young man mistimed his approach. The car had started to accelerate. I turned away from the waving fans to see it catch him at the hip, pen and paper flying from his hand which, as he was whisked up on to the bonnet, slapped hard against the windscreen. The car, which had not yet achieved speed, came to an abrupt halt and the young man slid from the vehicle into the road. Fortunately, he was soon on his feet again, clutching his hand. The chauffeur was quickly out of the car. The crowd gawped. Tonight's performance was not yet over.

I wound the window down myself; then, recalling the libel I had recently been subjected to, I opened the door and stepped out. 'Darling,' I breathed. 'You are so foolish to run to the car like that. You must be more careful.' The crowd came closer. 'Are you all right?'

'Yes, Miss Dietrich. I think so. I am very sorry.' He looked up at me and smiled, clutching his wrist. His young face moved me. I have always been vulnerable to young men in distress.

'Your hand? It is injured? Broken perhaps?'

'I don't know. No. I don't think so. I just hit it rather hard.' He spoke well. The crowd were close, but keeping a respectful distance between themselves and this unexpected drama.

'Here' – I moved towards him – 'let me see.' The audience hushed as I took the hand, gently moving each finger as I did as the young nurse in Von Sternberg's *Compassion* in 1926. I could hear distant traffic from the highway behind us. Headlights flashed shadow down into our narrow street.

The young man's face creased as I moved his hand. A combination of wince and smile. Enchanting.

He turned earnestly towards me. 'I really am sorry to have caused you so much trouble, Miss Dietrich. I only wanted your autograph.'

'And you shall have it, my darling. You will come back to the hotel with me,' I announced. 'There I will sign a photograph of myself for you. What is your name?'

'Kurt, Miss Dietrich.'

'Ah, Kurt. A German name. And when you are quite recovered, Herbert, my chauffeur, will drive you home.'

He smiled, a very open, charming smile. 'That is very kind of you.'

'Get into the car, Kurt. Beside Herbert.'

When the car doors were closed and we pulled away the audience broke into applause. I turned and waved to them through the rear window. Amongst the faces was one I recognized. Who was it? Of course. The dismissed doorman. He was not applauding.

Kurt's hand was fine. A little sore from the blow it received against the windscreen but not broken or even sprained. I took him to my suite, keeping Herbert on standby in his room on the floor below, ready to take the young man home when, or if, required. I use the word 'if' because there was just a glimmer of indecision in my attitude. Kurt was a very attractive young man. The child was still in the man's face. I like that. I have always found it poignant. Jean Gabin had such a face. Of course, there were years between us. But I am a legend. Isn't that as desirable as flesh? More rare. A man like Kurt could sleep with a different pretty girl every night of the week and I'm sure he did; he was vibrant with life. But would he ever again sleep with a star? To have slept with Dietrich when one was a young man – a story to last a lifetime.

It was this knowledge that was my motive in the war. The act of ultimate generosity – which many have used against me since. Constant touring, giving concerts to the Allied Forces – these were some of my greatest perform-ances. On an improvised stage with minimal lighting, I, Dietrich, sang out my heart for thousands of young men. Soldiers, airmen, sailors. American, British, Canadian, Australian. Yes, I sang my heart out, and it broke my heart: *This is the last song some of you will hear; this is the last time you will hear a woman's voice until the voice of your lover whispers gently in your ear as you fall; and for some she will whisper in my voice* – Gute Nacht, liebe. Gute Nacht. Liebchen.

But war was no more. Kurt would live a long life. The story of the night I drank champagne with Marlene Dietrich would be enough. And he spoke so well, of the world and how he would change it. For a time I lay on the chaise longue listening to Kurt's dreams; alas, I have for-gotten now what they were. No different from the other young men of the time, I suppose. To possess everything. I enjoyed hearing him talk, watching his face, feeling his restless energy as he paced, to the window to look out at the darkness of the sleeping city, around the suite, impressed by the luxury of each room, imagining what he would do when he was rich. Eventually he came to sit beside me, but I was tired. It was not, after all, to be his destiny to possess Dietrich – even for one night. I rang down to Herbert to return the young man whence he came. I gave him three souvenirs of our meeting: a photograph of myself that I signed, *To Kurt*, etc., the cork from the bottle of champagne we shared, and a kiss – on his mouth. A kiss from Marlene. His young mouth opened, a little at first, then more. It was a real kiss. Dawn could not have been far away when I called Beatrice to prepare me for bed.

It was a trick I might have pulled myself, back in my Berlin days. Name me a great star who didn't hustle at the beginning. I discovered, when I rose the next afternoon, that Kurt was a thief. He had taken a jewellery case – and its contents. A diamond choke, in a slim black leather case, my signature, *Marlene*, scrawled in gold across the top. Not real diamonds, of course. Paste. For performance. For the cameras and the lights. The real ones stay in Switzerland. But real enough to the unschooled eye.

Beatrice was distraught. Protested her innocence when I questioned her about them. Wept, poor fool; as if she would steal such things. No. It was the young man, Kurt. Herbert was phoning for the police, but I said no. I was not sure why at the time, but later I was glad.

When I arrived at the theatre that evening, the crowd was no more than twenty persons – too small to stop. But as I made to walk through them – they can tell when you will not stop and just part for you like the Red Sea, in awe – the face appeared, confidently breaking rank. The face from the rear window. The doorman who thought himself a comic. There were no words, but flowers – three white roses, a small envelope attached to their stems. He nodded, whispered, 'I'm so sorry,' most respectfully, and withdrew back into the crowd. Then I was through the door and inside the theatre.

More flowers were waiting for me inside. Each night I receive more flowers than a Mafia funeral, but despite the spectacular floral creations that lined the corridor, it was only the three roses I took into my dressing room that evening. The others would go, as usual, to local hospitals. Beatrice attaches a gold card bearing the legend, *With love, from Marlene.*

I receive countless gifts from my admirers, which is always touching. Chocolates, I give to staff; toys, to children's homes; cheap jewellery, to attentive hotel employees. Tonight, among the chocolates and toys and letters, a small black wallet, of very cheap quality. An elastic band attached a note to it: *Miss Dietrich, after you left the theatre last night, one of your fans handed this in. It was dropped by the young man who was hit by your car.*

I opened the wallet. *So, my friend! We will see!* It was almost empty. Some grubby coins in one compartment, two torn pieces of paper in another. The first was obviously the start of a letter, undated and without an address: *Dear Graham, there is no point going over the past. The thing to do now . . .* The rest had been ripped away – to provide material for my autograph? I read it again. The hand was ugly, uneducated. I turned to the second piece: a narrow strip of flimsy paper torn from the edge of a magazine page. Printed on this in blue biro pen was: 'Ask for Alf – CEN 9684 After 10'. I returned the papers to the wallet and put it to one side. He had been such a beautiful dissembler. Such a lovely face. Open and honest. I laughed to myself. So even the generation of love and peace has its crooks; things do not change so much.

I turned to my roses. Sniffed them. No perfume. Why do roses no longer carry their perfume? But their shape was exquisite – expensive blooms. Inside the envelope was a short letter:

Dear Miss Dietrich,

I write simply to express my sincerest apologies. I offer no excuses. It was very wrong of me to have spoken to your fans in such a way. I see that now.

I am shocked by my own behaviour, and what hurts me most is knowing that I have offended such a great star. That really hurts me.

Please accept my most sincere apologies,
Derek Richards.

I read it again. It was a good letter. I liked it. The paper was cheap, but the handwriting very good: well-formed letters curving just a little to the right. A firm, manly hand, I thought. Properly headed and dated. Written with a fountain pen too. Blue ink. White paper. Yes, I thought, this is quite good, it is the right tone, dignified; no embarrassing begging for reinstatement, no cringing descriptions of poverty and family commitments. It seemed a genuine expression of regret.

I lifted the roses again. Beautiful. A pity about the perfume. I sent for the backstage manager. 'I received these charming roses from the man I had dismissed last night.' I glanced at the name at the bottom of the letter. 'Dirk Richards.'

'Derek, Miss Dietrich.'

'Pardon, darling?'

'Derek. Not Dirk.'

'I see. Thank you, darling. Mr Richards was waiting outside when I arrived. Would you see if he is still there? If he is, have him brought to me.'

When he came in I was pleased by what I saw. He was wearing a good suit, a clean white shirt and a tie. It was rare to see a young man suited in such a way at that time; the vogue for informality had begun. Yes, he had made an effort with his appearance, as he had with his apology.

I did not stand to shake his hand. I had decided to forgive him – this was enough. Should I offer him a seat? No. Let him stand. Some women have told me they do not like looking up towards a man in this way; they prefer equal eye levels. All I can say is, they lack confidence. For me it has never been a problem.

'Miss Dietrich,' he started. 'I am –'

I lifted my hand to stop him. 'You have apologized very well in your letter, Dirk. It is not necessary to do so again. I was deeply hurt by your words, they were . . . But no, I believe your apology is sincere. I accept it.'

'Thank you, Miss Dietrich. I am grateful.'

I let him stand there. I said nothing. Let him feel discomfort. He was twenty-seven or twenty-eight years old. Not particularly handsome. Not a beautiful face, by any means, but a strong one; some echo of George Raft. He held himself well, was well made beneath his suit. I could see that. Sturdy. Like a peasant. And his eyes and mouth were good. The sort of man who laughs a lot. I like that; it shows confidence. There was none of the earnestness of my friend of the previous evening. He was not unattractive. Not at all. So, I sat there watching him. Quizzically he smiled his discomfort. Did I want him to go? He waited, his fingers rolling inward, nervously. He wore no rings.

Eventually I too smiled. 'Well now, Dirk, darling, I want you to do something for me. An act of reparation for the hurt you caused me.'

This surprised him. There are some people for whom the reaction to uncertainty is a smile. He was one of those people. Charming.

'You may sit down, Dirk.'

'My name is Derek, Miss Dietrich. Not Dirk.'

'Very well, darling. Now sit down. In that chair there.' I reached to the dressing table for the wallet and lifted it for him to see.

He listened attentively as I told him the story of Kurt. Then I pushed the wallet towards him. 'Here. Take it.' The confused smile returned. The foolish man thought I was making a gift of it. No, I regret using that word. He was not a fool, as I was to discover.

'Open it, Dirk. Yes. Now those two pieces of paper. I think Kurt may not be called Kurt at all. But this other name. What is it?'

'Graham.'

'Yes. Graham. Also, you see there is a telephone number. And another name. What does it say?'

'Ask for Alf.'

'And that is what I want you to do, darling. I want you to phone the number and ask for Alf. I want you to find out who this Kurt, or Graham, is. And if you can, what happened to my jewellery.'

'But surely, this should be given to the police?'

'I don't involve the police, darling. No. Are you saying you won't help me?'

He was confident again. Not looks, but a charisma, which is just as good; ask Bogart.

'Of course I will. I'll do everything I can to help you. It sounds fun.' I liked the way he said that.

I give everything in my concerts – a great star does, has to. In magazine interviews Beatrice reads me from time to time, some artists claim they can perform and think of something else at the same time – second-raters! Not Dietrich. Every particle of my being is concentrated as I perform. I live every song, am aware of my every movement, every gesture I make. At times of suffering in my life, and there have been many, performance has saved me. When the lights come up, I am the artist – my own life is gone. Is it any wonder I leave the stage exhausted?

When at the end of Tuesday's performance a member of staff told me that a Derek Richards sought permission to speak with me, for a moment I was not immediately aware of who he was. The words, *sought permission,* took my attention though. Then it came to me. 'Ah, yes. Dirk. Tell him I need a little time to recover. No. Just tell him I will see him in a few minutes. Tell him to wait.'

An hour or so later I was ready. 'Ah, Dirk, darling. More roses. How sweet you are to me. You may sit down. No, not there. Over here.'

Yes, he had charisma. It was the smile, I think. It often is with the peasant class. Think of Piaf. He had a sturdy self-confidence, but understood instinctively our relative positions and respected that – the ideal basis for a satis-factory relationship.

'Do you have anything to tell me, darling?'

'I do, Miss Dietrich. Your friend Kurt is really a Graham Borin.'

'Borin.'

'Polish. Or rather, his father is Polish. Settled here after the war. Graham is a Brummie.'

'Goodness! A Brummie. What is that?' It sounded like a member of some revolutionary group.

Dirk smiled. 'I'm sorry, Miss Dietrich. It is an expres-sion. The name given to natives of this city.'

'Remind me which city we are in, Dirk.'

'Derek, Miss Dietrich. Birmingham.'

'Ah yes.'

'Those from London are known as cockneys. From Birmingham, Brummies.'

'How charming.'

'The telephone number is of a bar called the Little Moscow. Very disreputable. A place where stolen goods can be disposed of. Half the criminals of the city hang out there. This man Alf is a fence for stolen jewellery.'

'A fence?'

'Another expression, ma'am. Criminal terminology. For someone who buys stolen goods and sells them on. I have talked with this man Alf. Explained what happened. Made it clear how hot this cargo would be once you inform the police and the press get hold of the story.'

'Just a minute, darling. You go very fast. What is this about "hot cargo"? More criminal terminology?'

'Yes, ma'am.'

'You seem very fluent in this language, darling. Tell me what it means.'

'That the items stolen – are known to the police. They're actively searching for them. Photographs exist and so these items are easily identifiable.'

'Thank you. That is very clear. So this Alf. What a curious name. He is no longer interested in fencing my hot cargo?'

'That's right. But he is prepared to help me get your jewellery back. I did hint that a small reward was likely for its safe return.'

'Did you? That is very generous of you.'

'I'm sorry, Miss Dietrich. Have I done the wrong thing?'

'The wrong thing? To promise a reward I must pay for the return of my own property.'

'I'm sorry. But with these people money talks.'

'Don't be deceived, darling. It talks to us all. It is the only truly international language.'

'Perhaps I was too enthusiastic. I wanted to make sure I got your jewellery back.' He looked so sad then. A disappointed child. That wonderful English word – crestfallen. It moved me. He had done well for me. I knew that.

'I am sure a small reward can be arranged.'

'Alf is going to meet this chap, Graham, tomorrow night. The bar stays open after hours, that means longer than the law permits. I guess the owner pays the police and they turn a blind eye. That is, they pretend –'

'Yes, darling. I know that expression. A blind eye.'

'A meeting has been arranged between Alf and Graham Borin for midnight. I will be there.'

'And so will I, Dirk. We will go together.'

*

It was curiously exciting. I left the theatre after only an hour and returned to my hotel. A black suit, like the one I wore in *Witness for the Prosecution*. Dark glasses. No jewellery. I am an actress; I can blend into any background. No, that is not right. I do not blend. I achieve a persona that is correct for any environment. And this bar, the Little Moscow – I have been in such places before. I am not unfamiliar with the criminal classes.

One descends stone steps to enter this place. I have trodden many such steps. The night was fine. At that time of year darkness is never dark. But of course, one must always be on one's guard; darkness is not essential for danger. There was a greasy canal near by. Oil-smeared, like an artist's palette. Oily circles of blue and green illuminated by lamplight.

I have never entered anywhere unnoticed. And this was no exception. Heads turned. It was my legs they saw first, the small-time crooks who sat plotting over their drinks. The legs of Dietrich. Legs more expensive than they could ever dream. Into this dingy pit the silver screen descended, the fabulous arrived and they did not know it.

I was not recognized as myself, but as the exotic. I do not believe a single eye saw anything else as Dirk escorted me to a table in an alcove. As private as was possible here.

Once I was seated, Dirk had to leave me to fetch whiskies from the bar. Whisky is the only drink tolerable in such places. 'They'd think Bollinger is a racehorse, here,' Dirk joked.

He returned with our drinks, accompanied by a tall, wrinkled lizard of a man, whose eyes twinkled with prison cunning. The blue of the petrol smear on the canal outside.

'Am I recognized?' I asked.

'No,' Dirk replied.

'Are you sure?'

'They think you are a whore,' the lizard answered candidly.

'Really. It is a mistake that has been made before.'

This amused the man who was now introduced to me as Alf. His weasel eyes continued to twinkle. Alf – what a foolish name to be known by; even now I cannot say it without thinking so. Carefully he explained to me that his correct name was Alfred Edward King. 'Alfred. Edward. Both English kings, you see, Miss Dietrich.'

Dirk told me that Alf would now leave us to wait at the bar for Graham. He would first ensure he had the cargo with him and then bring him across to my table.

Earlier I had considered contacting the local police force to place someone in the bar ready for the young thief. But I decided against such action. I was not particularly interested in whether he was arrested or not and I saw now that I was right. Such men as these might not recognize a Hollywood legend when she walked amongst them, but they smell police immediately, no matter how plain his clothes. And I was not uncomfortable. I was not unhappy sitting there drinking whisky with Dirk. With him I felt quite safe.

There was a jukebox. Two long-haired young men holding snooker cues like shotguns lounged against it chatting. A pretty song of the day called 'Always Something There to Remind Me' played as Graham descended the stone steps and moved towards Alf at the bar.

The two thieves, one old with lizard skin, the other beautiful with the complexion of a girl, ordered beer. There was conversation between them. Then the older man indicated the alcove in which Dirk and I sat. The young man looked over, looked straight at me. I removed my glasses. He was transfixed. It was a special moment for me.

Then, recovering himself, he swung away from the bar and up the stone steps. Immediately Dirk was after him. The drinkers took little notice.

Alf returned to my table and there we waited. He bought me another whisky and gave me a fascinating account of his working life. Please, I am not using that word facetiously. An artist should learn from all forms of life; it is our task to absorb all so that we can re-present it. Eventually, the lizard came round to the subject of a reward. I told him that there would be something for him, but at the moment the cargo was still just that, cargo; it could be sinking to the bottom of the canal outside as we spoke. If the jewellery were safely returned to me I would show my appreciation. Dirk would bring him something. He would have to trust me as I had trusted him. It is an irony that the word 'trust' gets used so much in bars like the Little Moscow.

Even for diamonds I will only wait so long; for costume jewellery half an hour was enough. When Dirk had not returned after this time I instructed Alf to arrange a taxi for me.

I was not surprised when I entered my dressing room the following evening to see the slim black case with my name glittering across its lid resting upon my dressing table. The jewellery was there, safe and sound. Everything was intact. More roses, an envelope attached. Out fell a strip of paper. Four photographs. Taken in a booth. It was the face of the thief. Graham. Kurt. Beaten and bruised. Swollen eyes. Across his cheek, a squiggle, like an autograph, made with a blade. On the other side, in blue biro pen, 'I'm sorry Miss Dietrich, Graham'. I turned to the photographs again and looked into the mangled face. Beauty broken.

Herbert was disappointed when I told him that I would no longer need his services. The travelling was too much for him. I intended to appoint a new driver, a younger man. I paid him off generously enough and gave him a photograph, signed *With gratitude, Marlene*.

Dirk looked very pleasing behind the wheel in his new uniform. His first task for me was to go to the bar known as the Little Moscow and deliver a similarly signed photograph in an envelope addressed, in my own hand, to *Mr Alfred Edward King.*

Bonebinder and the Dogs

M y name is Bonebinder. It is an ancient name, given to healers. There is no word in Chinese for irony.

I serve Hsinshu, Emperor of the Ninth Dragon. I fulfil many roles. There is nothing he could ask of me I would refuse. And he sets me many tasks.

The gambling is good business in Birmingham. 'Lucrative,' Hsinshu says. As he finishes the word, which he always pronounces slowly, breaking it apart to three syllables, a satisfied smile takes his mouth. I live to see that smile.

'Shuko, there is a market for another sort of gambling,' he said to me, 'that could be very lucrative.' He stretched the word 'very', dragging the vowel so it meandered like a river. Such pronunciation is unusual for a Chinese. I waited: a task was coming.

'Dogs, I think. There are those who prefer a more dangerous way to lose their money. They tire of cards, dice, the wheel.' He looked at me. Now the task: 'Dogs, I think, will take their fancy. Fighting dogs. To the death.'

I went to Fat Alex, who runs the Little Moscow. He was the man with the knowledge I needed. His eyes are like those of a fish when you take him by surprise. They bulge. Are still. Cold, while he thinks.

'Dogs. Fighters, you say?' He stroked the stubble on his chin, scratched down the side of his neck. He is not a clean man. There were stains on his vest. 'The Gordon brothers. They used to fight cocks. Over Brierley Hill. I think they done a few dogs as well. Or there's Diesel. Leave it with me, Bone. Come in Wednesday.'

It was Diesel who was waiting for me on Wednesday, sitting in an alcove drinking Guinness. Diesel is female. She is built like a sumo. I had heard of her. She keeps a snack wagon near the M40. It is called *Bite-Inn*. She is popular with lorry drivers, whom she resembles. Her grey hair is cut very short and she wears dungarees. She killed a policeman once and spent many years inside.

Sitting beside Diesel in the alcove was a woman in her forties with bleached hair, thin purple lips, and a boy of about sixteen, skinny, pimply, home-made tattoos up his arms, no more than scars, a nose ring, scabs on his shaved skull. Black circles around his eyes. A junkie.

Such people are scum, and I recognized these as such. But Fat Alex knows everyone. He is reliable. So I had to deal with them. When I meet with such people I remember the story of Kuransashi, who travelled through the bamboo forest to claim his kingdom. So close did each stalk grow, and so tall, that in their darkness he had to become bamboo, weave in and out, like a thread feeding a thousand needles, supple, patient and strong. When he claimed his kingdom Kuransashi had threaded a thousand slivers of bamboo, needle-thin, that he wore around his neck. When they drew blood, as they sometimes did, Kuransashi rejoiced in the memory of his journey to greatness. My purpose is to help Hsinshu retain and expand his kingdom.

'This is my girlfriend, Pauline,' Diesel said. 'And her son, Alan.' There were no handshakes or smiles, merely nods of the head. Pauline and Alan each had a pint of lager before them. All three smoked. Diesel came straight to business. 'Alex says you're after dogs. For fighting. Gambling.'

'That is right.'

'Dragons, is it?'

I said nothing.

'Well, you'll want to put on a good show. To the death, is it?'

I nodded.

'How many fights?'

'On the first evening, three. If the event is successful there will be others.'

Opportunity registered on Diesel's face. 'Pits is best if it's to the death. Or Tosas. Pauline breeds both. So we can supply what you want. But I'd say pits is best.'

I am a man who speaks few words. Most stay inside my head. Diesel talked. I listened. She could provide the dogs. Tell us which of each pair would be defeated so we could control the betting. The dogs would be three years old – at their most aggressive. Starved for forty-eight hours. It would be a good show.

'Premises,' she said. 'I can arrange them for you as well, if you want. A warehouse in Deritend, in the centre of an old factory complex. The whole place is derelict, has been for years. Falling down most of it. The warehouse is sound. Completely safe. Canal, railway, lots of roads. All make for easy getaways. I can get some lighting rigged up. A bit of music too, if you like. Keep the punters happy.'

'Will you do your own drink?' Pauline asked.

'Yes. That is something we can arrange.'

Diesel nodded. 'Fair enough. But I can do that as well if you want. A bottle bar. Snacks too. Basic or fancy. Think about it.'

The boy's eyes travelled from speaker to speaker.

'Now. Tell me, what is your price? For six dogs, premises, music, lighting?'

There was a problem. A look shifted between the three of them. Silence. A change in posture. They were preparing. The boy scratched his crotch.

Diesel raised her head. 'Not money.' She awaited my reaction. There was none: I waited too. 'A trade.' Still I waited. 'We want you to take care of someone.'

'Finish him,' Pauline snarled, her mouth mean and angry. The boy put his finger in his ear and twisted.

'Who?'

'Her old man.' Diesel nodded towards Pauline. 'He's a bastard. Won't leave her alone.'

'Wants money,' Pauline continued. 'Wants sex. Beats me up. And Alan.' Her thumb jerked towards the boy.

'I would prefer a cash deal.'

'No.' Diesel's hard eyes met mine. 'This is the only deal we're offering.'

I went to Hsinshu in the big red room above the casino and reported my meeting. He listened carefully, asked no questions. He knows I tell all. Hsinshu rose from the table and collected three arrows from the dartboard which hangs on the wall at the back of the red room. He paced back to the line and stood focusing on the board. This is often his way when making decisions. When he was ready he fired the arrows. Two secure in the House of Twenty. The third in the bull.

When he returned to the table he was smiling. 'It is good business. A price that means more to them than to us. Agree. Arrange it. But on the night of the dogfight. If all is in order we will settle the debt then.'

I used the telephone number Diesel had given me. We met in the Little Moscow again. The same alcove. Alex, in the same stained vest, waved.

I have the energy of Wood, Diesel the same. There are many with Wood energy, but it expresses itself differently

– in countless ways. Hers is twisted, the seed thwarted. Place a rock above a seed and its energy, the genetic code it contains, will force through, or travel round the rock until it finds a place. But the tree is deformed. It survives desperately. Gnarled and malformed but strong in its will to survive.

She had documents. Maps. Plans of the factory centre. A diagram of the warehouse space. Dimensions. The arena marked.

'We'll keep the dogs in the corridors over here. Bring em in from each side. More dramatic. The punters'll be all round here.' Her finger went to the centre of the diagram. 'All cordoned off, of course. But the dogs'll be leashed anyway. So no one gets hurt. Spotlight up here. Betting here. Booze here. You'll provide the lookouts? Security?' I nodded. 'Thought so.' She lifted photographs. 'I've brought some pictures of the dogs. Not the actual ones, but pits. To whet the punters' appetites. It's strictly invite only?'

'Yes.'

'Here's a couple of pictures of fights. You might be able to use them.'

'You have been very thorough. I think we can go ahead as arranged.'

She took out another photograph. A man. 'And here's my price.'

I looked at the photograph. The man was in a suit, his tie loosened, a drink in his hand. On the other side she had written information I might need. His name, address, even weight and height.

'You'll do it the same night?'

I nodded.

'Thursday. He'll be at the York Arms, but he always leaves early. About quarter past ten. Likes to watch *News-night*. I've made a map of the direction he takes. He drives a silver Focus. There's the reg.' She had written it below the map. 'I'm taking a big risk giving you these. My hand-writing. But I know you boys are professionals. I'd like all this destroyed though.'

'Of course.'

'Will you do it in the car park?'

'No. In his flat. While *Newsnight* is on.'

'Shooter?'

'Yes.'

'I suppose that's best. I'd have liked it to be slower. We thought about using the dogs on him. But it's too chancy.'

I checked it out. I leave nothing to chance. It is my nature and what makes me the valuable servant to Hsinshu that I am. I was impressed by the location. The warehouse was the perfect venue. A big, big room. Very high vaulted roof. Long narrow windows still intact. Yes, it would serve well. I went to see the dogs. They were fit, aggressive beasts. They would do the job. I drove to the price's flat, recognized him from the photograph. Followed his movements on two consecutive Thursdays. On the second visit I was seen, not by the price but by Alan. He had been waiting.

I opened the car door. He got inside. I said nothing, but waited for him to speak. When he opened his mouth I was taken aback. I did not expect this. Garbled, unintelligible sounds. The boy was mute, yet struggling to be heard.

Then the noises, repeated over and over, started to make sense. 'Don't kill my dad. Please. Kill Diesel instead.' Each word a forced sound, like wind from a tunnel.

'It is the contract,' I told him. 'The price.'

He was distressed. Tears in his eyes. Snot dribbling from his nose. He pulled at my arm and repeated his plea. I pushed him away.

'I'll warn my dad. I'll go to the police.' A screech in his noise now. An animal in pain.

This was a problem. 'Okay. Leave it with me.'

'Promise?'

'Leave it with me. Do nothing for now.'

I had to give this matter some thought. It is not my way to disturb Hsinshu with small difficulties. My task was clear – to set up the dogfight and that I must do.

'A cup of tea. Without milk or sugar.' Her surprise was obvious. I had waited for a quiet time. Two lorry drivers were eating bacon sandwiches, but they moved away to lean against their vehicle.

Diesel came round to the front of her wagon to stand beside me. She listened to what I told her.

'Stupid bastard,' she growled. 'You know he's a junkie?' I nodded. 'Suppose we could keep him supplied till this is sorted.' I said nothing. 'No. That's not going to work.' She wiped her hands down her dungarees. Made her eyes hard. 'The kid'll have to go with his dad. He's nothing but trouble anyway. They couldn't even manage him in care.'

I waited a moment, sipping the foul tea from its plastic cup. 'It will be a better solution if we revert to a cash deal for your services.'

'No.' Her response was instant. 'No way. It's this or nothing. The both of them.'

As I drove away I reflected how fast a seed might grow, how quickly barren land could become a forest. I had to husband this land, remain in control of it.

Pauline lives on the Kingshurst estate. A scruffy house. A long garden filled with cages. She was feeding the dogs when I arrived, throwing meat into the cages, pushing bowls of water beneath the wire.

She took me into the house. I declined the offer of tea. A television screen dominated the room. Two dogs occupied the chairs. She clapped her hands and shouted; the animals vacated the seats.

'These two are okay,' she reassured me. 'No more than pussycats, really.'

It is my way to be clear and direct in cases like this. I explained all to Pauline. 'You see, you now are the potential problem. If I go ahead with this deal as Diesel wants, you lose your son. I have to know what your reaction to this is.'

She had started to bite at her lower lip, using her index finger to push it into her mouth. I saw a physical resemblance between her and Alan, around the eyes and nose. The other hand patted one of the dogs.

I had the time, I let her think. Of course I was thinking too – assessing, but it was difficult to read this woman's thoughts from her face. There was only the gnawing of her lip.

Eventually she spoke. 'And this is what Diesel wants, is it? She thinks it's the best?'

There was no opportunity for me to reply, for outside the dogs started to bark. The door flew open. Alan stood there, swaying. Then shouting at his mother. She rose in an attempt to pacify him but he struck her. The two dogs in the room started to bark and snarl. The boy turned to me and I rose to meet him.

'Stop it, Alan,' Pauline yelled. Then to me, 'He's on something. Belt him one.'

Alan turned for the door and was out, Pauline following. I followed too.

He kicked and banged the cages, provoking the dogs to a hysteria of barking and foaming. Then he slips a bolt, pushes the cage door. The dog leaps out. Pauline shouts. Alan makes to move to the next cage, but not fast enough. The dog has him at the leg.

'Conga! Conga! Off, Conga!' Pauline roars.

Alan brings his hand down to push the dog away, but the beast sees it coming and leaps, closing its jaws over the fingers. Alan screams, twists. Still the dog holds the hand. Alan falls to the ground. The dog bites into his face.

Fearlessly, Pauline crouches. She takes hold of the dog's collar. 'Conga. Conga. Easy girl. Easy now.' Pauline strokes the dog's back. 'Come on now. It's all right.' The animal calms. Moves away. Licks Pauline's hand, leaving pink saliva foaming on it. Pauline leads the dog into the pen. Slips the bolt.

Alan, sobbing and bleeding, was crawling up the garden path. A voice from beyond the hedge called out to keep the fucking dogs quiet. Alan made for the shed. I followed him. He was bleeding profusely. Trembling. Silent now, he propped himself against a sack of dog biscuits.

'If you take him to hospital there will be too many questions.'

'I'll ring Diesel,' Pauline said.

I closed the door of the shed, followed her into the house. She kept her back to me as she explained to Diesel. They talked but there was little in Pauline's words, just 'Yes' and 'No', 'Okay', 'I suppose so'.

When the call was finished, Pauline reached into a vase on the window ledge and removed a pack of cigarettes and a lighter. 'I've been trying to give these up,' she said. 'But when you're upset.' Once she had lit her cigarette and inhaled deeply, she turned to me, but her eyes did not meet mine. 'Diesel says I should let you take care of him.'

'Are you sure?'

She nodded.

'I need some towels.'

'Just let me finish this.'

The boy was barely conscious when I returned to the shed, wrapped towels around his head and shot him. The dogs started to bark again. The neighbour called for quiet.

'Don't go into the shed,' I told Pauline. 'I'll be back later.'

'It's okay. Diesel's on her way.'

It is the sweetest thing to please your master. I saw pleasure in Hsinshu's eyes all that evening as he watched the dogs fight, the punters bet. 'This is very good business. We will have more.'

For the purpose of the fight the dogs had been given new names. Yellow Emperor. Confucius. Yangtze. It added interest for the punters. It was my function to destroy with a bullet the beaten dogs, put them out of their misery. Among them was Conga, renamed Red Devil, the dog that had bitten Alan.

Primitive Stain

Dowd looked down on the strangled girl. The last time he had seen her he had been shagging her. This was the time to get out. Have a quiet word with the Chief. Use a phrase like 'personal involvement' and cut loose. But he knew he wasn't going to do that. You can't afford to drop cases like this, not at this stage. And when it's a second murder: high profile. It'd be there on his record. The finishing post for his career.

He turned away from the corpse and took the information docket from Jack. The words danced before his eyes. He blinked to refocus. Still dancing. He blinked again – more than a blink: squeezed his eyes shut. When he opened them again the text was stable. He looked over it, nodded to Jack, handed the paper back. 'Let's have a drink,' he said. 'Talk this over.'

Dowd believed in luck. Not that it was just random chance, but that you made it. He didn't believe anyone reached the top without luck; he'd seen too many good people stuck in the ranks. He knew he was lucky. Believed that totally. He was lucky to have Jack Stevens as his assistant. He'd chosen him, groomed him. There was no one else in the force he trusted like Jack. So he didn't feel he was taking a chance now.

'Jack. This second murder, Stella Lyons. I know her.'

Suddenly he had to laugh. It was Jack's honest, earnest face looking across the table at him. 'I picked her up in Whites, a week or so ago.'

Jack swallowed. 'But . . .'

'I didn't pay for it, Jack. Whores fancy blokes too. Take a night off. They're not working all the time.'

'No.'

'I didn't know she was a whore. Well, not at first. When she told me she was a dancer I guessed it wasn't the Royal Ballet. When she said she worked at Pinks I more or less knew.' He smile-sighed. 'But her pants were in my pocket by then so it didn't make much difference.'

There was a pause. Dowd drank from his lager. Jack sipped his orange juice. A bloke in a tracksuit took the jackpot from a fruit machine. Coins churned out.

Dowd took a cigarette pack from inside his jacket. 'D'you mind?' A stupid question. The bar was full of smoke. But that was Dowd.

'No.' Jack watched him light up. 'Are you going to stay on the case?'

'I want to. Yes. Yes, I am.'

Then Jack understood. 'You bastard.' Dowd raised his eyebrows. 'You tell me so I have a choice: shop you, or carry on, knowing you shouldn't be handling this. If it comes out, I go down with you.'

'I guess that's about it,' Dowd said. Smoke left his mouth with the words and drifted between the two men. He lifted his glass and drank. When he put it down he looked at Jack. 'And?'

'I'm not going to shop you.'

He is listening to the water gurgle – above him and below him. The city above, he knows, is hot tonight. Here on the metal ramp it is cool.

The man's hands were cupped in his lap. Casually, it seemed. Jack looked at the fingers, white with pressure. There was sweat across his upper lip. He was scared, all right. But holding it together. Two hours ago he had walked into Harborne nick and explained to the desk sergeant that he had just heard about the murder of Stella Lyons. The night before she was killed he had slept with her.

Now he was in Interview Room 2 with Dowd and Jack. Dowd seemed to have recovered from his surprise. The physical similarity between himself and Brett Collins, the man seated across the table, was remarkable. Not just the face – the two men could have been brothers. Height and build, pretty much the same. Both expensively dressed in blue pinstriped suits, white shirts, black shoes. The ties were different – Dowd's red, Collins' grey – but both silk. Both had dark hair similarly cut. Both were tanned by the current spell of hot weather. And both had slept with Stella Lyons.

Jack had the tape running. Dowd was doing the questions.

'Perhaps you'll start, Mr Collins, by telling us what you told Desk Sergeant Long when you reported to Harborne Police Station at 9.17 this morning.' Standard.

Collins cleared his throat. 'Simply that I spent the night before she died with Stella Lyons.'

'And where did you spend the night?'

'At my flat.'

'When you say you spent the night with her, I take it you mean you had sex?'

'Yes.'

'Did you know Miss Lyons well?'

Collins sighed. Eyes on the desk. 'No. Not at all in fact.' He inhaled audibly as if he needed more oxygen to continue. Dowd waited. 'I picked her up. At a place called Pinks.'

'The lap-dancing club?'

Collins looked up. 'Yes.'

'And did you pay for the sex?'

'Yes, but not in the way you mean. There was no deal done. She agreed to meet me outside the club when she'd finished. I asked her to come back for a drink. She agreed. But in the morning, when I dropped her off in town, I gave her a hundred pounds. Told her to buy herself a present.'

Dowd was concentrating. There was a moment before he spoke. 'Tell me about the night.'

Collins was uncertain. 'How do you mean?'

'Tell me what happened when you took her home.'

'Well, we had a couple of drinks. I put on some music. We kissed a bit. Then went to bed.'

'And then?'

'Then?'

'In the bedroom.'

'We had sex.'

'In the bed?'

'Yes.'

'How many times?'

Collins looked across to Jack. His fingers turned in his lap. Then stopped. 'Three times during the course of the night.'

'Anything kinky?'

'No.'

'What positions?'

Jack shot a glance at Dowd but his attention was firmly on Collins.

'Missionary position. From behind. Her astride me.'

'Do you go with prostitutes very often, Mr Collins?'

The man leaned back in his seat, uncurled his lands, laid one on each knee, then sat upright again. He took a breath. 'As a rule, never. But my marriage broke up six months ago.' Dowd blinked. 'And over the past few weeks, yes, I have. I've been with three or four. Four in fact.'

Dowd considered. 'So, if I've got this right, in the last few months, since the break-up of your marriage, you have started going with prostitutes. You picked Stella Lyons up, and because of where she worked you assumed, although she didn't ask, that she would want money, so you gave her a hundred pounds.'

'Yes.' A sigh again. The head fell back, but only for a second. The fingers of the right hand started to tap the knee. The mouth opened. But no words came. Dowd and Jack waited. 'The trouble is,' he started. 'The trouble is. One of the prostitutes I went with. The first one in fact. It was Fortune Lawrence, the other girl who was murdered.'

He lifts the rifle to fence level. Follows the squirrel. It leaps to the branch. He fires. It falls.

'So. What do you reckon, Jack? Is this just some bloke who's got unlucky, or is he our killer?'

Collins was in a cell. The press had been informed that a man was helping with enquiries. Now they were on their way to Collins' flat, Jack driving. He was wearing shades against the fierce sun.

'If he is the killer,' Jack responded, 'surely it's pretty unusual for him to come in and admit knowledge of the victims?'

'Perhaps he's just trying to save himself.'

'Save himself?'

'From more. Serial killers are often horrified by what they do when they start. They want to stop. But then they come to terms with it. Immunity sets in. Or the drive is too strong.'

'But if that was the case wouldn't he have just confessed? He must have known he'd be a suspect, even with one girl, but *two*. No, I think he would've just come clean and got it over with.'

'Maybe you're right.' Dowd didn't sound convinced.

*

They sit on the steps. Encased in sound. The sluice-charge: ten minutes of roaring every four hours. It is how the city is kept clean. The noise resounds through the chamber. One holds the reptile, a yellow phase bearded dragon – finger pressure behind the eyes keeps its jaws apart. The other puts his hand between those jaws. The reptile's tongue licks at the hand. Like rough feathers. The two look at each other. If the one relaxes his hand, the other will lose his.

Dowd sat in a black leather armchair in the lounge of Brett Collins' flat, looking out at the canal glittering green below, the restaurants lining its edge; all the tables outside today. Metal and glass; they glittered too. Sun poured though the French doors.

The search was pretty much concluded when he and Jack arrived. Just a couple of rubber-gloved officers finishing off. Dowd had walked the flat several times. Silent. Thoughtful. Jack had never been to Dowd's house, but he imagined it was like this, like rooms in Sunday supplements. And he guessed, since Dowd's wife had left him a few months back, it probably felt as empty. Jack had watched Dowd stroke a glass head that stood on a plinth in the corner of the room.

'Crystal,' he muttered. 'An original. Expensive. Beautiful.' Then to Jack: 'There's an artist, you know, who has sculpted a head, his I think, out of his own blood. It has to be kept in a freezer.'

Dowd turned away from the window. Looked across to Jack. 'What do you make of the booty then?'

On a long low piece of rough-cut polished mahogany that served as a coffee table, the search team had placed the few items they thought might be of interest to Dowd. Four bamboo canes and a glass dildo. All turned up at the back of the fitted wardrobe. A jumbo box of condoms. A canister of lube.

'Open to interpretation, I would say.'

'Would you?' Dowd rose. Lifted a cane. Swished it through the air. 'Lives in a flat. No garden. These are hardly for supporting his hollyhocks, Jack.'

'No.'

Dowd replaced the cane. Lifted the glass dildo. Sniffed it. 'What do you think he uses this for?'

The lift doors open and she is face to face with him. He holds a rope. A push from behind and she's in the lift. The doors close.

It was the paperwork search that did it: PC Phil Drake, one of the uniform team, going through Collins' address book. Relaxor Sauna.

'It's a knocking shop,' Phil told Jack with a grin. 'Tries to be upmarket, but still a knocking shop.' Jack gave Phil a hard look. But the grin widened. 'Yeh, I've done a bit of relaxing there myself.' He winked. 'Don't tell the missus. A bit of a favourite with the lads from Henley Street that place is. CID specially.'

Dowd listened to what Jack had to say. A while back he would have been loudly critical of police officers frequenting such a place, but today he said nothing.

'Who runs it?'

'A woman called Julie Hannox.'

'I guess we'd better talk to her. Ring her up, Jack. Make an appointment. Don't want her to think it's a raid. And get a photograph of Collins.'

It's a familiar tactic. Once Geary, Collins' solicitor, was on the case, every interview died at birth. To Collins: 'You don't have to answer that question.' To Dowd: 'That has no direct relevance to the murder you are investigating.'

Collins again: 'That's an assumption of the detective inspector's. Don't respond, Mr Collins.' Geary was only a young bloke, late twenties, but sharp, going places. Blue pin-striped suit, immaculate. Green silk tie. 'I can't see that you have any reason to keep my client any longer, DI Dowd.' And he was right. Collins was released on police bail.

But Dowd had a hunch. 'Collins wanted to talk,' he told Jack. 'I'm sure he did. I'm not saying a confession. Not to the murders anyway. But you saw the way he was when we whipped the canes out. The dildo. Ashamed. He would have opened up if Geary hadn't stopped him. "Don't respond to that, Mr Collins."' Dowd mimicked Geary's clipped tone. 'Wanker. I think we should give him a chance to talk if he wants to. Just him and us. Off the record.' Dowd smiled. 'I'll give him a ring.'

Dowd was right. Collins invited them over. 'Tonight,' he said. 'About eight-thirty.'

Casual now – jeans, a polo shirt – but still smart. Jack couldn't imagine this guy ever looked scruffy. The windows were wide open but still the flat was filled with heat.

'Have you been to work today?' Dowd asked him. Friendly.

'Yeh. Trying to get back to normal, you know. Hard, though. This has been a real stress. Left early. A couple of hours in the gym.'

'Did it work?'

'I feel better.'

Collins offered them a drink. They refused beer, accepted fruit juice. Both police officers were pleased to see the pile of ice Collins heaped into their glasses. He took the armchair, they the couch. No air. Dowd loosened his tie, Jack did the same.

'I'll come straight to the point, Brett,' Dowd started. 'It's okay if I call you Brett?'

'Sure.'

'Look, Brett, you seem to have been straight with us. Coming in. But, I have to tell you, finding that stuff. Canes. Dildo. More rubbers than they keep in Boots.' He leaned forward towards Collins, elbows on his knees. 'I'm going to have to understand what all that's about if I'm going to eliminate you from enquiries quickly.'

Collins scratched his ear, seemed to wriggle in his chair. Embarrassed. Eyes to the floor. But Dowd was right. He wanted to talk.

'When Katie left me, it was bad. I didn't want her to go. I still hope she'll come back. But after a while I wanted other women too. I went to bars and clubs, like you do, learning to be single again. Chatted to girls. Pulled a couple of times. But it wasn't right. It felt like cheating on Katie. Then one night I went for a drive round Latimer Road. Told myself I was just looking. Curious. But I picked one of the girls up. Fifty pounds. Did it in the car. And I couldn't sleep all night thinking of how exciting it had been. Paying for it. I could do, get, just what I wanted.'

'And what was that?'

A pause. Dowd let it run. Kept his eyes on Collins. Collins kept his on the floor. Jack was uncomfortable.

'Did you ever cane your wife?' Dowd's voice cracked the silence.

Collins looked as if he might laugh. 'No. Our sex life was very conventional.'

'But you wanted to.'

'No.'

'But you like to use them on the whores.'

There was a pause. 'It was me that got walloped.'

Dowd didn't bat an eyelid, didn't miss a beat. 'What for, Brett?'

Another pause. Collins looked down. The sweat on his brow gleamed in the light. The room was oppressive.

'Being a naughty boy.' It was a whisper.

*

Blue. It attracts the python. The light means that every-thing is moving at the right speed and in the correct quan-tities. The city is clean. But the python cannot know this, cannot associate the colour with the efficient movement of effluent. The python sees only the colour and is attracted to it. It has no other meaning. The blue light appears and it slithers involuntarily towards it.

The receptionist was expecting them. That unmistakable sauna smell as she led them past white plaster statues of Greek goddesses, a jacuzzi, down a corridor of cubicles to Julie Hannox's office. Music playing softly. Eighties soul: Terence Trent D'Arby.

As soon as the door opened Dowd recognized her. 'Julie Bowen!'

'I've gone back to my maiden name.'

'Can't say I blame you.'

Dowd had put her old man away five years ago. Keith Bowen. Three life sentences for a string of offences that included robbery with violence, intimidation and murder. Dowd's first big case. Bowen didn't do his time though. Two years in, someone cut his throat. A crime for which no one had ever been charged.

Office – it was more like a sitting room, but no win-dows. Two pink couches, lamps, drapes, a repro-antique dark-wood table on which sat a laptop. Expensive job. And a printer. Some framed photographs. Underneath the table, a two-drawer filing cabinet of similar dark wood. A glass-fronted cocktail cabinet in a corner.

'You've been promoted. *DI* Dowd. Well done.' She turned to Jack. 'And who's this? Hutch?'

'DS Jack Stevens. My assistant.'

The woman gave Jack a blatantly appraising look, be-fore holding out her hand. More a caress than a handshake.

'Well, you make a pretty pair.' She sat on a couch. 'What can I do for you? I guess it's about Fortune Lawrence?' She saw the surprise on Dowd's face and smiled. 'You didn't know she worked here? Not for long, I'll grant you. But even so. I would have thought you would have known that. Not getting lazy are we, detective inspector?' A coquettish turn of the head, a mock-sweet smile. 'Never mind. No need to worry. I've printed out all the information you need. She wasn't here long. A bit of a troublemaker, but popular with you boys in blue. I get quite a few in here. Henley Street specially.'

'So I believe.'

'It's on the table.'

Dowd scanned the typewritten sheet. 'Thanks. This'll be useful.' He put it in his inside jacket pocket, swapping it for an envelope. 'Perhaps you'd have a look at this photograph, Julie. Tell me if you recognize him.'

'Brett Collins.' Now she was surprised. 'Is he the man you were holding? That was on the news.'

Dowd ignored the question. 'How do you know him?'

She laughed. 'He was a regular for a few weeks. But not when Fortune was here. She'd gone by then.'

'He told us he picked her up on the street. Is that likely?'

'More than likely. She came from the street, so I've no doubt that's where she ended up. Did a few other saunas from time to time, but she was the streets all right.'

'She was very pretty.'

'Yes,' Hannox conceded, 'she was a pretty girl. Like I said, she was popular. But greedy. Went for too much. And boasted to the others about what she got. In the end she was pissing off both the punters and the other girls.'

'Who did Collins go with? Did he have a favourite?'

'Me, mostly.' She waited for Dowd's reaction. Nothing. 'He liked to get his arse slapped first.' Still nothing. 'Not here, of course. Strictly routine stuff on the premises. That's the arrangement. With Henley Street. If the punters want anything individual they have to sort that out with the girls elsewhere. There are a couple of hotels some use.'

'And you?'

'I'm the boss. But I stick to my own rules. I went over to his flat once or twice and he came to mine sometimes.'

'Sounds like mixing business with pleasure.'

'Does it, inspector?'

'So is that your speciality? The cane?'

'Not particularly. But I won't miss an opportunity to give any man a good thrashing.' She looked towards Jack and smiled.

'And get paid for it as well,' Dowd added.

'Precisely.' She was still looking at Jack.

Sewer Boy is resting in his den on Ramp C. He watches the python making its way across the concrete curve heading upward towards the discharge outlet panels. It is attracted by the blue light that indicates 40%. A red light indicates 30%; orange, 50%; green, 60%. For higher levels there are combinations: white and yellow, 75%; green and blue, 80%. But it is only when the blue light shows that the python shows any interest.

Sewer Boy is waiting for Grant. It is Grant who calls him Sewer Boy, which is fair enough, for this is where he lives now. It is his world. Vicinity Unit 4. He has been here for months now and can count on the fingers of one hand the number of times he has been disturbed. Men in blue overalls descend the long metal ladder. Much more gingerly than Sewer Boy, who can swing down the entire length of all four ladders in seconds. They stop at the first gantry. Use it as their den, for toolboxes and flasks, sometimes radios. Before descending to lower walkways. They have never come this far down. One day they will, he supposes. When the effluent channel ducts start to roar the workmen climb out. Even with their ear-protectors they cannot stand the noise, but Sewer Boy likes it. He likes all the noises down here. The pings and clicks, the ticks and drips, all the roaring and swirling and gurgling sounds. This is his world now. And it is never silent. Nor is it ever really dark. The white neon strips are always on. So, too, are the green floor indicator circles that lead into part of the system where Sewer Boy has never been, where the pipes narrow so you would have to slide on your belly if you wanted to travel them.

Dowd tried to dodge past Trevor on the desk. If he caught him he'd never get to his office. But he was out of luck today. 'I hear you and Jack have been to see Julie,' he called across. Dowd halted. 'How is the old bag?'

'She's looking good. Very good in fact, for her age. Runs a sauna now.'

'Relaxor.' A look from Dowd. 'Not my type of thing, boss.' Trevor leaned across the desk. 'Don't know why she bothers. Loaded, she must be. Got all her old man's money. How's that son of hers? The weird one.'

'She didn't mention him.'

'Badly affected he was. By what happened to his dad. Screaming at everyone after the verdict. Mental hospital for a while. Private though.'

Dowd remembered the kid. About eighteen then. Completely hysterical at the end of the trial. Going for everyone. Unlike his mother. Very much in control Julie was.

'Then when his dad got topped, made things worse. We were called in a couple of times. Complaints he was killing things.'

Dowd's ears pricked. 'Killing things?'

'Rats. Squirrels. That sort of thing. Pellet gun. Neighbours were worried about their cats.'

'Well, if you're lumbered with Keith Bowen for a dad, I'm not surprised.'

'And Julie for a mom.'

It is after midnight. Sewer Boy stands beside the canal looking up for stars. There are not many tonight. Each time he comes to the surface now he likes it less. He is safer, happier below. There he can travel anywhere he wants. Travel the nowhere.

There is noise further along the towpath. Sewer Boy raises his hood and disappears into the bushes. The men pass, smoking and laughing. Grant is not one of them. There is a bar further along where Grant goes sometimes, where his dad used to drink. Sewer Boy does work for Grant. It is how he lives. Grant pays him or gives him things. Sometimes, late in the night, he will drive him to his mother's sauna, where Sewer Boy washes. It is where the slags shag the coppers. Grant brings him clothes sometimes.

He looks up again for stars. Pushes his head right back. Hardly any. He has more below the surface. He has the whole universe there. It is time to return. The night is hot and sticky. No air.

Grant hates coppers. He hates girls who shag coppers even more. Sewer Boy laughs when he thinks of the way Grant says that: 'Slags who shag coppers. We'll kill them.' It is because of his dad – the coppers framed him. Grant's words: 'The bastard coppers framed him.' Grant blames the coppers. His father went to prison for ever. And someone cut his throat out. Locked him in a toilet to bleed to death. 'Why don't you kill the coppers?' Sewer Boy asked Grant once.

'Maybe I will,' he said. 'But for now it's the slags.'

Except it isn't Grant who kills the slags, it's Sewer Boy. Grant tells him what to do and Sewer Boy does it. Sewer Boy will do anything for Grant. He is lucky to have found him. He looks up at the sky again. Thank your lucky stars. Sometimes Grant takes Sewer Boy to a pub where they play the fruit machines. Grant gives him pound coins and Sewer Boy plays the machines. They are always lucky together.

There was no shade outside the Smile of Fortune on Five Ways, at the edge of the city centre. All around, the looming glass towers of office blocks. There were girls in short skirts and skimpy tops, builders stripped to the waists of their khaki shorts. There was dust and the stink of petrol and diesel. Bright colours, like those of the flowers tumbling out of the barrels surrounding Jack and Dowd, were subdued in the glare, bland, not exotic. The sun, powerful and alien as it was, could not transform the city, only make it gasp and groan, tire it out.

Dowd was thoughtful. He drank from his lager, pulled on his cigarette, exhaled and spoke through the blue ring of smoke. 'More mysterious than the cosmos, if you ask me, Jack, the human brain. You never know what's there, waiting to be discovered. Wonders and monsters – they're all in there somewhere.'

Jack didn't know how to respond. He tried for a quizzical look. Lifted his water. The sparkle had gone out of it.

'Drives the same car as me, you know, Collins. Different colour though.'

'I've a job for you,' Grant tells Sewer Boy. He sits on the metal handrail that runs along the walkway. He is wearing the blue overalls he always wears down here. He swings his legs but is holding tight. On the surface he wears expensive striped suits, silk ties, designer leisurewear. Grant is smoking. He is tense. He always is when he brings a job. He tries not to show it but Sewer Boy knows.

'Another slag who shags coppers?'

'Yes.'

'When?'

'Soon. I'll take you there.'

Sewer Boy delves into the stuff he keeps beside his sleeping bag for a knife and the coil of rope. He cuts a length. Balls it. Slips it into the lining of his hood.

'Tomorrow,' Grant tells him, 'I'll take you out shooting rabbits, if you like. We'll go to Alcester again.'

'Is it dark outside?'

'It will be soon.'

Grant doesn't say anything about his father. This is unusual. In the past he has always talked about him before a job. He crushes the end of his cigarette beneath his boot. Sewer Boy collects it and puts it with the rubbish he takes away every day.

'I'm taking the python tomorrow. Two hundred quid for it. From a bloke in Atherstone.'

'Are the others staying?'

'Yes. For now. Till they sell.'

'I like Liam.' Grant gave the saharan uromastyx that name. Sewer Boy likes the colours he sees in the lizard when it crawls into the light. Yellow. Oranges. Reds. Like ore in rock.

'It's business, SB. Everything goes in the end.'

Jack was surprised to see Phil Drake at Stella Lyons' funeral. And in uniform too. It was form for the investigating officers to turn up. Pay their respects. Check everything out. But no one else from the team. He was talking with a group of whores, five or six, standing together on the crematorium steps. All were elegantly dressed in black or navy blue; dark colours anyway. Jack smiled; well dressed as they were, their stances – hands on hips, heads held at a certain angle – betrayed their profession. Drake seemed to know most of them. He must be here on his own account.

The heat was searing. Sweat ran down Jack's face as he listened to a vicar talk about how Stella Lyons was now safe forever within God's love. Afterwards he saw Dowd with Phil Drake over where the flowers had been laid out. Loosening his tie and carrying his jacket, he went over to join them. He was uncomfortably aware of the sweat patches under his arms. His shirt had stuck to his back, but he could not face putting his jacket back on. Dowd had his slung over his shoulder too. He had lit up. 'Look at this, Jack.' Dowd touched a wreath with his shoe. 'Read the card.' *With deepest regret and fond memories, Brett.*

They had come in Dowd's car because of the air con and it was a joy to be back inside it. 'Collins is our man, Jack. That wreath. It fits. Psychos do that sort of stuff. I wouldn't be surprised if he wasn't lurking somewhere, watching what was going on. Check out his movements.'

'Even if he was, it's not evidence.'

'Bollocks. Any brief worth his salt can use that for us. We know he goes with prostitutes, he admits it. What he told us about Stella Lyons was lies. It was another trans-action. The wreath is just part of his weird enjoyment. Check out the list of wreaths for the Lawrence funeral, Jack. Like his coming to us. All part of the thrill. Prosecu-tion'll get some psychiatric expert to explain to the jury that this is behaviour consistent with a certain type of serial killer. The worst kind. They'll get someone who'll scare the shits out of them. Verdict will be in within an afternoon.'

'But we've got no hard evidence at the moment, sir, that he is the killer.'

'Well, it's our job to get that. I've just got a feeling, Jack. It's part of being a good copper. More than good – better than the rest. The instinct. What the old boys called a nose for it. And the guts to follow that instinct. I know I'm right, Jack. He's our man. I feel lucky.'

'Bit of a surprise, Drake turning up.'

'He checked it out with me. Said he wanted to be there. So I said he could record the wreath messages. He seems to know a lot of those girls from Pinks.'

'How do you know they're from Pinks?'

Dowd laughed. 'Just a hunch. Look, Jack, Drake was quite straight with me. Said he goes there. And other places. But also said he never forgets he's a copper, always looking out to make contacts. See what's going on. He's hoping for the vice squad.'

'Well, he'll have the experience.'

Sewer Boy knows what Grant is doing. Now he can see only his blue legs and his boots as he slithers into the pipe. This is where he keeps his guns. Shotguns. Air rifles. And the little silver one he loves. The one he bounces from hand to hand. The one he places in his mouth sometimes. His eyes dead planets when he depresses the trigger. A hollow click, like the effluent gauge moving to automatic sluice. He groans when he does this, then grins. 'This is from Russia,' he told Sewer Boy once. 'It's killed people. It was my dad's.'

'I want you to go and see Julie Hannox again,' Dowd told Jack. 'Get a full statement from her. Make sure she goes heavy on the caning. And the dildo stuff. And anything else weird she can come up with. Make sure he sounds like the perverted little monster he is.'

'She might not be prepared to nail him like that.'

'It's your job to make sure she does,' Dowd snarled.

'Grant. You're not listening to me. This is serious.' Julie Hannox turned over on her lounger. Pushed her sunglasses up into her hair. He knew the look on his mother's face. Determined. She had something unpleasant to say. 'We're finished now. We don't need to do any more.'

234

'Okay.'

She reached for the ashtray on the lawn beside the lounger. 'This is red hot,' she muttered, stubbed her cigarette. Her lips tightened. 'So you can get rid of your friend.'

'SB? Get rid of him? What do you mean, get rid of him?'

There was no shade in the garden. She pulled her sunglasses back down over her eyes. 'You know what I mean. The jobs are done. We can't have him hanging around wherever it is you keep him.' Grant laughed. 'I mean it, Grant. It's too dangerous.'

'He's part of my business. He looks after the reptiles.'

'Look after them yourself. Or find someone else. Or get out of it. It only makes peanuts. They're all nutters anyway, the people that buy them from you. Loners who keep snakes in the airing cupboard, alligators in the bath. It's not worth the risks. Stick to the adventure holidays. At least they make some real money.'

'I'll do what I want.' He rose and walked across the lawn to the water feature: water bubbling over stones. Japanese. For contemplation. 'And getting rid of SB isn't part of it.'

'Well, it bloody well should be,' his mother shouted after him. 'I'm not going to make the same mistakes your father did. Going too far. We've both got what we wanted.'

'You have. You wanted to destroy Collins. And I helped you. Though it's a big price for any man to pay, just for rejecting a trollop like you.'

'You wanted it too. Perverted little fucker that you are. Someone had to pay. Slags who shag coppers, for Christ sake. Your dad got no more than he deserved. The coppers only did what they had to. They'd've had to be brain dead not to pick up on the trail he left. He was a bastard anyway. And stupid, which is worse. Sewer-life. Arrogant, just like you.'

She lifted herself from the lounger and came to crouch beside him. The purple gloss of her nails caught the sun.

235

'Brett got to me.' Her voice softened. 'He was different from any bloke I'd had. Vulnerable. Or so I thought. Then I find out he's shagging half the whores in the city.' She paused. 'Still. I've a new man now.'

Grant was surprised. 'Who's that then?'

'Never you mind. You won't like him. But Grant, you've to get rid of this SB. With him gone and Collins sorted we're in the clear. You must see that. We've both got what we wanted. Enough is enough.'

'Sure. Finish. I'm happy with that. But SB. I can't just turn him loose and forget about him. He couldn't cope. He'd be picked up in no time.'

'Which is why you have to get rid of him. You know what I mean. Once he's gone everything will be over. We move on.'

'But SB's like a brother. You don't kill your brother.'

'Don't be a prat, Grant. You get rid of anyone you need to.'

'Collins hasn't been convicted yet.'

'He will be.'

Sewer Boy is afraid. Grant can see it in his eyes. And the way he is crouched, pressed into the corner, the edge of his sleeping bag in his mouth. Grant is using a shotgun, but he has a Luger in the waistband of his trousers, hidden beneath the blue overalls.

There is only a blue-tongued skink left. These creatures rarely climb, preferring to scavenge and scurry at the bottom of whatever habitat they find themselves in. Now, however, this one is making its way up the concrete support to Sewer Boy's platform. All the other reptiles are dead, their blasted remains spattered around the tunnel. The winged head of a snow phase bearded dragon peers over the edge of the platform at the remnants of its body scattered below. The skink is moving steadily towards Sewer

Boy. Grant lifts the shotgun, finds aim and follows the creature's head as it moves closer and closer to Sewer Boy.

A bench outside the Country Girl on Raddlebarn Road. Dowd and Jack watching the traffic crawl past, the procession of people making their way to and from the hospital next door. At seven o'clock there was still no relief from the sun. They had gone over the case. Dowd was convinced they had their man. 'I'll talk to Geary in the morning. Then go for the charge.'

A group of nurses passed them on their way into the pub. Dowd's eyes followed them. 'Fancy another?'

'No, I'm all right with this, thanks.'

'This weather. It makes you horny, doesn't it?'

Jack said nothing; just smiled.

They are outside Palm Springs Spa. A health club. In the car park. They have been here for twenty minutes, in Grant's sports car. Despite the warm evening the roof is up. They are listening to music. Oasis. Grant tapping his knee. He has been on the phone. Sewer Boy does not know to whom. They are waiting, he knows that.

'Here it comes,' Grant says. A silver Peugeot turns into the car park and pulls up. A woman driving. 'Look at her,' Grant tells Sewer Boy. 'Remember.' His voice is husky as if his throat is sore.

Sewer Boy looks at the driver. She is blonde. Her hair tied back. He studies her face: the set of the eyes, the small mouth, the neat features. She is a little taller than he. She throws a sports bag over her shoulder. Looks at her watch as she alarms the car. Raises her head and he sees her face clearly in the evening sunlight. He holds that image.

Phil Drake knocked back the shot of brandy in one. His face contorted as he swallowed. He gasped.

'Take it easy, son,' Dowd told him.

Drake's body spasmed. Everyone froze. Waiting. For an explosion. Tears. Hysteria. Violence even. Something. He regained control.

'We'll get you home now, Phil. Jack will take you.' Jack had never heard gentleness in Dowd's voice before. He was touched by his boss's compassion. 'He'll stay with you until the family arrive.'

'They're on their way,' Jack said. Like talking to a toddler.

Drake was gaping. His eyes bulged. The tongue whisked the circumference of his mouth. He dragged the breath in, swallowed it, almost vomited it back again.

'Come on, Phil.' Jack put his hand on his colleague's shoulder. 'Let's get you out of this place.'

Dowd watched as they made their way down the corridor to the lift, then returned through the plastic swing doors to the mortuary. Helen Drake's body was still on the viewing table. He lifted the cover. The morticians watched. Facial damage. She had obviously put up more of a struggle than her two predecessors. The broken neck marked black and brown like stains in dirty washing.

Dowd looked down at the young woman. Looked hard. Almost looked through her, so that she became a kind of gauze beyond which he was able to see her final moments. The struggle in the lift with Collins. The rope destroying the pale skin of her neck. The contortions as her end came.

Grant has no record at all – so far. But it is inevitable. A father/son thing. He tries to concentrate. He's cleverer than his dad. His mom's always said so. 'You've got my brains.' As hard as fucking nails, the bitch. She never gave a shit about what happened to his dad. She got the money, made sure everything went in her name. Hardly visited him.

Grant tosses the little silver gun from his right hand to

his left, then back again. And again. At least they didn't get this. Circumstantial. Bollocks. The only real evidence was this. And it has been down here since the night before his arrest. 'Look after this for me, son.' And he raised his eyebrows, looked just like a little kid. Grant could weep when he thinks of that look. Bastard coppers. They nobbled the jury. Must have. Circumstantial. That look. The eyebrows. Grant saw it again when the verdict came. Will never forget it. Bastard, bastard coppers.

She'd never said. And he'd never asked. It was her he was interested in – only her. He'd spent a fortune on that girl. Fancied her like a forest fire. A hurricane. Irresistible.

'Leave him,' Grant said.

'I'm thinking of it,' she told him. 'He's cheating on me. Look. I found this in the jacket of his uniform. Relaxor.' A card for Relaxor. 'He said they all go over there. From the station. Said someone gave it to him. Swears he's never been himself, but I –'

'Station? He's a copper?'

'Course he is. Didn't I say?'

'You saw her at the gym.'

'No.'

'That's what triggered it. What happened, Brett? You can tell me.'

'I never saw her.'

'You were there. She was there. It's in the computer.'

'I arrived at seven. You know all this. Ten past eight she checked in. I told you I was there for less than an hour. Just a run. Ten K.'

'You were waiting for her when she got home.'

'No.'

'Yes.'

Collins ran his hands back through his hair. Sweat glossed his ashen face.

239

'Did you follow her into the lift, Brett? Or were you already in there?'

'I went home. I wasn't there.'

Dowd sighed and pushed the two tagged plastic bags towards Collins. 'Your cufflinks?'

'You know they are. But I told you. I've got lots of pairs. I lose them all the time.'

'One found inside Helen Drake's top, right down by her bra, the other in the foliage outside.'

'All this is circumstantial evidence, inspector.' It was Geary. 'There is no forensic evidence to implicate my client, despite all your tests. If he had gone into that building, gone into the lift and strangled Mrs Drake there, are you seriously telling me there would be no other forensic evidence?'

Geary no longer believed what he was saying. Dowd saw this. Result. He was patient. He spoke to Geary but kept his eyes on Collins. 'Yes, I am, Mr Geary. That's exactly what I'm telling you.' Said with such a force of certainty that Geary blinked. 'The lift was wiped. The door too. A lift without any fingerprints? This was a premeditated act, carried out by a man who knew the building, the victim and the process. A man who had killed before. And as for no forensic. Remember, hairs of Mrs Drake were found in Mr Collins' car.'

'He has admitted having an association with Mrs Drake but . . .' There was no conviction in Geary's voice now. The spinning wheel was slowing. Dowd could see it. And the ball was going to fall for him.

'Now, he has. But it took him long enough.' Dowd spat the words. 'When I interviewed him regarding the deaths of Stella Lyons and Fortune Lawrence he claimed that the only women he had been with since his wife left him were prostitutes.'

'I didn't,' Collins blurted. 'You asked me if I went with

prostitutes and I said I did. You never asked me about anything else.'

The beer is making Sewer Boy giddy. He looks around at the strange faces. Bald heads. Extended stomachs.

Grant plays darts with him. Sewer Boy likes throwing the arrows. Feeling the strength in his arm create speed. The unity of hand and eye, it's good. Sewer Boy does well with the arrows. But the two men who challenge him and Grant beat them. They like Grant. They knew his father. Grant has bought something from one of them. Sewer Boy thinks it is a gun.

The Little Moscow. Grant likes to come here when they have killed a slag who shags coppers. 'The safest place in the city,' he says, laughing. He is drunk. In the stinking toilet Sewer Boy takes a shit. Flushes. Thinks about the journey of his waste. The noises.

This had got to be the hottest afternoon of the year – for many years, probably. Throughout the station officers panted and groaned, complained; the water cooler was empty and desks were littered with plastic bottles of spring water. It seemed to Jack that all of the city's heat had coalesced in Interview Room 2. Dowd switched off the inadequate desk fan and Jack pressed the tape machine. He watched Collins as Dowd charged him – three counts of murder.

His eyes wide, dilated black pupils – a kid scared to death. His left cheek twitched. The chest heaved. The hands splayed on the desk before him pressed downward. He's trying to make sense of this, Jack thought. The cruellest nightmare. Collins' mouth fell open. The tongue lolled forward.

Dowd paused. Was the man going to collapse? Geary placed a hand on Collins' shoulder. Collins jumped. Regained control. Dowd continued, reciting the man's rights.

Tears sprang up in Collins' eyes. Trickled down his cheeks. As he lifted his right hand to wipe them away his body spasmed. Shook. Like electrocution. Dowd stopped.

Collins' mouth opened wide, his body convulsed forward, vomit fountained across the desk, hitting Dowd, Jack, covering the tape-recorder.

Dowd ignored it. He leaned forward. Collins tried to wipe his mouth with his hand, mumbling an apology. Geary, who had escaped, handed him a handkerchief.

'Don't worry, mate. It's understandable,' Dowd said.

Geary tapped Collins' shoulder, an attempt at comfort. The stench of vomit filled the room. Jack's own stomach rose. He wanted to get out and clean the mess off his suit. He wanted a bloody good shower.

Dowd reached across the desk and placed his hand on Collins' wrist. 'Come on, Brett. Why put yourself through all this? You need help, mate. I can see how unhappy you are. We all can.' Dowd's eyes went to Geary. 'I want to help you.' A sob took Collins. He shook again. 'Make it easy on yourself. We know you did these things. You might try to tell yourself you didn't, but you did. We have the evidence. It's all over, Brett. Make a confession. Would you like us to help you make a statement?' Geary said nothing. 'Come on, Brett. Help me to help you. It was you, wasn't it?' The room stank, rancid.

'Yes,' Collins gurgled. His eyes spun. 'Yes. I suppose it must have been.'

He breaks cover but they don't know he's there. Too busy rooting. Like rabbits. He raises the gun, takes aim and fires. Fires again. The legs of the male tremble. He watches until they stop.

'Come on, Jack, have something alcoholic. We're celebrating.' Dowd had nipped home to change.

'No. Just an orange juice. That'll be fine.'

Dowd shrugged and ordered. 'I can't get that puke off my suit, Jack. Fucking thing's ruined. All down the lapel. And a great big stain in the crotch. Six hundred quid down the drain.' They carried their drinks outside into the humid afternoon. 'I wish it would rain.'

Jack raised his eyes to the low ceiling of bruised cloud that covered the city. 'Looks like it should.' There was sweat on both men's faces.

They found a table and removed their jackets. 'I hate it like this. No sun. Fucking oppressive. What we need is a good storm. Clear the air. Wash the shit away.' Dowd took a hefty swig from his lager. 'That's better.' He grinned. 'We've pulled it off, son. Chalked up another victory.'

'You can't say that till the verdict is in.'

'It's a cert, Jack. Even if he changes his mind and goes for Not Guilty, which I don't think he will. The hair. The cufflinks. Even Geary's shut up.' He lay back in his chair and raised his glass. 'Our winning streak continues, Jack.' He drank, took out his cigarettes, lit one. 'How's Drake? I'll go over later.'

'Still pretty shaken. But he seems to be coping.'

'And he had no idea his missus was playing away?'

'None at all. A real shock to him.'

Dowd leaned forward. 'This trial's going to be a whopper, Jack. A real show. You realize that, don't you? Do us no end of good. The tabloids'll be all over it. Daily coverage. And the Beeb.' He took another drink, a long pull on his cigarette. 'I think I'll get a new suit, for the interviews.'

The humid stench of disgust. All over. Jack Stevens looked down at the dead woman. The last time he had seen Julie Hannox he had been shagging her. Her head was thrown back on the pillow then, as it was now, the mouth open just the same. The disgust he had felt with himself then, he felt again now. He forced his eyes down to the mess that was her breast, the blood and silicone swamp that had slithered down to pool and congeal in her belly. There was another hole, in her throat, ripped and yawning, echoing the open mouth above it.

Phil Drake's body had tumbled off the side of the bed. Dowd rose from examining it. 'Right through the back.' Then he looked into Jack's shocked and innocent face and beyond to the white wall where a perfect globe of blood had landed and streaked, like some primitive icon, a weeping sun.

Jack's hopeless eyes were upon him. Dowd met them brazenly.

A Tree for Andy Warhol

'You're really going to do it?'

'Course I am. There are the papers. I've got to. It's time. The hair. The glasses. The work. One further commitment.'

'It sounds like the ultimate step. You're being taken over by him.'

'I wish. No, I'm giving myself to him. I can feel his spirit. My ideas. His ideas. It's hard to tell. But I want his name. Not his name, or not just his name. I want to be a piece of his work. It's a dedication. Andy Warhol One – Blue. And if you're with me, and you've come this far, then you'll do it too. But another colour. Then we are joined with him through his name, but still retain our identities as separate works.'

'Pieces of art?'

'Extensions of his art. Carrying it on.'

'But why deed poll? We could just use the names.'

'Commitment. A statement. Like a vow in a way.'

'The Brotherhood?'

'A first step. Yes.'

'Okay. I'm with you. I'll do it too.'

'Brilliant. And so, Brother Andy Warhol Two, which colour will you take?'

'Well. Er. Wow. How to choose?'

'Think about it. It's important. It will define the rest of your life.'

'You choose. Yes. You choose my colour for me.'
'Okay. Green. You will be Andy Warhol Two – Green.'

I know everyone in Walton Towers. My little shop is at the foot of the block. Mr Blue calls it the cage. 'Good morning, Mrs Nayer,' he will say when he enters. 'And how is life in the cage this morning?' He calls it the cage because the front of the shop is protected by panels of wire mesh. Well, you have to. It's the area. Some very nice people, but there are some who are not.

Mr Blue and Mr Green come in often. Usually together, but not always. Sometimes Mr Green will come in with his girlfriend. Her name is Charlotte. They are artists, you know, Mr Blue and Mr Green. I don't know what Charlotte does but she is a very pretty girl. Mr Blue and Mr Green go each day to their studio to work. I have never seen any of their art, but I believe it is very modern. Not pictures. They do not paint portraits or landscapes. This is not the art that interests them, Mr Blue says. I think he feels that sort of art is very old fashioned.

There is not very much more I can tell you. I know they play sport on Saturdays because I see them leaving with sports bags. They wait at the bus stop over there, just as they do when they are going to the studio. And Mr Blue goes running early in the morning. Sometimes Mr Green will be with him, but quite often he runs alone.

No, I don't think either of them has ever had a car. Not many people do round here. Too much vandalism. Do you know one evening the police came to see someone in Walton Towers, they're often here unfortunately, and while they were in the flats their car was stolen? A police car. Now when they come, one of them always stays in the car.

Yes, I would describe Green as my boyfriend. Though that sounds more conventional than it is, our relationship.

Some weeks I might see him several times, other weeks not at all. It's like that. In the end it's Blue who calls the tune as far as Green is concerned. I accept that now. I didn't like it in the beginning, but . . . well, it's the way it is. So I'm cool about it now.

I met him, Green that is, when I was modelling. Life classes. At the Arts Centre. Wednesday afternoons. The students were mainly old people, you know, retired and that.

We just got chatting, Green and me, gradually, over the weeks. Well, we're about the same age. I'm a couple of years older than him, actually. Blue's older than him too.

We became sort of mates. Although I fancied him right from the start, really. Sometimes we'd stay behind for a coffee after the class. It just went from there. But it was me who had to do all the pushing. We'd never have got together otherwise.

This will tell you something about his character: he was a virgin. At twenty-three. But here's something I've discovered. The later a man loses his virginity, the better lover he is. You're blushing. Have I touched on something there? What's that look for? You need to know what I know and I'm sharing it with you. My knowledge. Which is personal. So please, show some respect.

It was when he took me to the studio that I really got interested in him. I knew he was unusual, but that place . . . Have you been there? All right, I know. You're asking the questions.

That old building, beautiful old building it is. Used to be the Water Board's offices. Years ago. Left to rack and ruin. All boarded up. Danger signs everywhere. And it's true. Looks like it could fall down any minute. I think that makes it more beautiful in a way. The decay.

There's this narrow path at the back, through a hole in the fence, and then steps to a cellar. That's how you get in. That door's not boarded. At least, not any more. And on the sixth floor they've got this great space. Beautiful. The window-boards aren't up that high. I was blown away when I saw it. And what they were doing in there. Serious art.

They're real artists all right. Blue went to art school. Painted abstracts for a while. Wild colours. John Turnbull he was then. Made a bit of a name.

The palm tree. So you have been inside. Brilliant, isn't it? They never stop working on that. Adding things. Removing things. The leaves take your breath away, don't they? All that bronze finishing. I could look at that for hours. And the trunk. Those tiny prints. Each one a Warhol. And names tucked in here and there. I'm on it. I think it's beautiful. Stunning. And I'll tell you what really impressed me: that it was just there. They had made it and kept on changing it because they needed to, because it needed to be made. Not to go in some poxy gallery. Not to try and impress Saatchi or the London monogobs. They made it for there. For them. Hidden away. This beautiful tree for Andy Warhol, right in the middle of some decaying old building in Birmingham. Brilliant. But I feel different now. It seems a waste. All that work in there that no one sees.

Dowd stood up and moved around. Slow. Easy. Carrow, the observer on this session, never shifted his eyes from the suspect. Dowd was pleased. He took long strides across the interview room, raised his shoulders to let the suspect know that he was taking a little exercise, loosening up; something *he* couldn't do. He strolled over to the window and stuck two fingers into the Venetian blind, extended them to make a gap, looked out into the station car park, let the blind go and turned to look down on the young man sitting on the far side of the desk. Short hair dyed almost white. Rimmed glasses. Shaw had the other suspect next door, with Jack.

'Now, let me get this right,' Dowd said, as if he was checking directions he had been given. 'You say you found him?'

'Yes.' There was impatience in the single word, which was how Dowd liked it.

'Go on.'

'Again?'

'Again.'

The man sighed. 'I saw him. It was nearly dark. I rang Green. He came over. We got him down and put him in an alley. Behind an old door that was in there. Then we got a van –'

'*Got* a van?' Dowd interrupted.

'All right. Stole a van. We stole a van, put him in it and took him back to the studio.'

Jack Stevens wished he was conducting this interview. Shaw was old-school. And try as he might, Jack couldn't suppress the contempt that was growing as he watched the senior detective at work. How the hell had he muscled in on this? It was embarrassing listening to him. This was Dowd's job. Jack his assistant. So why the hell was Carrow next door with the boss and he stuck in here with Shaw?

'You weren't surprised,' Shaw asked the shaven-headed suspect, 'when your mate rang you, told you he'd found a bloke hanging from a lamppost?'

'About the lamppost bit, yes, I suppose. But we'd talked about it. How we might get a body.'

'One of your projects?'

'Yes. We have a lot of ideas for projects. We record them all. You've got the notebooks. You must have seen it.'

'We've seen it.'

'So, you were prepared to help your friend –' he couldn't say the ridiculous name without looking down at the charge sheet, reading it, making it clear that he was only using it because it was down there in black and white 'Andy Warhol One – Blue, to steal a dead body?'

'Not steal. It didn't belong to anyone. The idea was to take it for fifteen days, then return it.'

'Fifteen days? Why fifteen days?'

I think they're all right really. They're good football players, I'll tell you that, both of them. When they first joined the club we thought they were really strange – in every way. A joke. The names for a start: Andy Green and Andy Blue. That's weird, isn't it? Two blokes turning up together to join a football club with names like that. Like characters from a kids' programme. And both wearing glasses, exactly the same. And Blue, his hair. You could tell straight away it was dyed. I thought they were gay. But they're not. Green, the one with the shaved head, he's got a girlfriend. Charlotte.

They never tried to fit in. You know, the way blokes do when they join a club. At first that was a problem. We're a friendly club, we've got a nice little bar and we like to get together. They never come in the club for a drink. And away games: on the coach, they read books. Fair play to them. They don't care what anyone thinks. But once you see them play, especially Blue: he's really talented, no doubt about it, and bloody ruthless. Look at him in the street and you'd think, what a ponce – but he's not. A real hard bastard when he needs to be.

I don't know whether to tell you this, cause I still don't know why you're asking me these questions. What they're supposed to have done. But something, well, something that really got me. Neither of them has got a motor. Someone always offers to drop them off after a game, but they always say no. I suppose it's because they'd have to stay for a drink and wait. They like to get straight off. Me, I need to wind down after a game, talk about it. Most of the blokes do. But not the Andies. Come, play and go. Fair play to them, though, that's up to them. Well, one Saturday, after a home game, we're all in the bar in the clubhouse, when Blue comes rushing back in, asking if anyone's got a plastic bag, a carrier, like. He's real insistent about this. In a bit of a panic, like. Anyway, one way or another someone comes up with a Sainsbury's carrier; I think one of the blokes had it to put his dirty knickers in after the game, something like that. Well, Blue's been making such a fuss about getting this bag and he's usually so cool and quiet that Dennis – he's the first team goalkeeper, we call him Bergkamp – he follows Blue out, to see what he's up to. And, well, apparently. There's this dead cat at the side of the road. We'd all seen it on the way in. Looked like it had been there for a couple of days, if you know what I mean. Anyway, the way that Dennis tells it, Blue scoops up this cat. With his bare hands. Puts it in the bag. Green's with him. Just standing. Watching. He doesn't touch the cat. But he's there, with him. And when it's in the bag, off they go with it, to the bus stop. As if it's shopping or something. Upset a lot of people that did.

What do they buy here? Not papers. Not regularly. Oh, sometimes they may pick up a daily paper, occasionally a Sunday. But nothing regular. Then last week. No. I think it may have been the week before. Mr Green bought three or four morning papers. Quite spontaneously I would say. He had purchased some chewing gum when he looked down at the papers laid out as they are here. Something must have caught his eye, because he picked up several.

Mr Blue buys cigarettes sometimes. But not so often now. He used to talk of giving up, perhaps he has succeeded, I shall have to ask him. It is groceries mostly that they come in for. From the back. Frozen meals, tins of soup, bread. Those sort of commodities.

I have to tell you they are both always very respectful. Unfortunately I cannot say that about all my customers. This estate is not as it used to be. Many of my best customers have moved away and now the council put in problem families. Yes, they are both very polite and respectful. I am always pleased to see them although they do not spend a great deal. Mr Green always strokes my dog, Sabre, here. He always stays here behind the counter with me. But when Mr Green comes in Sabre wanders round to be stroked and to have his ears played with. He likes that. Mr Green always rubs his ears and his tummy. There is something very playful about Mr Green. Even when he is alone. With him there is always a smile. Mr Blue I find more serious. There is a sadness about him, I think. But when they are together, they are always laughing. Like two small boys.

'Are you religious?' An old trick. The unexpected question suddenly snapped out.

It worked. Blue was taken aback by it. He thought for a moment. 'I don't know what you mean.'

'What do you think I mean? Are you religious?'

'I'm an atheist.'

'Were you brought up in a religion?'

'Catholic.'

'Is that why you've got all those statues?'

'Religious iconography.'

'Come again.' Dowd sneered. He knew perfectly well what this bloke was up to.

'I – we – are interested in icons. Inanimate objects that inspire religious devotion.'

'So you go round churches nicking statues, candlesticks. Or are you going to tell me these are on loan too? You were going to take these back like you returned Martin Burrows.'

'No.'

'No. So. Tell me.'

Before I say anythin I wanna know that I'm not goin to get in any trouble over anythin I tell you. Right? This is about they, not me. Right?

The firs thin to say then: okay, they a lil bit crazy, but they good guys. In me book they very good guys. Right? Yes, man. They help me good when I came outa the prison. I first seed Green at social security. We chat a lil bit. Nah mean? After a few time I give he a lil weed. Now I wanna stress here the word I jus use – give. Okay? I no supplier, man. It a gift, man, an that no illegal no more. Am I right?

I always a curious type an I aks Green questions. First he close, nah mean? But then he open a lil bit. He say he an artist. I say blow, man, tell me. Can I see, man? He a lil sheepish firs. Perhaps. One day. Close. But I persistent type, an I keep aksin, an one day he take me to studio. An, I can't believe it, man. In this crumblin ol heap they got this lil world. Blow! Then I go often. Drop in, nah mean, man?

Thing bad for me when they throw me off rehab. Blue. Green. They let me sleep there a time. Man. Otherwise I been a streetkipper. All the brethren. Promises. But ony promises. These guys different. 'Oh, man,' they say. 'You in trouble, Charlie. Stay here, man. We help you.'

It winter. When it rain and it hit that ol roof and it echo down all those corridors an big rooms, man, the noisiest place in the world. I know how Noah feel, man.

Shaw tapped his fingers on the desk, eyeballing the suspect in front of him. It was a familiar technique, but Jack could see it wasn't working for Shaw. Green was giving him a sympathetic look as though sorry he had bad nerves.

Eventually he pulled the notebooks towards him. 'I'd like to talk about these notebooks.' He lifted the top one, flicked the pages. 'There are some things in here that, well, quite frankly, I find them rather alarming. Particularly this. Where is it? Yes. Here. Now I know this isn't your handwriting. Blue's, I guess. "Can killing be a work of art?" Question mark. What sort of bloody question is that? No. Let me read you another. On the same page. Same handwriting. "Criminals are the true celebrities of our age!" Exclamation mark. Then there's this list of names. "Donald Neilson, Fred West, Ian Huntley, Luke Mitchell, Jeremy Bamber, Ian Brady." I won't go on, but there are more of the buggers.'

'Fifteen,' Green said.

'Yes, that's right. Fifteen names. Of terrible criminals. People who have committed horrendous crimes. And in here they are regarded as the true celebrities of our time. I have to tell you, son, that I find all this very disturbing indeed. Sick. Makes me want to puke, as a matter of fact. And added to the matter we are investigating, it poses, for me, some very worrying questions about you and your friend, Andy Warhol One – Blue. You can see my point, can't you?'

'I think . . . I think that if you looked in the notebooks of lots of artists, writers, film-makers too, you'd find things that you could say that about. That they're disturbing. That's our job. To think about things. To ask questions.'

'That's my job too.'

'Look. Those notebooks record ideas, all sorts of random ideas, talks we have. The celebrity criminal list came out of an idea for a series of screen prints. But you look through and you'll see lists of lots of celebrities. Singers, footballers, boxers, cartoon characters. Fifteen of each.'

'Yes, you're right, they're all in here. List after list. Weird drawings. And who's this lot? Never heard of them. Marion Ryan, Dennis Lotis, Eve Boswell, Yana, Dickie Veli Vel . . .'

'Dickie Valentine.'

'So who are they, then? Modern artists or bloody serial killers? I don't think any of them ever played for Villa.'

'British entertainers of the 1950s. They were all household names once.'

'Which is what you and your mate will be if you're guilty of only half the things I'm beginning to suspect you of. I'm sorry, son, but you'll have to forgive me if I wonder about minds that don't seem to distinguish between Bart Simpson and Myra Hindley.'

'It's –'

'Don't tell me. I know. It's art. Leaving the criminality of taking this corpse aside for a moment, can you just explain to me. A genuine question. I'm interested. Just explain to me, man to man, how can taking photographs of a corpse, every day for fifteen days, recording its process of decay as you say, how is that art? How can it possibly be? What's that got to do with Van Gogh, Rembrandt, Goya. They're real artists. Surely?'

'Look, all this has got nothing to do with –'

'Just answer the bloody question.'

'If you look back over the history of art –'

'Oh yes, it changes, sure. But what's the stuff you're doing – and others, I'll grant you – what's it got to do with art? Really. I don't understand. What about that bird with the bed? I suppose you think she's good. A great artist. An unmade bed. Knickers and tampons all over the place. I suppose you reckon that's art too. Give me the Mona Lisa any bloody day.'

'Tracey Emin is following a tradition that started with Marcel Duchamp, in the 1920s. Dadaism. He took a urinal, an ordinary, familiar object, into an art gallery; therefore it became art.'

'Bollocks.'

'Yes, they can be art too. It depends on the context.'

'Don't come the funny bastard with me, son. Right. This'll take the smile off your face. Now on this page here. This fair turned my stomach, I have to tell you. This is a blank page, right? Nothing on it at all. Except. Here. On the top line. In your handwriting. Yours, mind. These words: "Three little kids for flavour". Given me bloody nightmares, that has. Exactly what sort of perverted animal are you? "Three little kids for flavour". What are you two? Bloody cannibals or something? What you bloody laughing for? Are you having a turn or something?'

'It's a line from a song. By Dean Martin. "Memories are Made of This". I just thought it was funny. There are other lines from songs in there too. Lines I think are odd or funny or really clever. I thought that one was funny.'

It individuality, man. These guys – they individuals. They make their own mind. Me, I like that. They dress cool. They safe.

Guns at de studio? I never seed no guns. No time. No way. I saw every sorta shit in that place. But never no guns.

De statues? They just old statues, man. Plaster an paint. Nah mean? You talk guns. There people swapping guns in this city for fifty poun a go. True. I take you there. There people, people I know, pickin up protection, right – hundreds every week. Lil shopkeepers. They no escape. They have to pay jus like the big boys in clubs an bars. There spiv and whore and businessman who pay no tax. A few statues, man. I know a girl. White. Three thousand pound of clothes, man. First offence. She tell, 'I get a migraine. Ooh, so bad. The pain. I didna know what I do.' She white girl. She speak very well. I know she junkie. She go to court all smart, like receptionist. Father, he stand there, by her. Smart suit, man. She weep a time. 'Ooh, the migraine.' Conditional discharge. She still pullin in de clothes. An all this fuss over statues. It make me blow, man. They make a sorta chapel anyway. Candles. All nice an quiet. That what statue for – chapels.

Dowd sat alone playing the tape, listening to Blue's words. Fascinated. He'd heard all sorts. But this. We all live in different worlds – side by side, but different worlds. And we know nothing of each other. He must get Jack to listen to this, he'd know what this guy meant. He pressed Play again.

'And where did you keep the guns?'

'Guns?'

'Come on, Blue. Two men were blasted in Burrows' bed. Probably on the day he died. Blown all over the walls. Half the police forces in the country are looking for Burrows and all the time he's propped up, rotting away, under your palm tree. Surely you can see that we might consider the possibility of a connection?'

Dowd listened to the burr of silence on the tape.

'I know you artists feel you have to cross boundaries.' Dowd noted the change in the tone of his voice. Softer; not friendly, but understanding. That was good. 'I can't say I understand it, but it occurs to me that possibly this shooting was some sort of performance art. Something that in your mind, or creative vision, if you like, was part of your work.'

'No.' Dowd recalled how frightened Blue had looked at that moment. 'No. There was nothing else. No killing. Honestly.' Dowd replayed the tape. Listened hard to the voice of the suspect. Saw in his mind's eye the face across the desk. 'No. There was nothing else. No killing. Honestly.' And Dowd believed him.

'Blue wanted a sort of spiritual space. Not religiously spiritual. He hates religion. But something to reflect the camp of religion – Catholicism, it is mostly. But there's some Buddhas in there, a Ganesh and a Hanuman.'

257

'So you thought you'd insult every bloody religion in the community while you were at it, did you?' Shaw foamed. 'Anything Jewish in there?'

'No. It started off with Bernadette Soubirous. The girl from Lourdes. It was, like, she became famous in the days before celebrity. That interested us. And the belief that her body never decomposed.'

'Not like Martin Burrows, eh? So Bernadette. Which statue is she?'

'The girl kneeling before the Virgin.'

'Sounds like the start of a Bernard Manning joke.'

'And you say I'm sick.'

'Sick. Yes.' Shaw banged his fist on the desk. 'Yes, I do say you're sick. Most definitely I do.'

Jack watched Green watching Shaw. Of the two men it was definitely Shaw who was exhibiting stress. Green seemed relaxed.

'According to our records, Green, two statues were stolen from the grotto situated at the front of the Roman Catholic Church of Our Lady of Lourdes. One a six-foot statue of Our Lady herself, the other a four-foot statue of the saint, Bernadette, in kneeling position. Well?'

'Yes.'

'You admit it was you? You and your weird mate?'

'Yes.'

'In that case presumably you also admit that you were responsible for leaving a papier-mâché model of Sir Jimmy Savile in the grotto in the Virgin's place. Well, her statue's place, anyway.'

'Yes. It was a sort of joke.'

'A joke. How did you expect Father Derwent to feel when he saw that? You expected him to burst out bloody laughing? No wonder the poor bastard had a breakdown. Disappeared off the face of the earth.'

*

Dusk was settling over Birmingham. Lights were coming on all over, but without real darkness their glamour was insipid. In an hour or two they would come into their own and define the geography of the city in white and yellow and blue. But for now they had to wait.

In the crumbling old red brick building that used to belong to the city's Water Board it was much darker. In the Statue Room Blue lit the candles. Charlie, who had been hanging around all day, lit a spliff. Blue joined him, lolling on the floor.

'It look real cool here now, man. Holy cool. With de candles lit.'

'The colours look great, don't they? Look at the glow in that face.'

'She de mother of God, ent she?'

'Yeh. The Virgin Mary.'

'And who her friend?'

'That's Bernadette Soubirous. A French peasant girl. The story goes that the Virgin appeared to her. Several times. It made her famous. Lourdes. You've heard of Lourdes?'

'Sure. Madonna's kid.'

'Yeh, well, she's called after the place in France. Lourdes, where the visions were supposed to have happened.'

'Oh, yeh. De place where cripples go. Right? For miracle?'

'That's the one.'

'You ever bin there, man?'

'No. Never.' Blue passed the spliff back to Charlie. He inhaled deeply. Exhaled a halo of smoke. Both men watched it float through the room. Disintegrate slowly.

'Man. Dese statues. In de candlelight. They look like they jus about to breathe.'

'That's their power. Desperate people have knelt before all of these images and prayed for help. They represent thousands of realities; yet there's nothing real about them. Just images. Dreams made plaster. Andy was brought up a

Catholic, you know. His mother was very devout. He never went to her funeral. Didn't tell people she was dead. When they asked how she was doing, he just said, "She's fine. Doesn't get out of bed much these days."'

Charlie found this sad. 'What happen to de Bernadette girl? De peasant girl?'

'She was made a saint. She became a nun and was world famous. Just by the story of Lourdes. What's interesting, though, is that when she died she was buried in the convent grounds. They dug her up after thirty years. And nothing. She was exactly the same as the day they closed the coffin lid. Hold on there, Charlie, I'll show you something.'

From the shelf by the door Blue fetched a pile of postcards, flicked through, selected one. 'Look at this, Charlie. We've got this enlarged real big in the Decomposition Room.'

'There no way I go in that room, Blue. You have the best picture in the world there, still no go. Never no way.' Charlie moved the card towards the candlelight.

'That's a photograph of Bernadette taken in 1936. Nearly fifty years after her death. People say that it's a miracle that she's been preserved like that.'

'Sure look like one big miracle to me. She lovely woman. Dreamin. Sleepin.'

Jack watched Dowd examining the tree. Vague traffic sounds drifted in from the city outside. The thick bronze fronds of the Phoenix palm glinted in what little light the long, narrow grimy windows let into this space. The fronds were perfectly shaped and carved and spoke, it seemed to Jack, of a glamour from long before his and Dowd's time, glimpsed now only in old films.

Dowd was stroking a frond. 'Perfect art dec,' he said, more to himself than to Jack.

He stooped to look more closely at the trunk. Each triangular layered bump that formed the bark bore an image.

Most were miniature copies of Warhol's work, but not all. There were pictures of Warhol himself, a priest, some motorbikes, a milkfloat. Some were just individual letters in various fonts: a G above Warhol's image of the electric chair, an L above that; an N on each side of Jacqueline Onassis. And text too.

'Look at this, Jack.' Dowd crouched to the base of the tree. 'These names: Crawford, Burrows, Kieran, Office.'

'The Little Moscow crowd.'

'Not all. Father Derwent. Lottie. Any idea who that is? Charlie.'

Dowd rose and turned to Jack. 'You're not saying much.'

'I'm just thinking. A bit awed by it all actually. Impressive, isn't it?'

'Oh, yes. This whole place is.'

'It's the line, though,' Jack said, feeling his way through his thoughts, 'between creativity and criminality.'

'Absolutely.' Dowd recognized something in his colleague's words. 'I'd throw madness in too. You probably have to be a bit mad, to be so creative. You have to see things differently, and maybe that's the first step.'

'And that's where criminality creeps in?'

'*Can* creep in, Jack. Can. When it goes too far. When the ideas, the search for originality, become more important than the lines society draws. Artists like these guys – and they're artists all right, there's no denying that – they get off on breaking through convention, but that buzz can be so strong they fail to distinguish between convention and law. They see themselves, or their art, as immune from any form of restraint.' He turned to the tree again.

This is police work, Jack thought. The sort he wanted to be doing, anyway. Not just the mechanics of cases – crime, evidence, conviction, end of story – but to delve beyond these. It was rare, this capacity to look beyond. Dowd had it. It was why Jack wanted to work with him. It was happening now. Here. Jack hoped Dowd would achieve his ambitions and get right to the top. Okay, he wasn't perfect by any means, he could be as pig-headed as any copper, but Jack would feel happier with Dowd running a force than anyone else he could think of.

Jack recalled his day with Shaw. Dowd must have read his thoughts, for he turned from the tree to Jack, a wide grin on his face. 'How did it go with Shaw today?'

'Nothing new. I'm not sure why he's been brought in.' Jack heard a sullenness in his tone. Disliked it. 'I could have conducted the interviews with Green just as well.'

'Better.' The single word, delivered so definitely. Jack was pleased to hear it. The grin was back on Dowd's face as he explained. 'I want him on this for now, Jack. Going through the motions. Until we see how big it's going to be. Blue's the engine of this little team. I'll handle him. I want you with Shaw, listening, thinking – getting the picture for me. However big or not this turns out criminally, it's already very public and it'll get bigger. These are the cases that will make our names, Jack, the high profile ones. And the more senior DIs who've assisted us – and I mean *us* – the further ahead of the pack we move. When the time is right, if arrests are imminent, you'll get your time alone with Green and I'll make sure Shaw's out of the picture when the charge sheet is drawn. If, on the other hand, it looks like turning into an embarrassment, we can slink away and leave him to it. He's a tosser. Won't know his throat's cut until his head falls off.'

Moving away from the tree, he reached inside his jacket for his cigarettes. He settled himself in a modern chair made of tubular steel and strips of blue leather. Motioning Jack to take the green one, he lit his cigarette. 'Now. What have we got?'

Jack smelt the smoke Dowd exhaled with his words. 'The definites?'

Dowd nodded.

'These guys were in possession of Martin Burrows' body for fifteen days. No argument about that.'

'Burrows had been murdered.'

'Not quite a definite. He died from the hanging, we know that, but. Was it murder or suicide? That's the question.'

'And if it was murder, was it our boys? Or did they merely find him, as they claim?'

'Sounds a bit far-fetched, doesn't it? Finding a body hanging from a lamppost.'

'Jack. Don't even go there.' Dowd poked his cigarette. 'Animal rights supporters terrorize an entire village and dig up the corpse of a woman from her grave. A well-respected family doctor spends thirty years murdering three hundred patients. Neilson grinds human flesh down the waste disposal. If you'd read about any one of those a few years ago you'd have said it was far-fetched.'

'Okay. They find the body. It's a one-in-a-million chance, but they find it. What makes it even more remarkable is that they want a body. They have this idea of recording decay for their art. They've already done it with animals. Now they want a human. They keep the body for fifteen days and are in the process of returning it when they get pulled over by traffic.'

'Good old traffic. Never lets us down. Gave Maurice a bit of a turn, I believe.' Dowd laughed.

'He's on sick leave. Applied for counselling. Says he can't get rid of the smell.'

Dowd rose and looked again at the tree. Circled it. 'Y'know it reminds me of Las Vegas. The posh hotels.' He walked away into the Spiritual Room. Jack followed. 'Look at all this,' Dowd said. 'Artists. Criminals. There comes a point where you can't tell the difference.'

Dowd went up to the statue of Bernadette Soubirous, looked carefully at the saint, as if she herself were under suspicion. Then he put a hand gently on her shoulder as if she was a girl in a bar. He sighed and turned back to Jack. 'I don't think these guys are killers, Jack.'

'Nor me. Why would they choose Burrows?'

'I think they're telling the truth. They've not denied taking the body, using stolen materials, stealing the van, using Charlie Donovan to nick stuff for them. They know they'll go down.'

'And Burrows had plenty of enemies. Crawford. The Panyatskis. He'd swindled both. Plus half the Moscow crowd would have liked to string him up.'

'Now we come to the statues or – shall I use your term? – religious icons. Six pieces in all, the most significant of which is a six-foot statue of Our Lady of Lourdes, and a four-foot statue of Saint Bernadette. Said statues comprising a pair. From the outdoor grotto of the Church of Our Lady of Lourdes. Then the theft of a Transit van from outside the yard of J. Cochran's Builders' Merchants, and property of said builders' merchants. I think we can add to this the illegal connection of electricity and water supplies at Freer Street.

'Also, in your little Aladdin's cave, we've found a whole lot of goodies: cameras, computers, lithograph equipment. All very expensive stuff. And you two are both signing on. Though God knows why. You're both perfectly capable of working. Just bloody layabouts. Thieving layabouts, in my opinion. And also in my opinion, you're going to be nicking more funds off the state in an hour or so to pay for your legal aid. Though much good will it do you.'

'So you're charging us?'

The veins bulged in Shaw's temple. 'You're more intelligent than I thought. Were you bloody listening to that list? Of course I'm bloody charging you. But I'm not finished yet. Oh no. Our search of the old Water Board offices in

Freer Street has revealed evidence that cannabis has been smoked on those premises and among the fingerprints we found –'

'Fingerprints. You fingerprinted the place?'

'If I had my way I'd have exploded the bloody place, not just fingerprinted it. If there was any justice I'd have been inoculated before being required to set foot anywhere near it. You've got dead animals in there. Five or six of them.'

'But they're all together in one room.' Green's tone was reasonable. 'The Decomposition Room. You make it sound like they're just lying around all over the place. We photograph them. Turn them into images.'

'It's disgusting. And to top it all. To add insult to injury. You've got a picture of a nun in there. Sacrilegious. A beautiful nun. Asleep. With all those decaying animals.'

'She's dead too.'

'What?'

'Saint Bernadette. The nun. It's a photograph of her in her coffin.'

'A fucking saint. That's even worse. A saint. How low –'

'The idea is to look at the contrast between what is claimed to be a miracle of the literal preservation of flesh and decay and –'

'Forget it, Green. I'm not interested. The only miracle you need to be concerned about right now is getting a short sentence. And here I can offer you a little hope. As I was saying, we found prints in there of someone known to us, someone with form.'

Green sighed. 'Charlie!'

The sigh pleased Shaw. It showed he was getting somewhere. 'Precisely. Charles Philip Donovan. A number of convictions for theft, two for supplying. Was he supplying you with drugs?'

'Charlie? No.'

'Was he doing some of the nicking for you then?'

'No way. Charlie had nothing to do with anything. He just used to come round sometimes, that's all. For a chat.'

'About art, no doubt. And who's his favourite artist then?'

Look. Now they've been charged we need to get things sorted. Quickly. I've given you this story. And if you do it right it'll be major. No. Don't tell me, I know, you're the journalist. But it was me who put you on to this. Gave you the real story. The one your readers will want. The police weren't giving anything away. It was me who gave you all the details, their address in Walton Towers, the football club; it was me who got Charlie to talk to you. Okay, so you turned him a few quid. He wouldn't have come anywhere near you if I hadn't persuaded him.

Just think about what we've got here. The shooting connection – that's headline stuff on its own. A stolen body. Left to rot and photographed every day, all in the name of modern art. Your paper will love dishing the dirt on that. Then there's theft from churches. And the stuff I told you about Blue being abused as a kid by that old priest. Okay, allegedly. But he told Green that. And he wouldn't lie to him. He's probably the only person he's ever told. Obviously led to his obsession. You could get an expert psychiatrist to do a piece on that.

This story has got the works. Blue's dream of forming an artists' brotherhood in Warhol's name. Think what you can make of that. And all the time they're on benefits. You can keep this going for a week. But. You buy my story. And for a fucking good price. Then you get sex too. Remember, I'm the one who knows it all. Knows these men. Was the lover of one of them; I'll say both if you like. And there's the modelling angle. Nude-model girlfriend. Very tabloid. And I can say we made love in a room next to the corpse. The shock. The disgust. How I threw up. It was abuse, really.

But I want photos. Of me. I'll do nude, glamour, distress, anything you want. Pictures of me visiting Green in prison, if you like. The broadsheets will cover it too, because of the art angle. A nice bit of seediness dressed up as being about modern art. I want photos. This is my chance and I'm not going to lose it. If you don't want to work with me, or can't come up with the goods, I'll go to another paper. I know the value of what I've got.

That tree's going to end up world famous. You know it is. Ten years from now it'll be in a gallery somewhere. New York, most likely. Which is where they'll probably be when they get out. You know how these things work.

'At least we got bail.'

'Still got to go back though. Shit!'

Blue and Green walked slowly away from the court and across the city to Freer Street. The sun was shining but neither man wore shades.

'God. Look at this. They've boarded it up again.' Blue kicked impotently at the boarding. 'They've done a good job too.'

'Blue. We shouldn't even be here. You know we shouldn't. The bail conditions.'

'Our work's in there. Andy's Tree.'

'No, mate.' Green clutched Blue's shoulder. Held him. 'They've cleared everything out. You know they have. It's as empty as the day we first saw it.'

'That stuff's ours. We made that. The statues and stuff, well. But that tree is ours. Shit! How did all this happen? Come on. Help me get this down, I want to know what's left in there.'

'Nothing. I've told you. Everything's in the police compound.'

Blue went to the side of the building. The broken fence: repaired. 'Shit.' He broke away. Crossed the road. Sat on the steps of another derelict council building. Green joined him. The sun had disappeared.

Blue looked up at the grey sky. 'It's going to rain in a minute.'

'I suppose we should have known we couldn't get away with it for ever.'

'Andy did. Perhaps that's the nature of genius: getting away with it.'

'It's over, Blue. We have to face it.'

'All that work. The happiness of it. The nicking. The making. The thinking. The sheer bloody fun of it all.'

'Nothing in my life has been as good as this. With you. Nothing even comes close.' He let his arm fall. Clutched his hands between his knees. Suddenly he felt very cold. 'They're going to send us to prison, aren't they?'

'No doubt about it.'

'I'm not sure I can handle it, Blue.'

'You'll be all right.'

'Will we be together? In the same jail? It won't be so bad if I've got you.'

'I don't think so. Joint convictions usually end up in separate nicks.'

Then it had to be said: 'The tree. Will they destroy it? Break it up? Find him?'

'Father Derwent. No. The bastard's in there for ever. Like a pharaoh. It's too good. Ornate. Beautiful. It's art.'

'I wish I was so sure, Blue.'

'Greed'll save it. Our story. Andy's Tree. It'll mean bucks for someone, even if it's not us.'

'Christ! How did this happen?'

Blue put his arm round his friend's shoulder. 'You'll be all right.'

'*You* will be. Whatever happens. I know you. You'll have

Andy. You'll be able to take him with you. I only have you. I'm scared, Blue. Scared of being locked up. All those hard blokes. Psychos. And I'm cute. I'm scared of being buggered every day. Buggered to . . . buggery.' There was hysteria in the way the men laughed at this. Swaying. Slapping their thighs. Then it was gone.

Green reached out for Blue's arm. 'Blue, I –'

'Don't say it. I know.'

'But I do.'

'You'll be okay.'

It started to rain but they were protected by the red brick arch of the old building. They brought their feet up onto the step, so they were sitting cross-legged, like Buddhas.

'Here, Green. Give me fifteen Hollywood –'

'Not now, Blue. I can't.'

About the Author

Photo: Ian Davies

Mick Scully lives and works in Birmingham: a city whose underworld inspires his fiction. His 'Little Moscow' stories have been published in a range of magazines and anthologies including Tindal Street Press's bestselling *Birmingham Noir* (2002) and *Dreams Never End* (2004).

Acknowledgements

I would like to express my gratitude to Joel Lane, Kevin Grant, Christine Moysi, Polly Wright and Peter Foggan for their encouragement, and to all at Tindal Street Press for their patience, hard work and support

Tindal Street Press

The Concrete Sea
John Dalton

Dalton's 'new mystery consolidates his high standing on the urban noir map and sees him emerge as a poet laureate of Midlands bleakness. Crime writing is at its best when it summons an unmistakable sense of place, and Dalton proves a master, conjuring a malevolent palette of grey city streets, urban desolation and sociopathic life. British dirty realism at its strongest'   *Guardian*

ISBN: 978 095479 132 2 • £7.99

Jakarta Shadows
Alan Brayne

An unsettling and topical mystery that captures the unease of a westerner adrift in South East Asia.

'There are echoes of Graham Greene in this stylish, thought-provoking thriller that reeks of the damp heat, violence and corruption of Indonesia.'   *Bookseller*

ISBN: 978 095358 958 6 • £7.99

www.tindalstreet.co.uk

Tindal Street Press

The Executioner's Art
David Fine

Set in Sheffield, city of steel, this menacing debut
begins with a murder that has reduced the layers of
human identity to a few scraps of flesh.

'A hard-edged new voice for fans of strong regional
crime' *Bookseller*

ISBN: 978 095413 031 2 • £7.99

The City Trap
John Dalton

This masterly noir debut resonates with the tense atmosphere of corruption and betrayal of Birmingham's
underworld.

'Dalton evokes a strong empathy for the down-
trodden, taking pride of place among British crime
writing's dirty realists. The slick tale unfolds like a
whiplash, with thin glimmers of redemption shining
out . . . A powerful new voice' *Guardian*

ISBN: 978 095358 956 2 • £7.99

www.tindalstreet.co.uk